GLUTTONY

THE DAMNING BOOK 3

KATIE MAY

EXPRESSO PUBLISHING, LLC

Writing these, I realize I don't have that many friends. So...I suppose I'll dedicate this one to my cat, Carol. Love you, sweet girl.

CONTENTS

RECAP OF PREVIOUS BOOKS

When Z wins the Damning—a competition that pits the best assassins against each other—her world is overturned. Suddenly, she's forced to be the assassin for the exact kings she wishes to kill.

Fortunately, she has the seven princes to help her with the tasks ahead, each prince one of the seven supernatural species descended from the Seven Deadly Sins... and her fated mates. There's a prophecy surrounding the seven princes that they'll either save the world or destroy it. They despise their parents and their inhumane treatment of humans.

At the end of the first book, Z had been poisoned by a competitor of the Damning named Zack at the order of Aaliyah. Her mates are completely unaware that she was poisoned...and that the poison is slowly killing her.

The kings assign seven tasks, seven games, Z has to complete to prove her loyalty. Despite her hatred for them, a spell administered by the mage king prohibits her from harming any member of the royal family.

She completes the first task, assigned by the mermaid king. In the process, Dair kills his evil older brother, Tavvy, who'd attempted to rape and kill Z. Just before he dies, Tavvy tells Dair that he and the rest of the Z's mates weren't born—they appeared out of thin air.

Meanwhile, a mysterious female named Aaliyah is sending extinct supernatural creatures after Z, including a gorgon, kraken, and fae. She instructs her monsters not to kill Z, but to bring her to Aaliyah alive.

At the end of book two, Z discovers that Jax, her vampire mate, has gone missing.

CHARACTERS:

Z — Member of the Alphabet Resistance that advocates for human rights, assassin, mate to the seven princes, and winner of The Damning. She is poisoned at the end of book one

Dair — Z's mate, mermaid, and descended from Envy. Like all mermaids, he's forced to live as a mermaid for twelve hours a day and a human the other twelve. His father constantly cuts his legs off, grows them back, and then cuts them off again each night.

Devlin — Z's mate, genie, and descended from Greed. He has a soul trapped in his lamp that he accidentally lost. He's Z's childhood sweetheart.

Killian — Z's mate, incubus, and descended from Lust. As a child, he was forced to watch his father rape and kill his nanny. Currently a virgin.

Lupe — Z's mate, shifter, and descended from Wrath. His father implemented the first human concentration camps. He prefers to fight with words rather than violence.

Ryland — Z's mate, shadow, and descended from Pride. He hides his face in his shadows to hide his hideous facial scarring. He was the first to know all of the princes were mates with Z.

Jax — Z's mate, vampire, and descended from Gluttony. He's facing madness because he refuses to drink human blood and is only coherent around Z. Currently engaged to Atta. He was kidnapped by Aaliyah at the end of book two.

Bash — Z's mate, mage, and descended from Sloth. He distrusts the mate bond and the lack of free will, so he struggles with his affections for Z.

Atta — Shifter and descended from Wrath. She's Lupe's younger sister and the mate to Mali, but is currently engaged to Jax.

Mali — Vampire and descended from Gluttony. She's Z's best friend who unwittingly betrayed her, leading to the death of the mage, Diego. Mate to Zack (now dead) and Atta.

Diego — Mage and descended from Sloth. Z's best friend and mate to HH. He was murdered by Zack protecting Z after Mali betrayed them.

T — Z's friend from the Alphabet Resistance and brother of S.

S — Z's deceased ex-boyfriend who was killed by shifters and T's brother.

B — Leader of the Alphabet Resistance.

A — Z's former mentor before he died.

Aaliyah — Main antagonist of the series who wants to capture Z for reasons unknown.

Zack — Mage and evil assassin who killed Diego and poisoned Z. He was Mali's mate, but now he's dead.

Axel — Shadow and ex-assassin of the kingdoms.

PROLOGUE

JAX

I knew pain intimately and greeted it like an old friend or lover. The pain broke through the dissonance. Steady and reliable, the only constant in my chaotic life.

For that brief moment, as fire ran through my veins and set me aflame, my mind was coherent. I'd been staring at my life through a distorted mirror, but now, the vision was clear. My mind flashed to Z and her golden hair and willowy frame. The fire in her eyes. The way she felt in my arms as I held her through the night.

A lump formed in my throat.

My mate.

My love.

My life.

And I would die before she realized it.

My eyes flickered down to the stake protruding from my chest. It had fortunately missed my heart, but I had no doubt that this wound was fatal. Already, the ground was covered in a slick sheen of blood.

A beautiful face peered down at me, alive with glacial fury. Red locks framed her rosy cheeks. But while she was beautiful, she was nothing compared to Z. It was a beauty earned through hours in front of a mirror. A predatory type of beauty, cold and empty.

My mate, on the other hand, rolled out of bed the epitome of perfection and beauty. It was effortless.

"You're going to die, Jax Vampire," Aaliyah whispered in a singsong voice.

I tried to speak, tried to protest, but only blood managed to gurgle through my parted, chapped lips.

She stood, the hem of her gown catching in the thick puddle. Seemingly unconcerned, she moved to stand directly behind me, a manicured hand stroking my hair. I flinched at her unwanted touch, a ferocious roar somehow able to escape, despite my fatigue. The crazy bitch chuckled.

"But..." she continued, wiping her hands on the sides of her skirt. "There's a way you can live." She allowed her words to settle between us like thickening syrup. They were just as sickly sweet. "Denounce the human girl and become my lover."

I narrowed my eyes and attempted to glare up at her menacingly. A surprisingly difficult feat, considering I was weak from blood loss and rapidly losing consciousness.

"I would rather die," I managed to stutter out.

Pain. Pain everywhere. It set my skin on fire.

Aaliyah's face twisted with disgust, and she huffed as she turned away.

"Then you die," she announced snidely, stalking out

of the cell. She didn't bother shutting the door behind her. Why would she? I was too weak to even lift my hand.

At that moment, I knew with an unwavering certainty that I was going to die. I only wished I could see Z one last time.

I'm sorry, I whispered in my head weakly. Darkness pressed in on all sides of me as my hold on life rapidly waned. *I love...*

And then, darkness.

ONE

Z

The punching bag rattled under the force of my assault. Each punch did little to calm my frayed nerves.

Punch.

Jax.

Punch.

Dair.

Punch. Punch. Punch.

A fine sheen of sweat coated my skin, and I angrily brushed at a strand of curly hair that'd escaped its binding.

It had been a week since I'd returned home from the Mermaid Kingdom. A week since I discovered my vampire mate, Jax, had gone missing.

Punch.

My knuckles were cracked and bloody, but I barely noticed the pain. How could I? All I could focus on was Jax and Dair.

The golden-haired mermaid prince hadn't made an

appearance since we'd arrived back at the capital. According to the others, he was with his father, but that only made my worry ratchet up another dozen notches.

I didn't know his father well, but what I did know was that the King of Mermaids was sadistic and evil. His son, Tavvy, had attempted to rape and kill me before Dair had killed *him*. Still, Tavvy's ominous revelation reverberated in my head.

"...you and those men you call your brothers magically appeared. Out of thin air."

The words had been spoken at Dair, meant to hurt my kind prince. But what did they mean? Was it true, or were they the false words of a dying man?

Punch. Punch. Punch.

When I won the Damning and became the kingdom's official assassin, I'd thought the games would be over. I didn't realize how fucking wrong I was.

The games had only just begun.

The kings used me, twisted me, to befit their malevolent schemes. I was nothing but a human female, a bug meant to be squashed beneath their feet.

Hundreds of years ago, humans ruled this world. That all changed when the Seven Deadly Sins descended on this Earth and gave birth to the original nightmares.

Shifters, descended from Wrath.

Incubi, descended from Lust.

Vampires, descended from Gluttony.

Mages, descended from Sloth.

Genies, descended from Greed.

Mermaids, descended from Envy.

Shadows, descended from Pride.

Each of these supernatural factions embodied the characteristics of their sins. Take shifters, for example, the most volatile beasts of all the nightmares. When they became angry or emotional, they shifted into their animal form with no cognizant thought. They were entirely focused on the hunt, the kill.

Punch. Punch. Punch.

The final punch caused the bag to fall off its chains, hitting the ground with a thump. I remained standing over it, breathing heavily, as my hands clenched and unclenched into and out of fists.

"Z?" a soft voice questioned. A moment later, the door to the workout room opened the rest of the way and Killian stuck his head in. "You feeling punchy?"

Killian was sexy. There was no getting around that. His red hair was stylishly tousled, longer on the top than the sides. His face was perfectly proportioned, not a blemish in sight. With a strong jawline, high cheekbones, and abundant tattoos, he was every female's wet dream. The ultimate bad boy incubus. Only certain people knew the truth—Killian was an awkward, adorable nerd wrapped up in a sinfully delicious package.

"I'm feeling *very* punchy," I replied, shaking out my sore hands. Killian's red brows furrowed in concern as he rushed towards me, tenderly grabbing both my hands in his own.

"You need to be careful," he said.

"I'm fine." I pulled them away, bending down to grab the fallen punching bag and propping it against the wall. Killian's palm on my shoulder stopped me from moving again, my muscles bunching at the menial contact. "Seriously, Kill, I'm fine. I don't need you to baby me."

Almost reluctantly, he dropped his hand from my shoulder and released a heavy sigh. Snapping at Killian was the same as kicking a puppy. I would rather sever my own limb than hurt him. Frowning, I turned back towards him, just in time to see the flash of hurt in his gemstone-like eyes. Fuck. I really sucked at this whole mate thing.

"Kill..." I began, trailing off. How could I say *I'm sorry for being a shitty mate. I just sometimes don't know how to human?*

They didn't make enough cheesy greeting cards for that.

"Don't apologize." Flames entered Killian's cheeks as he sheepishly ducked his head. "You're dealing with a lot of stress. The kings have been unusually silent, Jax is still missing, and we have no idea what's happening with Dair. You have every right to be punchy and angry." He flashed me a small smile, revealing twin dimples in both his cheeks, and heat traveled straight to my core. How could something as innocent as a smile cause such an instinctive reaction?

Maybe it was because Killian was Killian and his beauty ensnared me as effectively as a hunter trapping his prey. It wasn't just his incubus allure, though that was certainly a part of it, but the kindness that seemed to emanate from his eyes.

Before I could stop myself, I pushed up onto my tiptoes and pressed my lips to his. He had a sweet taste, one I associated distinctly with Killian, and it caused an inferno to blaze in my stomach.

At first, his kiss was hesitant and unsure, but soon his lips were feverish against my own. He tangled his hands in my golden hair, pulling just enough to sting. Killian was sweet, almost shy, but when we were intimate, he turned into a completely different person. I wasn't even sure he realized he was doing it. He was just...Killian.

"You're so fucking sexy," Killian murmured, trailing kisses down my arched neck. His hands traveled down my sides to my ass, cupping both cheeks and giving them a squeeze. "Do you want me to make you feel good, baby?"

Does a dog shit?

And...

I shouldn't be thinking of shit when I'm about to get naked with my mate.

Instead of answering, I managed to release a strangled squeak. Very sexy, if I did say so myself.

"Kill..." I whispered breathlessly, eager for his lips. His taste. A small smile blossomed on his face, and somehow, it was able to embody both sin and innocence. It was something only Killian would've been able to pull off.

"Get on the ground," he said, still flashing that disarming smile. Seriously. It should've been illegal to look as sexy as him. Everywhere he went, he killed brain cells. Well, mine at least. I didn't know how to function around him.

Eagerly, I dropped to the ground, uncaring that I was sweaty and gross. It probably wasn't an ideal time for sex, or whatever Killian had in mind, but I wasn't about to complain. Orgasms were a must for survival.

Killian's hands traveled from my ankles to my inner thighs, the path he took causing heat to migrate straight towards my core. I was burning for him, for my mate, and only his touch could alleviate the ache.

Helplessly, I clenched my thighs together, but that only made Killian smile wider. Placing one hand on either leg, he shifted them until he could comfortably place his head directly above my pussy.

Fuck, I needed him. His lips. His tongue. His—

"Kill! Z!"

Fuck me in the vagina with a barbed wire dildo.

Killian jumped to his feet as if his ass were on fire, cheeks burning and head ducked sheepishly. Normally, I would've laughed at his flustered reaction. However, I was too pissed off at the lack of orgasms to muster even a smile.

For a moment, for a brief fucking moment, I'd forgotten about all the shit currently piling up on me. It was burying me in a steel coffin that none of my mates had a chance of accessing.

"Errrr...coming!" Killian stuttered, arranging his cock in his pants. He helped me to my feet, diligently wiping dirt and grit off of my clothes. I swatted his hand away impatiently.

"You're *not* coming," I teased, staring pointedly at his still erect dick. When he blushed crimson, I couldn't contain my giggles.

Yup. Apparently, I *giggled* now.

The door to the workout room opened, and Lupe

entered, his head buried in a thick book.

My shifter mate, as always, took my breath away. The man was positively giant, almost brutish in appearance, with a sweep of brown hair and stubbled jaw that gave him a dissolute look. I'd never found overmuscled men attractive before, but somehow, Lupe was able to pull it off. Seeing him made my mouth water and knees go weak.

A pair of glasses sat on his nose as he pored over the open book.

"Lupe?" I queried, garnering his attention. He glanced up from the tome with an unreadable expression. My stomach twisted and turned painfully. "What is it?"

"Bash allowed me to access some of the mage king's books," he began, rubbing at his stubbled jaw. His muscles clenched, shoulders bunching to nearly his ears.

"Did you find anything?" I was unable to contain the eagerness in my voice. The hope. It pierced the painstakingly constructed bomb shelter surrounding my heart.

Fucking hope.

Only fools believed in it.

"Bash believes he can perform a tracking spell to find Jax," Lupe declared, and my entire body deflated in relief. For the first time in days, it felt like I could breathe again. My lungs were finally capable of taking in air.

Jax.

"Wh-wha-at's th-the-e prob-b-blem?" Killian managed to ask. I noticed that his stutter always got more pronounced when he was experiencing a strong emotion. When his cheeks darkened in embarrassment, I rubbed my hand up and down his back soothingly.

"The problem is the spell." Lupe cast me a pointed look. "It requires something from his mate."

His ominous words sent a chill racing down my spine. However, it didn't deter my resolve. I would give anything to find Jax. *Anything.*

"The others are already in the library," Lupe continued, snapping the book closed and removing his glasses. With a delicateness that belied his muscular frame, he placed them into his shirt pocket. "I was sent to grab you two so we can discuss it as a family."

"Is Dair with you?" I inquired, but Lupe's hesitation was answer enough.

No. No, he was not.

Killian grabbed my water bottle off the ground and smiled shyly at me before he and Lupe led me towards the library.

I coughed once, quickly covering the noise with the inside of my elbow. When I pulled my arm away, I saw a splatter of blood on my skin.

Fuck.

Memories of the Damning bombarded me. Zack, one of the competitors, had poisoned me before I killed him.

Fucking shit.

"Z?" Killian asked, oblivious to my horror. He and Lupe stood at the doors, holding them open. I was grateful Lupe didn't have his enhanced sense of smell flipped on, or else he'd have discovered the blood. "You coming?"

Managing a shaky smile, I strutted towards them. "Of course. Let's get my mate back."

Z

I was unsurprised to find all my mates—minus Dair and Jax—huddled around a table in the library. I took a moment to survey them uninterrupted, memorizing their breathtaking features.

Devlin, as always, was bedecked in a formal business suit and cufflinks. His violet tie accentuated the purple of his eyes, a common trait in every genie. With his olive-toned skin and curly brown hair, he was as familiar to me as my own reflection. I'd once stared at his face for hours, never tiring of his perfection. He'd been my childhood sweetheart, my best friend, until he broke my heart. And even though he'd apologized and explained he'd left to protect me, it would still take time for the ache to completely heal.

Bash stood opposite him, blond hair tousled and dark green eyes hooded. He leaned back indolently in the chair, kicking his legs up with a sneer playing on his sensual lips. Mages, descended from Sloth, were naturally lazy and languid. It was why they had a surplus of power—to do the work they refused to do themselves.

Finally, my eyes landed on a shadow crouched on the windowsill. His features were obscured, but I knew him to have dark skin, onyx colored hair, and pouty lips. Scars marred the skin of his face, the wicked white lines somehow making his beauty even more captivating. However, he chose to remain hidden in the shadows, too prideful to show his face in public.

"Took you long enough," Bash muttered. His shrewd eyes narrowed on me, expression unreadable, before he abruptly turned away. His jaw clenched with tension.

Devlin immediately stood from his seat, striding towards me and wrapping me in his arms. He released me only long enough to press his lips to my forehead before sitting once more in the seat and placing me on his lap.

"So, what's this about a spell?" I queried, leveling my gaze on Bash. He pursed his lips as if he'd eaten something sour before sighing heavily and nodding towards Lupe. The shifter immediately dropped the ancient book onto the table, dust wafting from its brittle, yellow pages.

"It's a powerful tracking spell, capable of finding anyone anywhere in this world," Bash explained. He brushed his thumb over the cursive words.

"And it involves me?" Though I'd phrased it as a question, I already knew the answer. When did shit not involve me? I swore I was swimming in a pile of poop at this point.

"It involves a sacrifice," Bash countered. "A sacrifice from the person Jax loves the most."

All five men turned to stare at me, eyes piercing. I just barely resisted the urge to scoff.

"Oh, please. Me? Really? I know I'm his mate, and I even accepted it, but that doesn't mean he loves me the most. You guys are his brothers, his best friends. I'm just...me." I shrugged helplessly.

"Z, you're Jax's entire world," Devlin said. "I'm pretty sure he masturbates to a piece of your hair."

I scrunched up my nose. "That's disgusting. And that only proves that he feels lust for me, not love."

"Can't he feel both?" Bash retorted. He gave me an indecipherable look before turning back towards the book, thumbing through the pages.

"So, what do you need from me? A blood sacrifice?" Honestly, at this point, I was only half joking.

Lupe growled, a low and menacing sound, as if the mere prospect of my blood being drawn filled him with dread. I wondered how he would feel when he discovered I was dying.

"An object," Bash interrupted before Lupe's growls could intensify. "The object you treasure the most."

"The object I treasure the most," I repeated dumbly. It was almost comical. There were very few things I cared about, and even less that were tangible.

Bash's eyes turned pained as he dropped his gaze to something in Lupe's massive paw. It took me a moment to recognize the pendant held in his hand.

The necklace Diego had given me, the one that transformed me into a badass assassin when I was competing in the Damning. Though I hadn't used the necklace in a while, it held tremendous value. It was the last thing

Diego had gifted me before he died. Before he was murdered.

Tears flooded my eyes before I could contain them. They were asking me to sacrifice the necklace, the last piece I had of Diego, in order to save Jax.

I knew I was going to give it up. There was no doubt about that in my mind. Jax was worth everything and then some, but it didn't negate the intense pain unfurling in my chest. It felt like offering up the pendant was saying goodbye to Diego.

"If there was any other way..." Devlin insisted softly, his lips grazing my earlobe.

Even Bash, the moody asshole, was staring at me in pity. Fuck, I hated pity, especially coming from him.

"Do it," I managed to stutter out through clenched teeth. My muscles were taut and rigid, like the string on a bow before an arrow was released. Any second now, I would be let loose on the unsuspecting population. Heaven only knew what that would entail.

Bash continued to study me, a muscle in his jaw clenching, before he nodded once. Grabbing the necklace from Lupe, he scooped the book up and settled it under his arm.

"I'm going back to my room. The spell has to settle," he explained. His mossy eyes settled on me once more before dropping to my arm where I'd coughed up blood. His blond brows furrowed, but he didn't comment.

Surely he didn't know the truth, right?

Without another word, he turned on his heel and stomped out of the room.

"When are you going to remove the stick up his ass,

Z?" Ryland purred, his silky voice coming from directly behind me and Devlin. I didn't bother to turn around, since I knew by the time I looked, he'd be gone.

"The least Bash could've done was butter his ass up with lube so he's not in so much pain," I snarked.

Devlin chuckled softly, and even Killian flashed a timid grin.

"You should shower." Devlin squeezed my waist once, and I whipped my head towards him in mock horror.

"Are you saying I'm stinky, Lin?" I asked, quirking a brow.

"Not at all," he answered immediately. "I love the smell of your sweat. It reminds me of some of our more... pleasurable activities." At his unrepentant smirk, I smacked his shoulder.

"You're horrible." Sighing, I reluctantly got to my feet, immediately missing Devlin's warmth. When he made a move to follow me, I shoved at his shoulder until he fell back onto the seat. "Nu-uh. You called me stinky. No shower sex for you."

My other mates chuckled as I wiggled my fingers at them in goodbye. Smiling softly, I exited the library and moved down the twining halls of the capital.

I was always in awe of the building that served as the neutral ground for all seven nightmare kingdoms. It was a mismatch of architectural styles and cultural symbols designed to evoke connotations of wealth and status. Hundreds of windows allowed a copious amount of sunlight to enter, and paintings lined the walls. The portraits depicted everything from blue-skinned genies to incubi in the throes of passion.

I made it back to my bedroom easily enough. Honestly, I expected to be assaulted by at least one king. Those men were ruthless assholes.

In my room, I stripped out of my sweaty clothes and threw them into the laundry bin. One of the human servants would arrive and wash them later today, despite my protests that I could wash them myself.

I turned the water dials on, watching the steam mist up the mirror. Fuck, I loved this shower more than life itself. It even had an ass massager.

Stepping under the spray, I made quick work of scrubbing pomegranate bodywash into my skin. I'd just put my shampoo in my palm, prepared to rub it into my curly blonde hair, when the bathroom door opened and closed.

"Lin?" I asked, expecting to see my violet-eyed mate. Instead, a familiar broad-shouldered male stared back at me through the glass, eyes ablaze with banked heat. "Lupe?"

The shifter rumbled, the sound carnal and primitive, before he took a step closer. The mist from my shower was molding his shirt to his perfectly sculpted body. Fuck, Lupe was a work of art.

"I'm sorry," Lupe murmured, but he didn't step away and his eyes didn't leave my body. "Fuck, you're gorgeous. Your hair reminds me of liquid gold. Of fine silk I long to purchase and covet. And your body...all of your supple curves and flawless skin..."

His breath hitched, pupils dilating with desire, and I

couldn't help but smirk. "You're quite the poet, aren't you?" I teased, enjoying the way his cheeks darkened. It always struck me as strange that a man as large as him, a man that evoked fear in others, could be such a hopeless romantic. He had journals of poetry beside his bed. "So, what do you say, poet? You wanna join me?"

Lupe didn't need to be asked twice. He quickly ripped his shirt over his head, being mindful of his glasses still in his pocket, before sliding down his jeans. The boxer briefs he wore left very little to the imagination. Lupe was packing, there was no other word for it. I could see the outline of his cock through the thin material of his underwear. When his thumbs hooked under the waistband, I thought my lady parts were going to explode.

Wouldn't that be a way to die.

Here lies Z the assassin, died of cock before penetration.

I would never hear the end of it.

My breath caught as he wrenched them down his muscular, shapely legs, his cock jutting to attention.

Fuck, it was massive. I shouldn't have been surprised, since Lupe himself was a beast of a man, but *fuck*. That thing could kill a girl...or at the very least, her vagina.

My smile slipped as I thought about that monstrosity in any hole other than my pussy. Nope, not going there. I would become, as Killian put it, stabby.

"You like what you see?" Lupe asked with a carnal grin. He slid open the glass shower door and joined me beneath the spray.

"That...*thing* is not entering me," I said immediately.

Fuck, did Lupe have to register that with the kingdom as a deadly weapon?

He rolled his eyes heavenwards as if looking for patience.

Tough luck. He wouldn't find any help up there.

"My vagina is capable of a lot of things," I continued slowly, seriously, hoping my words would penetrate that thick head of his. "It pops out babies, for one. *Babies*, Lupe. But that python? It'll fucking break me."

He scoffed. "It won't break you. This isn't the first time—"

I placed my hand over his mouth. "Don't you fucking finish that sentence, Lupe Shifter, or so help me God, I'll cut that big ass penis off and shove it up your anus. Then you can understand my pain." I stared intently at his throbbing dick. "It'll be like putting a bazooka through a donut hole. We'll need to work up to that very, very slowly. I've had a lot of cocks, Lupe, but that is something else entirely."

"First of all, don't talk about the other cocks you had prior to me." His tone darkened considerably, as if he was imagining the brutal murders of all the young men I'd fucked before him. "Second, your donut will be fine."

"You know what you do with a donut?" I asked snidely, stepping up on my tiptoes to push down on his shoulders. "You eat it."

"Maybe if you're a good girl and ask nicely," Lupe teased, but he obediently dropped to his knees. Fuck if that wasn't the sexiest sight known to mankind. He stared up at me through his fluttering lashes. "Say please."

"Please," I gasped, my core aching, throbbing,

wanton.

"Please...?" His smile was sinful, exuding an aura that nice girls ran from kicking and screaming.

But I'd never been a nice girl.

And this man? He made me want to be bad. Very, very bad.

"Please, sir," I said with a huff, and I was greeted by his glorious smile.

With a show of impressive strength, he grabbed both of my legs and threw them over his shoulders. His hot breath wafted over my naked core, and I groaned, dropping my head back against the slick shower wall.

"Do you want my tongue in you, baby? Do you want me to lick all of your cum? Do you want to imagine it's my fat cock in you?"

"Yes..." I groaned, jerking my hips in an attempt to ride his face. He chuckled deliciously, the noise vibrating through me, before he lowered his face to my pussy and began eating me like I was his last fucking meal. Like he was dying, and only my juices could sustain him.

I gasped incoherent praises as he licked and sucked at my sensitive bundle of nerves. One of his huge fingers entered my channel, joined quickly by a second one. I didn't know how he was capable of holding me up while his fingers fucked me, but I no longer cared. All I cared about was the impending orgasm coursing through me and setting me aflame.

His mouth left my core, leaving me feeling bereft, before he returned with a vengeance, attacking and biting at my clit.

"Fuck!" I cursed as his hand smoothed over my backside. One of his fingers entered my puckered hole, using my own juices as lubrication. "Fuck! Fuck! Fuck!"

"Nope." Lupe pulled his head away from my pussy, lips glimmering with my juices. "You said I couldn't fuck you."

"I'll fuck your asshole with a sword if you don't let me orgasm," I threatened breathlessly, grabbing his hair and pulling him back towards my aching mound. He chuckled darkly.

"As you wish," he whispered. Two of his fingers entered me at the same time his teeth clamped down on my clit. I came with a scream that echoed in the bathroom, riding his face through my pleasure.

"Fucking hell!" I screamed. I was falling blindly off a cliff, but I knew for certain that Lupe would be at the bottom to catch me. He always caught me.

I stared down into my mate's light blue eyes. The scruff on his jawline. The tousled brown hair. He was gorgeous, both inside and out. I remembered when I first met him—back when I'd been mistaken as a contestant of the Matching. I'd been terrified of the burly shifter with cold eyes. Who would've thought we'd end up here?

Lupe dropped me on my feet, keeping his hands on my waist to steady me, and I smiled up at him.

"I'm not going to fuck you," I said, grabbing his cock and stroking it gently. "However..." I dropped to my knees, batting my eyelashes in what I hoped was a seductive manner. I probably looked more like I was seizing than anything else.

My tongue darted out to taste the pre-cum on his tip. The salty flavor assaulted my tastebuds. Not delicious, but not horrible either. I could definitely swallow if I needed to.

"You ready, poet?" I questioned, lifting a brow. When he opened his mouth to protest, I stopped him with a slap to his ass cheek. Fuck, he was ripped. He could probably cut diamonds on them. "Nope. If we're playing again, we're doing it my way this time. You're no longer sir."

He eyed me carefully, deciding, before he relented with a pained groan. "Yes."

"Yes, what?" Two could play at this game.

"Yes, ma'am."

Smirking with satisfaction, I traced the vein on his cock with my tongue. It jerked beneath my touch.

I curled one of my hands around his ass, holding him steady, while I cupped his balls with the other.

With a wicked grin, I opened my mouth, being mindful to relax my jaw, and took him as deep as I could. He wasn't only thick, he was long as well. I couldn't even swallow half of him.

But fuck if I wasn't going to try.

I removed my hand from his ass to wrap around the length I couldn't reach with my mouth.

"Your mouth feels so good," Lupe hissed. "So good."

Smiling around his length, I released his balls and slapped his muscular ass. When he groaned, I decided to take it a step further.

I swore Lupe jumped five feet in the air when I stuck a finger into his anus. Wimp.

"What the...?" he growled out, but the sound came out more husky than he intended. The kinky bastard liked it.

Adding a second finger to the first, I breached his tight hole as he moaned in delight. My mouth and hand continued to pleasure his cock in tandem.

"I'm gonna..." He grabbed my hair, holding me still so he could fuck my mouth relentlessly. "I'm gonna come."

I allowed him to use my mouth for his pleasure. Everything I had was his at that moment. When he came, it was like an explosion. He roared his release to the heavens, back arching, as stream after stream of cum shot down my throat. Like a champ, I swallowed it all.

I really deserved a reward for that.

"That was amazing," Lupe murmured, helping me back to my feet and kissing me feverishly. The water continued to pelt us, wiping away the evidence of our activities, but I could've sworn I tasted myself on his lips.

"You definitely impressed my pussy," I teased, stroking his neck. "She wants your cock." At his knowing grin, I amended, "Almost. Not yet. She's still a little frightened. I'm pretty sure when she first saw it, she boarded up all the windows and placed a 'closed' sign out front."

Lupe threw his head back and roared with laughter. The sound made me giddy. Sure, it was just a laugh, but it almost felt like...more.

"Let me wash you," Lupe insisted, grabbing my soap and washcloth. He gestured for me to give him my back.

"I already washed myself." But despite my protests, I obeyed immediately.

One of his fingers touched the lips of my pussy.

"Let me wash you, baby girl," he purred in my ear. "You won't regret it."

ATTA

I smiled demurely at the maids passing me. They bobbed their heads respectfully, their expressions a mixture of adoration and worship. One sniff confirmed they were both human.

When I turned a corner, leaving them behind me, my smile dissipated. I knew my brother was still with Z. Hopefully, I would get in and out before he noticed I was gone.

Three guards lined the doors to the capital, but they didn't bother to try and stop me. What could they do? I was the princess, and they were lower-class shifters. Normally, the hierarchy of life gave me a splitting headache, but even I had to admit that my position came in handy. People feared me, and that fear often translated into respect.

Leaving the guards behind, I exited the capital and walked briskly towards the gardens. I'd always loved this particular area. The green shrubbery was dotted with perennials and roses, and gnarled vines created a tapestry over my head.

I glanced over my shoulder once, assuring I hadn't been followed, before moving farther into the maze-like structure. A stone bench sat directly below a small gazebo highlighted with gold accents.

Smoothing out my dress, I perched at the very end and watched a bird flap its wings overhead. The creature was majestic in appearance, ethereal. What would it be like to fly high over the sky, not a worry directed at the tiny creatures below?

My wistful musings were interrupted by a body plopping down on the bench beside me.

"Mali," I greeted, fisting my hands to keep from touching her. The mating bond pulsated between us, a living entity, and I wanted nothing more than to lunge for her, take her face between my hands, and kiss the shit out of her. Instead, I remained silent. Stony.

"Atta," she said just as softly.

Silence descended between us.

"How's Z?" she asked immediately, swiveling to face me. I kept my gaze straight ahead, unable to ignore the stab of pain that her question brought me. I was her mate, her other half, yet she still always asked about the assassin first and foremost. Mali missed Z immensely, and I had to wonder if she missed the friendship or something else, something more.

"She has seven cocks to keep her company," I said pointedly, ignoring the way Mali blanched. "But she's alive and well."

Before I'd even finished speaking, Mali was shaking

her head. "Not well. Alive, yes, but not well." She nibbled anxiously on her lower lip as a flash of pain distorted her beautiful features. "Before Zack died, he poisoned her."

Zack had been a competitor in the Damning, but he had also been Mali's fated mate. He wasn't mine—so far, Mali was my only one—but I knew losing him would be like losing a limb. She wore that pain on her sleeve for the entire world to see.

"Zack poisoned Z," I parroted. Fucking hell. "What's the cure?"

"There isn't one," Mali said despondently, lowering her head. Her dark hair spilled forward, shielding her face from view.

"Every poison has a fucking antidote," I snapped, my patience splintering. I didn't know how I felt about Z, if I loved or hated her, but she was my brother's mate. The love of his life. He wouldn't recover if he lost her, which meant *we couldn't fucking lose her*.

"It's common in the Mage Kingdom," Mali mused, tapping at her chin. "It's usually used for executions."

"And I'm sure they have an antidote," I pointed out, already mentally planning my trip to the magical kingdom. Slowly, like ice melting on a hot summer day, my hands stopped clenching and relaxed on the stone bench.

We were both silent for a long moment, the tension thrumming between us like a live electrical wire. Mali broke it by releasing a heavy, disgruntled sigh.

"I miss you," she whispered brokenly. Her pinkie touched mine on the stone bench. I knew I should pull away, I wanted to pull away, but my hand remained stubbornly in place. My pulse skittered in reaction to her touch.

"You don't act like it." I couldn't hide the snark in my voice. The jealousy.

"You know I love you," she continued, ignoring my outburst. Finally, *finally*, I turned towards her completely. Her eyes glimmered with unshed tears. She reached for me at the same time I reached for her.

Her lips were soft against my own. Soft and familiar, eliciting goosebumps down my spine. Her hands tangled in my red hair, pulling to the point of pain, while my own hands kneaded her heavy breasts. Holding her, being with her...it reminded me of all the reasons I fell in love with her in the first place.

But like with any fairy tale, the clock had to strike twelve and the magic had to end.

She pulled away with great reluctance and rested her forehead against mine. Her breaths sawed in and out.

"You have to go," I said. It wasn't a question.

"She's waiting for me," Mali admitted, voice choked. She squeezed her eyes closed, tears suspended from her lashes, before she pressed a tender kiss to my nose. "I love you, Atta. Never forget that."

Feeling as if I'd lost a crucial piece of myself, a piece I could never get back, I watched Mali disappear in the opposite direction of the capital. It almost appeared as if the vines were eating her alive.

I would find a way to free my mate, or I would die trying.

FOUR

Z

I found Slippy in the freshwater lake adjacent to the capital.

My tiny kraken immediately crawled out of the water when I arrived, adorable cooing noises reverberating through his body.

With one eye, slimy gray skin, and dozens of tentacles, Slippy was a sight to behold. Originally, he'd been sent to kidnap me, but Bash had performed a spell that shrank him to the size of a large cat.

Some bitch named Aaliyah had sent him—as well as other extinct supernatural creatures—after me. They'd been told to bring me to her alive for whatever reason. Personally, I would've ordered them to shank the bitch. Having hostages was fun and all, but it involved a lot of gray area.

"How's my favorite man doing?" I cooed, extending a hand for my pet to nuzzle against. Some people loved dogs and cats, others preferred krakens. I fell firmly into the latter category.

As I rubbed Slippy's slimy head, my belly began to churn angrily, and Slippy released a distressed sound. Before I could comfort my ugly pet, I was leaning over the rocky shore and losing what little food remained in my stomach. Tears filled my eyes at the intensity of the assault. It felt as if my insides were twisting and tightening, every organ knotting.

Fuck.

My vomit was red with blood.

Slippy pressed his wet face against the backs of my knees, but I couldn't pull my gaze away from the disgusting liquid getting washed away by the waves.

Fuck. Fuck. Fuck. Fuck.

At Slippy's whine, I turned towards the kraken and held him in my arms. "I'll be okay, little man," I assured him, peppering kisses on his head.

Movement in my peripheral vision diverted my attention from the kraken. Frowning, I placed Slippy back into the water and crouched on the balls of my feet.

The mermaid king was exiting a small house neighboring the capital building. There was nothing particularly exciting about the building, one of dozens of servant huts that lined the perimeter, but his appearance still caused unease to skitter down my spine. Why was he visiting the servant quarters in broad daylight?

His golden hair was brushed away from his face and held back with a crown. Blue robes swirled around his body as he walked, his gait deceptively casual.

Even from this distance, I could see the blood speckling his face.

What the hell?

Slippy, seemingly able to sense my unease, disappeared beneath the water's surface. I quickly pressed myself against the trunk of a tree, my harried heart pounding in my ears.

The king glanced in both directions, expression carefully impassive, before stalking up the path that led to the capital. The guards allowed him through with respectful bobs of their heads.

"What are you up to?" I whispered, debating whether or not I should follow him. Instead, I turned towards the building he'd left.

Indecision flared within me. If he discovered I was snooping where I shouldn't, he wouldn't hesitate to kill me. Or at the very least, send one of his men to do the job. However, I couldn't ignore the nagging voice in the back of my mind propelling me forward.

Fuck it.

Remaining low, I stealthily moved through the weeds dotting the shoreline until I reached the modest building. It appeared to be some rickety shed, the wooden logs dilapidated and cracked from age and weather. There were no windows, and the single door was padlocked shut.

What are you hiding, asshole?

I didn't have the strength to break the padlock, but I *did* have twenty years on the streets as an assassin and thief.

Silently, I removed two bobby pins from my hair and placed them into the hole. I made quick work of the lock, and a moment later, the padlock snapped off.

Casting a glance in both directions, I pushed the door open and stepped inside.

The pungent smell permeating the air barraged me the second I entered. I was a trained assassin, so I knew what that smell was.

Blood.

The room I stepped into was nothing more than a cement cell. With no windows, I had to rely on the single hanging bulb swinging up above. It illuminated everything in a soft, golden glow. The ground was mostly hard-packed, compacted dirt, as most of the floorboards had rotted away.

The stench got stronger the farther I walked. I was practically gagging on it, my stomach swirling in disgust.

"Fucking hell," I cursed, plugging my nose.

I moved on silent feet down an empty hall, one hand holding my knife and the other pushing open doors as I went. The majority were empty of anything besides a simple bed. It was only when I entered the final room that I keeled over, vomiting once again.

My mate—my precious, perfect mate—was lying unconscious on a dirty cot. His golden hair was matted to his face with sweat and blood. From the knees down, his legs had been severed.

"Fuck!" I screamed, lunging forward. I placed a shaky hand on Dair's ashen cheek. It was cold to the touch. Fuck, he was so cold. So lifeless. "Dair? Dair? Can you hear me? I'm here. I'm here." I didn't know if my inarticulate ramblings were able to penetrate his unconscious mind, but I was hopeful. "What the hell did that sick fuck do to you?"

When I met Dair, he'd been in a wheelchair. His father and brothers, in a fit of jealousy, had cut off his legs. They were envious of his good looks and benevolent nature, and like with all nightmares, they'd sought to rectify the situation. When we traveled to the Mermaid Kingdom a few weeks earlier, his father had given him a potion to regrow his legs.

Obviously, it wasn't a lasting gift.

Horror cascaded through me, setting my veins ablaze, as I stared at my mate, my love.

"I'm going to kill him," I whispered resolutely, envisioning the mermaid king's disgusting face. I had no doubt in my mind that he was behind this. "I'm going to cut him open and feed on his innards."

"I love it when you get protective of me," a sleepy voice murmured. Dair opened up one eye and offered me a droopy smile.

"Dair," I sobbed, cupping his cheeks. His brilliant blue eyes, the color of a roaring sea, met my own. His hand went to cover mine, holding me to him. Holding all of my broken pieces together.

"I'll be okay, Z," he assured me with a wobbly smile. Blood coated his lips and teeth. "He gave me a potion. I won't die."

"He cut off your *legs*," I hissed in horror. What type of parent did that? Obviously, one that deserved to die.

I'd killed men for less.

"I know what you're thinking," he whispered, stroking my hand. "He's the king, Z. You can't go after him. Not without an army."

"Then I'll get an army." I ground my teeth together,

worked my jaw, and flexed my hands. "He'll pay for what he did to you."

Dair continued to stare up at me with a dopey smile, and it was that expression alone that made me have my next revelation.

"How often?" I whispered hoarsely. At his quirked brow, I added, "How often does he cut off your legs and then grow them back?"

I knew that the mermaid king and Dair's brothers had done it before, but I'd wrongly assumed it was a one and done type of deal. I hadn't expected *this*.

The pain he must've endured...

The torture...

I wanted to scream and cry. Punch something. I wanted the world to bleed.

Dair's smile diminished as quickly as it appeared, a bloated storm cloud moving in front of the sun, and my heart shattered into thousands of pieces.

"A lot," Dair admitted, lashes fluttering against his high cheekbones. "A lot."

It took every ounce of willpower within me not to rush out of this prison, find the mermaid king, and eat his fucking fishtail. The man didn't deserve to live, not after what he did to Dair.

"How can we fix this?" I asked desperately. I knew the capital had healers on hand. I could ask one of them to help...

"He uses a potion to grow my legs back," Dair explained with a sad smile. "A potion he made with the mage king by combining their blood."

"Then I'll grab you that fucking potion," I hissed, but Dair was already shaking his head.

"Z, it's fine."

"It's not—"

"I've dealt with this for years now. *Years*. I'll deal with it now." He captured my hand with his own, giving it a reassuring squeeze. "You have to trust me, Z. Please. I know what I'm doing, and I know what we're up against." He nodded towards the corner of the room, where his wheelchair was folded against the wall. "Grab me my chair, please."

Tears of indignation and anger trickled down my face, but I knew arguing would be futile. Dair could be as stubborn as me when he wanted to be.

Didn't he understand that I needed to defend him? Protect him?

I was beginning to believe that my purpose in life, my purpose in coming here, was to protect these seven men who'd drilled holes in my heart, filling the cavernous space with gold and jewels. For so long, I'd been letting the tides carry me away, but these men were giving me the motivation to swim and resist the current. To adhere to a purpose that went beyond simply killing.

Hands trembling, I opened the chair and helped settle Dair comfortably on it. Sweat continued to bead down his face, but he still offered me a tenuous smile.

In a rare moment of vulnerability, I pressed my lips to his in a tantalizingly soft kiss. Errant fireworks exploded from that menial connection.

"I'll fix this," I vowed, straightening. Sadness

descended in his expressive azure eyes, the sight strangling me.

"You can't fix everything, Z," he whispered. "You're amazing and I love you, but you're only human. You're only one person. But fuck, if anyone can bring this world to its knees, it'll be you." He flashed me another tiny smile, and though it was strained, it wasn't polluted with anger or fear, just grim acceptance and a love that stole my breath.

"Will the sick bastard hurt you again if you leave?" I questioned, already pushing him out the door. I rolled him down the hallway, my stomach tightening now with each glance I directed at the various rooms. Knowing what they were used for clawed at something raw and bleeding in my chest.

"He's done with me," Dair assured. I didn't need to see him to know that he would have pasted on a feeble smile. Fucking hell. He shouldn't have to fake a smile with me.

"He'll pay for this." We stepped out of the building and into the glaring sunlight. The grounds were miraculously deserted. I spotted Slippy's gray head bobbing in and out of the water, his one eye blinking at me. "I'll make him fucking pay."

I would drive my knife into the mermaid king's throat, even if it was the last thing I did.

FIVE

I moved with the shadows.

I was so in tune with them that there were times I couldn't demarcate where they ended and I began. They pressed in on me from all sides like a disgusting sludge. In the shadows, I could see everything and be anything. There were no limitations, no pain.

Shadows were renowned spies for the Nightmare Council. According to my father's numbers, over three hundred were currently on the kings' payroll and stationed throughout the kingdoms.

We embodied a stealth and grace that exceeded that of the other supernaturals. As a descendant of Pride, we were notorious for our secrecy. Very few shadows showed their faces out in public. I would be the first to admit that I was one of them, preferring the darkness over the light. I liked to remain unseen. I saw the rest of the world, but the world itself remained oblivious to me.

Pulling the shadows tight around me like an onyx cloak, I glided down the hall and to a servants-only door.

Men and women, the majority of them human, were bustling in and out, their hands overflowing with plates and goblets. The kings were feasting today. One final meal before the majority left the capital and returned to their respective kingdoms.

One final attempt for me to learn what they knew about Z.

I knew some of them, if not all, suspected that she was our mate, and that thought alone caused icy fear to skate down my neck. In this world, information was power that could be dangled over people. There were no winners in this fucked-up game. There were only losers and even bigger losers.

None of the servants spotted me intermingling within their ranks. How could they? I was nothing more than a silhouette on the wall.

A door at the very end of the musty hall led to the dining room. I knew better than to go directly there. No doubt, my father would be able to sense me the second I entered, and I still wasn't positive of his allegiance. I trusted my father more than I trusted the other men, but even that trust was tenuous at best. Trust was a fragile thing. One wrong move, one misspoken word, and it could burst into tiny shards, never to be mended together again.

I turned into a different room, opposite the dining hall, and stopped directly behind a knight in shining armor. Only then did I drop the shadows.

There was already a small hole in the wall, and I didn't waste any time leaning forward and pressing my eye to it.

The kings and some of their wives were spread out at a large table. I spotted the mermaid king sitting beside his twin sons, Idol and Manchester. His fated mate, Elise, sat on the other side of him, her lips puckered into a snarl. Elise wasn't Dair's biological mother, and thank fuck for that. Elise was just as cold as the grinning king beside her.

The mage king was already asleep, head lolling against his shoulder and soft snores filling the room. The incubus king sat beside him, two women kneeling between his legs and giving him a blowjob. How they were both able to do it at the same time was beyond my comprehension.

Across from them, my father sat in a cloak of his own shadows, providing much needed anonymity. The vampire king was sipping from a golden chalice, his lips coming away red with blood. He seemed entirely unconcerned that his only son was missing. The genie king sat next to him, dressed in his usual suit with his hair slicked back.

Finally, my eyes rested on the shifter king.

He was the largest in the room by far, exuding an aura that made me want to run in the opposite direction. With his shoulder-length hair, broad shoulders, and numerous scars, he was a terrifying sight to behold.

He was also the epitome of evil.

Already, he had created over two dozen human work camps throughout his territory. Humans there were considered nothing more than cattle to be sold and traded. Some of the other kings were well on their way to implementing his horrific, bigoted policies. Actually, I was nearly certain all of them were, sans my father.

But even he could be bought.

I watched them for more than an hour, but all they did was make idle small talk.

But what the hell did I expect? The mermaid king to get to his feet and announce his evil aspirations to the world? For the shifter king to rub his hands together, cackle malevolently, and explain his plans for world domination?

Instead, I discovered that Cheryl from accounting got a new boob job and Richard was cheating on his mate.

The horror.

I was just about to leave when the door to the dining hall opened and closed, and a familiar man stepped through. I recognized him instantly, though I couldn't recall where I'd seen him before.

He stopped directly beside the shifter king's chair and bowed once.

"Your Majesties," he said respectfully. A smile blossomed on the mermaid king's face. That, more than anything, scared the shit out of me. That man did *not* smile. Unless he was killing someone.

Well, fuck. This did not bode well for us.

The newcomer had cropped black hair, piercing eyes, and a form that rivaled Lupe's in the muscle department. Despite his subservient tone, there was something testy in his dark gaze, something I couldn't name.

While he was large, I didn't get the sense he was a shifter. No, the way he moved, with a grace and agility that belied his lumbering frame, made me believe he was a shadow.

"Have you thought about what we talked about, Axel?" the shifter king demanded. He barely spared the man a glance.

Axel...

A lightbulb went off in my head when I realized where I'd heard that name before.

He'd been the previous assassin...before Z won the Damning. He was known throughout the world for his ruthlessness and butcher-style killings.

Why the hell were the kings meeting with him?

After the Damning ended and a new assassin took over, the old was given a life of privilege tucked far away from the capital. A life of wealth and prestige and fucking mansions. By all standards, the kings should've been talking to Z, not Axel.

Trepidation clawed at my heart, destroying something I couldn't name.

Axel pounded his fist against his chest, lowering his head once. "I would be honored."

Honored? What the fucking hell were they talking about?

The shifter king grinned, his white teeth gleaming, before clasping the assassin's arm.

"We'll start making arrangements immediately," he said, releasing a jovial laugh. Axel nodded once more, but there was a tightness to his face that hadn't been there before. His jaw was clenched so tightly, I was afraid it would break.

With that, Axel turned on his heel and stalked out of

the dining room. He didn't seem at all concerned that he was giving his back to a bunch of deranged, sociopathic nightmares.

When it became apparent that nothing else interesting would happen, I pulled the shadows to me once more and exited from my hiding spot.

I felt like I'd witnessed something monumental, but what that thing was, I wouldn't have been able to tell you. I had the distinct feeling that Z's life was in danger yet again.

But this time, I'd be damned if I didn't do everything in my power to save her.

SIX

Z

I brushed at a strand of Dair's golden hair, highlighted from the sun. He looked peaceful in his sleep. Serene. The tightness once wrinkling his face and clenching his jaw was nowhere to be seen. I wanted him to stay like this for the rest of time.

I'd brought him to my bedroom and helped him onto my bed. The second his head had touched the pillow, he was out.

Fuck, what type of parent did this to their kid?

It didn't take long for Devlin to find me. I swore he had a sixth sense that focused solely on me. Whenever I was distressed or frightened, he would come running.

His eyes honed in on me first, assessing me for injuries, before lowering to a sleeping Dair.

"Fuck," he cursed, scrubbing a hand through his loose brown curls. He moved to stand behind me, hands resting on my shoulders. "What happened?"

"What do you think?" I didn't mean to snap, but my emotions were running rampant within me. All I wanted was to make the mermaid king bleed for what he did to my mate. My love.

The brutality of nightmares never ceased to amaze me. They lived their lives with an abandonment most humans didn't possess. They didn't think about consequences before they acted. Instead, they only saw the rewards.

"I always knew he was a twisted fuck," Devlin murmured, referring to the mermaid king. His hands tightened imperceptibly on my shoulders before he abruptly released me. "When they first cut off Dair's legs, many years ago, I wanted to kill them. Tavvy. The twins. His father." He paced in front of the bed, repeatedly running his fingers through his disheveled hair. The dark strands stood in all directions like he'd stuck his finger in an electrical socket. "I didn't even think... I couldn't imagine..."

"That they would do it again?" I queried, focusing once more on my unconscious mate. "Over and over and over again? Fuck, how many times have they grown his legs back just to cut them off? How many times?" Tears distorted my vision, but I refused to let them fall. It wasn't my story to cry over.

Yet I couldn't help but think about all the times he'd had meetings with his father. Was he enduring unbelievable torture while I was only a hairsbreadth away?

My stomach twisted and tightened, slithering like dozens of snakes.

"I came to retrieve you," Devlin finally said. "Bash completed the spell. We know where Jax is."

"Jax?" I whispered, spinning towards my genie. His

violet eyes were anguished as he stared at Dair before focusing on me.

"We'll meet with the others," he said, grabbing my hand. Before he could pull me out of the room, I pressed my lips to Dair's sweaty forehead. Already, I could see color returning to his ashen cheeks. He was right earlier—the mermaid king must've given him a special potion to amplify his healing capabilities.

"I'll be back," I promised my golden-haired prince. Giving him one last kiss, I followed Devlin out of my room and down the hall. His hand was tight in mine—a reminder that no matter what it seemed like, I wasn't alone.

"He'll be okay," Devlin vowed as we turned right at the fork in the hall. "Dair's strong. Resilient. I swear the asshole's made of steel." There was a smile in his voice. I could sense how much he loved his brother, how much he respected him.

The princes weren't related by blood. However, they'd forged unbreakable bonds at a very young age. They were brothers in every sense of the word. Besides, look at Tavvy, dead by Dair's own hand. Despite believing they were blood-related, they were nothing but enemies. Blood didn't equal family.

We stopped at an unfamiliar room at the end of the hall. Devlin didn't bother knocking before he stepped inside.

"Bash-hole! We're here!" he called, kicking the door shut behind us, and I couldn't help but smirk at the nickname. I hadn't planned for it to stick, but I wasn't complaining. Anything that annoyed Bash was a win in my book.

Huh. This must've been Bash's room.

It was larger than mine and bedecked in masculine, monochromatic colors. The black bed was a startling contrast to the white carpeting and beige painted walls. Two nightstands flanked the bed, one holding a lamp and the other a television remote. There were no dressers, but the closet was practically spilling clothing out. I wasn't surprised that Bash had a fetish for designer jeans.

The ass himself was sitting at a desk in the corner of the room, a black cauldron emitting a murky green mist in front of him.

Seriously? A cauldron? If that wasn't a cliché, I didn't know what was.

Killian was already sitting on the bed, his long, lean legs crossed at his ankles. The first few buttons of his shirt were unbuttoned, revealing a myriad of tattoos and a splatter of chest hair. Fuck, he was gorgeous. A work of art.

I didn't see Ryland or Lupe, which surprised me. Before I could inquire about their noticeable absence, Bash spoke.

"He's in the Vampire Kingdom." His voice was the snappy, no-nonsense one I was beginning to hate. I sometimes wanted to replace the giant stick up his ass with a dildo. Maybe then he'd be content.

"Jax?" I clarified, and he shot me a look that made me feel like an imbecile.

"No shit," he retorted curtly.

"Don't be a dick, Bash," Killian said. He sat up on the

bed, eyes narrowed into thin slits and hands clenched. Out of all my mates, Killian was the least confrontational. It was surprising to see him so pissed off in my defense.

Bash glared at the incubus, chest heaving, before he turned towards me. The harshness in his eyes immediately dissipated, and he placed his head in his hands.

"I'm sorry, Z. It's just... He's my brother."

I wasn't angry at his snarky outburst. Bash coped with stress and pain differently than my other mates. Frankly, I understood him better than I did the others. His prickly exterior hid a compassionate, gentle soul. His heart was surrounded by coils of barbed wire and thorns. But every rose had thorns to protect it from harm. He was a beautiful, broken man, and I sought to replace the holes in his heart with beautiful things.

"It's okay," I said sincerely. "You're scared, and you miss him. I do too." I gulped, remembering how I'd found Dair only a few hours earlier. I didn't even want to think about Jax enduring the same treatment.

Taking another ragged breath, Bash held up an old, yellowing map. A trail of green slime extended from the capital to the Vampire Kingdom.

My eyes devoured the map eagerly, memorizing the trail. It appeared to end directly beside a forest, ominously named Killer's Hallow.

Totally not a terrifying name.

"We need to go after him," I said immediately, already planning which route we would take. We had to be careful about venturing into the vampires' territory. They saw humans as nothing more than food. I once heard a rumor that the vamps created slaughterhouses and captured unsuspecting humans from neighboring towns. The mere thought of it made me sick to my stomach. Male. Female. Young. Old. They didn't discriminate. Every human was a target, regardless of demographics.

"We can't," Devlin sniped from behind me. When I gaped at him in disbelief, he ran his fingers through his hair. It was a nervous tic he'd had since we first met, when we were sixteen. "You're the kings' assassin now, Z," he explained reluctantly. His voice was potent with pain. "You can't just leave. The spell they placed on you when they inducted you won't allow it."

"What the fuck are you saying?" I snapped, my agitation physically manifesting itself. I began to pace the large room, no doubt wearing holes into the carpet. Bash and Killian watched me warily, but neither of them spoke up. "I need to ask for fucking permission to rescue my mate?"

Devlin's tightened jaw was the only answer I received.

"They'll agree," Killian assured me. "There's no love between Jax and his dad, but he's still the bastard's heir. If you offer to go after his son, he'll agree."

I wanted to punch something. Stab something. Anything.

It fucking gutted me that I had to rely on the permission of seven sadistic assholes. What if they said no? What would I do then? I had no doubt that the potion they forced me to consume would kill me if I tried to disobey their direct orders.

"Fine," I said through gritted teeth. "I'll ask them."

"Today," Bash broke in, turning back towards the

map. His finger idly traced the trail his magic created. "They leave tomorrow, so you need to ask today."

"They should be in the throne room," Devlin added. He sounded reluctant, pained, as if he would rather have me do anything else but talk to those men. I didn't blame him. I was pretty sure carving my eye out and eating it would be more appealing than pleading with the kings.

"Then let's go," I said curtly, already walking towards the door. I would beg the kings if I had to, losing what little dignity I had left. However, it would be worth it. Jax was worth that and more.

Come hell or high water, I was getting my mate back.

THE KINGS WERE AN INTIMIDATING BUNCH.

The power they exuded was almost staggering. It wrapped around my throat like a wire, pulling until I could no longer breathe. Even if I didn't know what species they were, the way they sat would tell me.

The mage was sleeping, the incubus was winking seductively, the shifter king was coiled with unrestrained tension, and the mermaid king glared enviously at the vampire's golden goblet.

All seven of them immediately turned towards me when I entered. I noticed, somewhat distantly, that the previous assassin, Axel, was standing just behind the shifter king's throne, watching me as intently as the others. Ignoring his obsidian gaze, I directed my attention to the vampire king. I knew that would piss off the others, particularly the mermaid king. Fucking drama queen.

"Your Majesty," I said, addressing the handsome vampire. He looked a lot like Jax, but unlike my eccentric mate, his face was hard and his eyes were cold. Still, both men had light brown hair grazing their foreheads and lean, muscular bodies. The red robe anointing him as a member of the vampires flared around his ankles as he reclined in his throne.

"What's the meaning of this, assassin?" the shifter king demanded. I ignored his outburst, keeping my attention on Jax's father. Did he feel any love for his missing son?

"I've heard that Jax Vampire has gone missing," I declared. There was no use beating around the proverbial bush. I'd learned long ago that I needed to be direct with what I wanted, especially when it came to these seven men. Anything else, and they perceived it as a weakness.

I stared at the arresting man, searching for any indication that he cared about Jax's disappearance. There was no surprise on his face, no worry, no fear. It could've been hewn from stone with how expressive it was.

"And?" he drawled lazily.

A long, potent silence descended between us, only broken apart by the incubus king's fingers thrumming against the arm of his throne.

"And," I began, taking a fortifying breath. "I would like your permission to go after him."

The asshole didn't even blink. Instead, he continued to stare at me with an unnerving clarity that made goosebumps blossom on my arms.

"Why?" the vampire king inquired at last, canting his head to the side.

My eye began to twitch. Literally twitch.

If there weren't a spell prohibiting me from hurting them, I would've jabbed my knife in all of their throats.

"He's royalty," I explained, repeating the line I'd rehearsed with the others. "It is my sacred duty as the kingdoms' assassin to protect him and the others."

"Ridiculous," the mermaid king said with a huff. "Why should we waste our valuable resources to save a dim-witted boy?"

My hands curled into fists as anger pulsated through me. Smug, idiotic asshole.

Fortunately, the mermaid king's outburst had the opposite reaction he'd hoped for. The vampire king leaned forward in his chair, eyes penetrating the side of the other man's head.

"You can't talk about my son like that," he hissed, fangs elongating and piercing his bottom lip. Red rims appeared around both of his pupils as his nightmare floated closer to the surface. "He's my heir. If I want our assassin to retrieve him, she will."

I just barely resisted the urge to smile. Who would've thought that their own internal rivalries would aid me with my request?

"I agree with the vampire," the shadow king retorted from his throne. Shadows hugged his skin, obscuring his features from view. "I vote the assassin retrieves the missing prince."

"All in favor?" the vampire king asked. All the kings, sans the mermaid and shifter ones, raised their hands in solidarity.

"Don't be so upset," the incubus said with a tsk,

turning first towards the shifter and then the mermaid. "We could make this another game for our little human assassin. Her next task to prove her worth. She does have six more, does she not?"

Oh, fuck.

The shifter king's eyes gleamed maliciously.

"A scavenger hunt," he declared to the murmurs of approval from the other kings. To me, he said, "You will find the vampire prince and bring him home. You have five days. If you fail, you will die." His smile grew until it practically cleaved his face in two. There was something evil lurking just beneath the surface. Something that made fear trail an icy finger across the nape of my neck.

"Axel," the mermaid king interjected, nodding towards the stone-faced assassin. "Would you accompany Z on her quest for the missing prince?"

If it were possible, and I didn't think it was, Axel's face hardened even further. Lips pressed in a solemn line, he nodded once.

"Perfect!" The vampire king gleefully clapped his hands together. "You leave tonight. If you return, Z, we have a special surprise for you. A reward, you could say, for completing your mission."

Fuck. Me.

SEVEN

My jaw cracked with my next yawn as I scrubbed a large hand through my hair.

I didn't know how long I'd been in the library, only that the sky was turning a metallic gray outside. Books covered the oak table, pages loose and strewn across the wood.

I'd been at this for hours now, and I still had yet to find the strange symbol in any of my books.

During the Damning, numerous assassins had gone after Z and my brothers under Aaliyah's orders. Each one had had a tattoo etched into their skin, on the back of their right shoulder. It appeared to be thin black lines morphing into thicker red ones in a makeshift circle. The symbol had to mean something. My analytical brain refused to accept anything else.

But what?

My eyes flickered towards a history textbook praising the kings and their generosity. I actually scoffed as I read a paragraph detailing my father's contributions towards "improving shifter and human relations." The man had placed them in work camps, killing those he deemed too weak to survive. If that was what history called generous, then I didn't want to know what they considered brutal.

The textbook also briefly described a prophecy. *The* prophecy. The one that had been hammered into me from a young age.

According to some ancient mage hundreds of years ago, seven descendants from each species, with a relationship resembling that of brothers instead of enemies, would either bridge the divide between nightmares and humans...or ruin it completely. Our powers were supposedly more potent than that of our parents or any nightmares that came before us.

Slamming the book closed, I tilted my head back and stared intently at the ceiling. A mural was painted across the gilded wood. Seven demons encircled an angel. I could only tell they were demons from their grotesque appearance—horns protruding from their scalps, veiny tails wrapping around their clawed feet, and skin that varied in colors. Red, purple, blue, green, white, pink, and gold. The hues of the sins. The angel, however, was a combination of all seven of them, her skin comparable to a rainbow.

I'd been in the library hundreds of times, but I'd never noticed the painting on the ceiling before.

My thoughts were interrupted by a throat clearing behind me. I jumped in my chair, startled by the intrusion.

My father glided forward with Atta following closely behind him. He was a tall man, handsome in an untraditional sort of way, with muscles that gave him a towering, imposing stature. His piercing brown eyes focused first on me and then on my books.

He never understood my obsession with reading. He believed shifters were good for two things—fucking and fighting.

"It's our sin," he always said. "We're wrathful, not studious. Don't be a fucking dumbass."

My father wasn't a good man. I knew that. The world knew that. Z knew that. However, my father had never hit me. Not really. He was cruel and domineering, always staring at me like I was a bug on his shoe, but he never physically hurt me. I often wondered if it was because he was as afraid of me as I was of him.

"Father," I greeted, nodding respectfully. I hated that I had to play nice with the murderous asshole. I wanted nothing more than to slash my claws across his throat. "Atta." I turned to my sister next, my hard eyes warming marginally.

My sister had received our mother's vibrant red hair and freckled face. With her soft, dewy features and bright green eyes, she was the light to my father's darkness.

"Lupe," Atta replied. Her voice was reserved, terse, and her eyes flitted from book to book without ever sticking. My hackles immediately rose.

"What can I do for you, Father?" I questioned. Every muscle in my body was rigid, bracing for a fight, and my stomach swirled and tightened uncomfortably. Daddy dearest rarely called for me. Actually, I could count on one hand the number of times he had.

Did he know about my mating with Z? I knew that he, along with the other kings, suspected as much. It was dangerous knowledge to have. Threatening her would have all seven of us on our knees, begging for mercy. The mighty would fall and the world would burn before we'd let anyone hurt our mate.

"Come with me," he demanded briskly, turning on his heel and stalking out of the library. I exchanged an anxious glance with my pale-faced sister before following after him.

"Where are we going?" I asked, racing to keep up. I was easily able to match my long strides with his.

I could feel my bear prowling just beneath the surface, demanding to be let loose. He sought to protect his mate from all harm, including from his father. If I released the fragile grip I had on my animal, hell would reign.

We entered an unfamiliar portion of the capital where the number of servants hurrying about became lesser and lesser. Still silent, my father led us both down a rickety staircase. The distressed wood creaked with every step we took, and I questioned if it would be able to hold our combined weight.

The farther down we descended, the staler the air became. A musty smell barraged my enhanced senses.

"Where the hell are we?" Atta grumbled, tripping over the hem of her gown. I reached out a hand to steady her before pulling it back just as quickly. If my father were to see me help my sister, he would perceive it as weakness. From both of us. She should never need help, and I shouldn't offer it without expecting something in return.

The hall was lit by hanging bulbs evenly spaced down the long corridor. Iron cages were on either side, consisting of nothing but hard-packed dirt, rusty chamber pots, and worn cots.

A dungeon.

My dad had brought us to a dungeon.

My unease ratcheted up a dozen notches as I stood protectively in front of Atta. I had no idea what my dad's plans were, but I'd be damned if she got hurt because of him. Did he intend to lock us down here? I would fight tooth and nail before I ever allowed that to happen.

Atta, sensing my anxiousness, dug her fingers into my shirt from behind. Her touch grounded me, causing my muscles to relax incrementally.

I wanted to assure her that we would be okay, that I would get us both out of this mess alive, but I couldn't get the words out. Especially with my father only a step in front of us.

We turned down a second hall, our footsteps echoing on the cement floors, before stopping in front of the final cage.

It was smaller than the others, devoid of a bed or any blankets. Only a single bucket rested against the far wall, overflowing with piss and shit.

I plugged my nose instinctively at the repugnant smell, and Atta released a strained cough.

A man sat in the cell, his back to us.

"We caught him a couple of days ago, attempting to kill a council member," my dad bit out scathingly. His eyes hurled daggers at the man's back. "A leader of the fucking human resistance."

My eyes widened before I quickly blanked my expression.

Surely, it wasn't the same resistance that Z once worked for. There were dozens, if not hundreds, of groups across the globe that sought to end the kings' rule. The Alphabet Resistance was only one small faction.

My pulse skittered with fear and trepidation.

"If we get him to talk, we'll find where the others are," my dad continued, an eager, malicious glint in his dark eyes.

"I'd rather you kill me," a familiar voice drawled lazily.

Oh, fuck.

He finally turned, the single bulb casting strange shadows on his face. His auburn hair was greasy and stringy, speckled with blood, and a jagged gash ran down the length of his cheek. When he smiled, revealing bloody teeth, he appeared more nightmare than human.

T.

One of Z's closest friends and a member of the Alphabet Resistance.

Fuck. Fuck. Fuck. Fuck.

"Kill you?" My father laughed, the sound so cold and chilling that my blood turned to ice. "I'm not gonna kill you. But by the time I'm done with you, you'll wish you were dead." Turning towards me, my father grabbed a knife out of its sheath and held it out as an offering. "Would you like to do the honors, my dear boy?"

EIGHT

Z

What did you bring on a mission to the Vampire Kingdom to save your missing mate?

Pursing my lips, I surveyed the small pack I'd stolen from Devlin. So far, I had a water bottle, fresh underwear and bras, two changes of clothes, and a few hunting knives. I didn't know what I expected, but I was hopeful that the mission would be successful. It had to be. I refused to accept anything less.

I didn't want to weigh down my bag with canned food and other non-perishables. If worse came to worst, I would hunt for food. I'd done it before, numerous times, when I worked for the resistance.

With a sigh, I slipped the bag over my right shoulder, slung a bow and arrow over my left, and sheathed knives to both my thighs.

"You ready?" Killian stuck his head into the room, expression anxious, despite the hard, determined glint in his eyes.

"You don't have to come, Kill," I murmured, exiting my room and locking the door. I then dropped a red tablet Bash had given me, which was supposed to prevent any man or woman with ill intentions from entering my room.

"I'm coming." Killian clenched his jaw and fisted his hands. "We all are."

I knew that arguing with him would be futile. All of my mates were immensely protective of me, despite the fact I was capable of kicking their asses in a fight. Still, the backup would be much appreciated, and all of the princes had been to the Vampire Kingdom enough times to lead me.

When we exited the capital, my mates were standing beside a sleek black car. Devlin was leaning against the hood, and Ryland's shadowy form hovered just above the hood of the car. Bash was silently fuming, arms crossed with a petulant pout to his lips.

"Where's Lupe?" I questioned, noticing his absence immediately. Before any of them could answer, the door behind me snapped open and my burly shifter emerged. His tanned skin was pale, ashen, and dark circles surrounded each of his eyes. Ignoring the others, he stalked forward until he was directly in front of me, his hands on my shoulders. "What's wrong?"

"Z, I need you to trust me," Lupe pleaded, eyes intent on my face. At my furrowed brow, he leaned closer until his forehead was against my own. "I can't explain everything right now, but I need you to trust me."

"I don't understand," I replied honestly, searching his eyes. What the hell was he going on about?

Lupe sighed, dropping my shoulders and taking my bag from me. "I just need you to trust me," he said at last. "I have a plan." Those ominous words sent goosebumps up my spine. A niggling voice in my head demanded that I question Lupe, but before I could articulate one of the thousands of questions clamoring for attention, the shifter opened the car door. "Let's go save Jax."

WE TOOK TWO EIGHT-PASSENGER CARS. One consisted of me and my princes, sans Jax and an unconscious Dair, and the other had Axel and a few guards and servants. I didn't know why we needed them, but the kings were insistent.

Lupe sat beside me, jaw clenched tightly. When I tried to ask him what was wrong, he pressed his lips into a grim line.

"Trust me," he whispered, and there was a hint of pleading in his growly voice.

The road through the mountains was twisty, the rocky cliffside closing in on all sides of us. The beauty of the capital never failed to amaze me. Even from this distance, peeking through the boughs of trees, I was utterly captivated. The large building sat in a valley created by the mountains. Floor to ceiling windows revealed a copious amount of artificial lighting, and a large body of water sparkled like thousands of diamonds directly beside it.

The farther away we drove, the smaller the capital became, until it was merely a speck of dust. I found it ironic, in a demented way, how we perceived our government to be larger than life until we were no longer in its thrall. Only then did we realize how small it actually was.

"How long is the drive?" I questioned Lupe. When he remained taut and tense, I rested my head on his shoulder. He seemed to physically deflate with my contact, his body sagging in something akin to relief. He pressed a tender kiss to my forehead.

"We'll drive all day," Killian answered from the passenger seat. Devlin, of course, was driving. I didn't expect anything else from my genie, since he always had to take control when the opportunity arose. It was what made him an amazing leader.

"There's an inn just before we enter the Vampire Kingdom," Ryland added. His shadowy form hovered in the seat in front of me. "We'll stop there for the night and discuss strategies."

"Perfect," I murmured, yawning. The events of the past few days were already catching up to me. My eyelids were leaden, unbearably heavy. It proved how much I'd grown to trust these men that I was even considering falling asleep.

"Rest," Lupe murmured, stroking my curly hair away from my face. "We'll wake you up when we arrive at the inn."

I wanted to protest, but my mouth was incapable of forming the words. Instead, I snuggled deeper into his side, his rhythmic breathing lulling me into a deep, soundless sleep.

I KNEW I WAS DREAMING, yet *I didn't know where I was. Weren't dreams supposed to be an extension of your subconscious? Wasn't it true that you only dreamed about things you saw in real life?*

It was unbelievably dark, a single candle sitting in the middle of the room. The orange and yellow flame flickered, casting strange shadows on the wall and floor. It appeared to be a cell of some sort, with gray stone walls on three sides and iron bars on the fourth.

As I stepped forward, my eyes latched on to the single figure lying on his back. A black liquid seeped out of a wound on his chest. It almost appeared to be tar. No, not tar.

Blood.

My heart hammered as I knelt down before the painfully familiar male. His light brown hair was longer than I remembered, matted with blood, and his skin seemed gaunt and pale.

"Jax," I gasped in horror, running my fingers through his hair.

His eyelids fluttered against his high cheekbones before they snapped open, honing in on me.

"You're not real," he murmured, blood drizzling from his parched lips.

"Jax..." All I could do was stare at him in numb horror. This wasn't the eccentric man I had grown to care for. This broken, defeated man was a stranger. I continued to smooth back his brown locks, tears distorting my vision. My breaths were choppy, harried, as I stared at the vampire. "Here, take my blood." I attempted to press my

wrist against his lips, but he turned away from me with an animalistic snarl.

"You're not real!" he screamed, shaking his head adamantly. "You're not real! You're not real! Go away! Go away!"

Ignoring his outburst, I removed a dagger from my sheath and sliced the skin of my wrist open. Blood welled, dripping onto his dirty white shirt. His fangs extended at the enticing smell, and his pupils turned red.

"Jax, you need to eat. You need to heal."

"No!" he roared. Before I realized what was happening, my back was pressed against the grimy stone wall and his lips were inches from mine. "I'm not going to allow you to trick me again, bitch."

My heart thrashed at the feral, unhinged glint to his eyes. Emotion gripped the organ in an impenetrable, steadily shrinking vise. I didn't know if it was fear for myself or worry for him.

"Jax, please. You're injured."

"No! Go away, Aaliyah! Go away!" Spittle flew from his mouth as he screamed.

"I'm not Aaliyah! It's me. Z. It's me!"

"Don't lie to me again!" he screamed. "I hate you!" His hands wrapped around my neck, no doubt leaving bruises, and tightened. My breath lodged in my throat as I struggled futilely against his impressive, enhanced strength.

"Jax," I wheezed, clawing at his hands. "Jax, please."

"Get out of my head!" His voice was anguished, a broken cry, and caused my heart to crumple.

"Jax..." Before I could finish, I was wrenched away

from my crazed vampire mate. I had one final moment to see his eyes, tainted with darkness and pain, before his features dissipated like smoke.

"Z, WE'RE HERE." Ryland shook my shoulder until I groggily opened my crusted eyelids. There was a pain in my neck from the awkward position I'd fallen asleep in, and my limbs felt like spaghetti.

"Huh? What?" I murmured, rubbing at my eyes. My skin felt raw and blotchy, as if I'd been crying. All I could recall were the snippets of the strangest dream...

Try as I might, I couldn't firmly grasp the elusive memory. It trickled through my mind like water in cupped palms.

"You okay?" Ryland asked worriedly. His shadowy hand touched my forehead and then my cheek. I swatted it away in irritation.

"I'm fine. Just a strange dream."

A dream that I couldn't remember, no matter how hard I strained.

Frowning, I stretched my taut muscles and surveyed our surroundings for the first time since I awoke.

Both cars appeared to be stopped in front of a modest, two-story log building. Numerous windows allowed a copious amount of light to escape through, illuminating the darkened parking lot. I didn't see the rest of my mates, and my worry increased instantly. I didn't like having them out of my sight. I knew they were big men and could protect themselves, but I liked the responsibility of watching over them falling solely on my shoulders. It made me feel...needed. Important. Somehow worthy of these seven men who'd clawed their way into my heart.

"We're at the inn for the night," Ryland explained, lazily running his fingers through my tangled hair. "We've been driving all day."

"Why didn't you wake me?" I demanded immediately, already pushing open the car door and grabbing my bow and arrows from my pack. Ryland chuckled darkly, placing a restraining hand on my shoulder.

"Because we're in the Vampire Kingdom now, my little dove. They don't take too kindly to humans." There was a bite to his tone that I hadn't heard before.

"Not even the kingdom's assassin?" I retorted, crossing my arms over my chest.

"Not even her," he replied easily. "Devlin is checking us into a couple rooms, and Killian is contacting Dair. When he wakes up, he's going to be livid that we left without him." There was a warning and a reprimand in his voice. Instantly, guilt flooded me like a ten-foot-tall tidal wave. I hadn't wanted to leave my mermaid mate behind, especially when he was still healing, but I didn't have a choice. We only had five days to find and rescue Jax. Defying the kings would lead to my inevitable death. I knew Dair would understand, but that didn't negate the crippling guilt and hurt.

"And Axel and company?" I asked dryly. I hadn't seen the ex-assassin yet this trip, thank fuck. I didn't know what I would do if I ran into him. Stab him with a spoon? Probably.

"Already checked in." Ryland's voice was tight, heady with tension, but before I could comment, he gripped my hand and pulled me towards the inn.

We'd just reached the front entrance when muffled voices reached me.

"...fucking dumbass," Bash hissed vehemently. "You need to fix it."

"I'm trying," Lupe snarled. The sound was so unlike my sweet bear shifter that I paused mid stride.

"You should tell her," Bash continued, ignoring Lupe's outburst. "Before she finds out—"

"Hello, boys," Ryland purred, interrupting my eaves-dropping. I knew he damn well did that on purpose. Stupid, sexy, shadowy asshole.

He dragged me towards the door where Bash and Lupe were huddled together, deep in conversation. Both men sprang apart, flashing me identical, sheepish smiles. Well, Lupe's was sheepish. Bash's just appeared annoyed, as if he couldn't decide whether he wanted to stab someone or stab himself.

"What's going on?" I queried, glancing from one man to the other. Ryland tightened his grip on my hand almost imperceptibly, tension thrumming through his body.

"Nothing," all three men said instantly. Bash threw Lupe a dirty look, eyes scathing, before turning towards Ryland.

"We need to talk about Z," Bash told the others, changing the subject.

"What about Z?" I asked, cocking my hip to the side and raising my eyebrow. Again, the guys exchanged wary looks.

"You're human," Lupe began, fumbling over those two words. Twin red splotches erupted on his cheeks.

"Wow. Do you want a reward for your detective skills?" I snarked. His blush deepened before he took a fortifying breath.

"You're human, Z, in a kingdom that considers humans food. You need to be careful and smart."

I glanced from one face to the next, but Bash refused to meet my inquiring gaze. And Ryland, the coward, remained in the shadows.

"What exactly do you mean?" I asked, my thin patience splintering. My hands balled into fists. "Spit it out."

"Oh, what the hell," Bash murmured before he lifted his head and met my gaze directly. His green eyes were speckled with flecks of gold, somehow making the color even more enticing and beautiful. "You can't be Z our mate while we're here. For your own protection. If they knew what you mean to us, if they knew you're our mate, they would kill you." He took another deep breath as if bracing himself for war. "While we're here, you need to be our servant. Our slave."

Could you really blame me for punching the asshole in the face?

NINE

DAIR

My sleep was restless. I tossed and turned all through the night, only to be woken by streaks of yellow from the moon penetrating the closed window.

Groaning, I rubbed my freshly healed cheek against my pillow. It smelled vaguely like my body cologne, though I would've much preferred to wake up beside Z's sweet, pomegranate smell.

Pain gripped my sore muscles as I stretched.

The last couple of weeks had been hell. I'd known my father would retaliate after I killed Tavvy, but I hadn't expected the extent of his delusions. Immediately upon our return, he strapped me to that disgusting bed in the slaves' quarters and removed both my legs. His blade had cut through tendons and bones, muscles and skin. His fist had been the only thing I saw as it repeatedly bashed into my skull. Blood ran down my cheeks in rivulets, staining my skin.

I'd seen my father mad hundreds of times before, but

never like this. Never this...enraged. As he destroyed me, flayed me, I didn't recognize the man looming above me. There was something distinctly manic about his smile and laugh. Before, his torture sessions had always been carefully controlled—a way to assert his dominance over his "disobedient son." I truly believed that killing Tavvy sent my father over the edge. He didn't love my older brother, but he did see him as an investment. His perfect, malevolent heir.

Now, Tavvy was dead, and he had to rely on my idiotic younger brothers to carry out his evil will.

Well, not my blood brothers, if Tavvy was to be believed. I didn't know if I could trust his incessant ramblings. He'd claimed that my brothers and I appeared out of thin air, but that sounded like rubbish to me. I didn't want to admit—even to myself—that Tavvy's words had stabbed at me, flaying me open until I was standing before him damaged and unloved. That I felt like the anomaly he'd always accused me of being. People didn't magically *appear*. I hadn't told the guys what he'd said, and I knew Z hadn't either, trusting me to follow my gut instinct.

No doubt, Tavvy had been lying, attempting to get one last rise out of me before he died.

But if it was true, if I truly wasn't related to my sadistic father and brothers, then that could explain why I was their favorite punching bag.

Fuck, I ache.

The last thing I remembered before unconsciousness mercifully claimed me was Z's angelic face. With her golden hair framing her heart-shaped face, she could've been an angel sent straight from heaven. An angel sent to save me and protect me. To smooth down my jagged edges and be the balm to fix my tattered soul.

I smiled wistfully at the thought of my perfect mate, stretching out my muscles once again. Father had given me a potion designed to accelerate my healing, but it healed everything except my severed legs.

Tears of indignation flooded my eyes. Those days with Z in the Mermaid Kingdom had been some of the best of my life. For the first time in my life, I'd felt like a man, someone worthy of Z. I still remembered the taste of her as she rode my face. Her pussy clenching around my cock. Her hands tangled in my hair.

My cock jumped to attention as pleasure bombarded me. What I wouldn't give to be balls deep in my perfect, beautiful, frightening mate...

"Control the tent in your pants, mermaid, before I cut it off," a familiar voice snarked. Atta flipped the lights on, instantly blinding me.

"What the hell are you doing here, Attie?" I questioned, using the nickname we all gave her when we were kids. Biologically, she was Lupe's sister, but we all loved her like she was our own. And pestering the feisty redhead was always a highlight of my day.

Her delicate lips pursed in distaste as she surveyed me on the bed. I didn't know what she knew about my condition, if she'd heard the full story or only parts of it, but either way, she wasn't pleased.

I was surprised to see her here. Don't get me wrong, I loved the girl fiercely, but I would much rather have woken up to my beautiful mate.

"Where's Z?" I asked. When her expression shuttered, the muscles around her eyes clenching, I felt my heart stutter. Worry pulsated through me like an electrical current. I sat straight up in bed, ignoring the slight sting as my muscles protested the sudden movement. "Is she hurt? Where the hell is she?"

"She's fine," Atta said immediately, worrying her lower lip with her teeth.

"And?" I searched the room until I found my wheelchair, resting against the wall. Atta, noticing the direction of my gaze, hurried forward to open the chair. "Where is she?"

"You're not going to like the answer," she admitted, stepping away as I used my arms to pull myself onto the chair. It was the one perk of being handicapped—I had arm muscles that most guys envied and most girls swooned over. I was strong enough to hold Z up and eat her out without breaking a sweat.

Yeah, I was smug, but could you really blame me?

"Where is she, Attie?" I repeated, turning towards the shifter princess.

Her lips curved downwards as she fiddled with the front of her dress. "She's with the others."

My eye fucking twitched.

"And?"

"And..." She blew out a raspberry. "They're traveling to the Vampire Kingdom to find Jax."

"What?" I exploded, already wheeling out of my room and into the makeshift kitchen. Sure enough, my tablet—powered by both magic and technology—was beeping with dozens of messages from my brothers.

I scanned through them all, my irritation at them and my fear for Z growing with every consecutive second. The Vampire Kingdom was notorious for their blood banks and human carnivals. I knew my brothers would protect her with their lives, but that knowledge didn't alleviate the worry pounding through me. I should be with them too. Me.

Instead, they had left me behind.

All of my earlier insecurities returned with a vengeance. Z had made me feel like I wasn't less of a man because of my handicap. Two legs or no legs, I was worthy of her love.

Still, she'd left me. I understood that they didn't have a choice, but worry still corroded away at my organs.

"They didn't want to leave you," Atta whispered, moving to stand behind me. She placed a hand on my shoulder and gave it a squeeze.

"I know," I replied with a nonchalance I didn't feel. I felt nothing but worry for Z and my brothers. Had they found Jax yet? Were they hurt? Fuck.

Scrubbing a hand through my golden locks, I focused once more on Atta. "Anything else?"

She wrung her hands together guiltily. "The kings made her take Axel."

"Axel?" I raised a brow. "The former assassin Axel?"

Atta nodded slowly, eyes cautious as she surveyed me.

If the kings wanted him to accompany Z…

That was a shit ton of bad.

"Anything else?" I asked through gritted teeth, and once more, Atta appeared indecisive. She chewed on her lower lip anxiously as she rocked back and forth. Finally, she shook her head once.

Yeah, like I fucking believed that. She was hiding something from me, but I could only pray that it didn't have anything to do with my mate.

Turning away from Atta, I focused once more on the glowing tablet. Killian had messaged me a few minutes earlier to tell me they'd arrived at an inn on the outskirts of the Vampire Kingdom. I didn't recognize the name, and my worry only intensified.

Unease skittered down my spine as I switched the tablet off and tossed it across the room. My breathing was heavy as I clenched and unclenched my hands by my sides.

"Your reaction is completely understandable," Atta assured me softly. "Your sin is envy. You're envious that Z's other mates are capable of doing what you can't. You're jealous that they're with her right now and you're not."

"What the hell are you trying to prove, Attie?" I snapped. "Make me feel bad? Make me feel like a shitty mate?"

"No." She shook her head, a whimsical smile playing on her lips. "I have an idea."

"And what is this idea? Go after her ourselves?" I'd considered it, but I knew I wouldn't be able to reach the inn before they left again. I could demand that they wait for me, but Killian had explained Z's strict time limit. Fuck the kings. Fuck them all to the deepest pit of hell, where they could rot with our ancestors.

"There's a pill that the resistance uses," she said,

lowering her voice to a whisper. I gaped at her, slack-jawed and shocked. Her words were very, very dangerous.

"What do you mean?" I tossed her a wary look that warned her to tread carefully.

Her smile was positively carnal, like the cat that caught a canary.

"It's a little green pill that a powerful mage can make. I know Diego used to make them for Z. It creates a portal to your home."

My confusion only grew. "But I'm here...and she's there."

"But is this place your home?" She cocked her hip out. "Or is that pretty mate of yours your home?"

I considered her words for a moment in stunned silence. Giddy glee cascaded through me as I looked up at my devious sister.

"Can you get me one of those pills?"

Atta's smile was capable of shriveling a snake into nothing more than a husk.

"What are sisters for?"

TEN

Z

"What the hell was that for?" Bash groaned, clutching his cheek.

"What the hell do you think?" I snapped back vehemently. "Are you seriously asking your *mate* to act like your slave?" Beneath the growing anger was something akin to hurt and frustration. I didn't like being considered less than my mates. Not at all. "Are you going to make me crawl on my hands and knees? Give you a blowjob?"

His eyes widened in horror before narrowing. "Fuck, no! You know we don't have an option."

"That's the stupidest thing I've ever heard," I retorted, glaring first at Bash, then Lupe, and then Ryland. "You're the princes, for fuck's sake. You can set a precedent." I was panting, my chest heaving, as I implored them with my eyes. Change started with one person, one brave soul willing to defy societal laws and norms.

"Not at the risk of your life," Lupe responded at last.

At my penetrating glare, he held his hands up placatingly. "I'm sorry."

"No, you're not," I hissed. When Bash procured a leash from his backpack, I just about fucking lost it. I knew my eyes were hurling daggers, but I couldn't find the words to articulately express how pissed I was. In a matter of minutes, they had belittled me and shamed me. I didn't feel like their mate. I felt like their property.

Annoyance and anger warred for dominance in the pit of my stomach, but shock kept them adequately subdued.

What type of world were we entering that made my mates behave like cavemen?

"Don't punch me again," Bash warned as he held up a sea blue collar. When I remained stubbornly silent, too angry to speak, he sighed. "We'll take it off of you as soon as we enter our rooms. We're doing this to protect you."

"And what about the hundreds of other humans experiencing the same treatment?" I bit out, allowing him to fasten the collar around my neck.

I felt like a fucking dog. A pet. I'd never experienced anything more humiliating.

Bash's lips pressed into a grim line, but he didn't respond.

When the collar was secured, he hooked the leash to it and wrapped the end around his fist.

"I know you're mad," Bash began, but again, all I managed to do was level him with a glare capable of freezing lava. "Do you think I like doing this? Do you think I enjoy seeing my mate on a fucking leash?"

"Oh, so now I'm your mate?" I said with a scoff. The

collar was dreadfully uncomfortable, scratching at my skin. Anger in the form of liquid heat sizzled through my system. "I thought you didn't believe in mates."

He gave me a long, indecipherable look. After a moment, he sighed and turned towards the lobby.

"Let's get you to your room. The sooner we get there, the sooner we can get this damn thing off of you."

I swore my anger was a living entity. It had festered in my belly like a tiny seed and gradually began to grow and grow. Now, there was a decent-sized hate plant blooming throughout my body. Its thorns rubbed against my heart, pressing down on the organ until blood seeped out.

With Bash leading the group, we entered a surprisingly modern and elegant lobby. The white flooring tiles had been polished so meticulously, I could see my reflection in them. Golden cherubs, each one with long fangs, lined the ceiling. Each cherub was laced with white veins that bled into the cream paint on the wall. I didn't know if I found it terrifying or beautiful.

A bored clerk sat behind a desk, his head resting on his hand, but he sat straight up when he caught sight of us. Leering, he gave me a critical once-over that instantly put him on my kill list. It was a really fucking long list.

"Your Highnesses," he said with a reverent bow of his head. Bash's expression was glacial as he tugged me along.

"I believe Prince Devlin already checked us in," he said as Lupe stood on one side of me and Ryland took the other.

The innkeeper's eyes flickered from me to the mage

prince and then back to me again. To my disgust, the fangs poking his bottom lip were coated in a strange, yellow substance. There was nothing I hated more than a vampire who couldn't keep up with basic hygiene.

"He didn't register a human," the innkeeper stuttered out. Despite his obvious unease, he gave me another lecherous look.

"She's with us," Lupe growled possessively. I just barely held in my snort. If he didn't want people knowing I was their mate, then he needed to tone down the mine claims.

"Humans go to the stables," the vampire countered with a haughty smirk. I had the distinct feeling that if I traveled to the stables, I wouldn't be coming back.

"She's with us," Ryland reiterated, tone almost indolent. He wrapped a shadowy arm around my shoulders. "Ours to do with as we please."

Oh, yeah. I was gutting that asshole as soon as we were alone.

The vampire seemed flustered, but thankfully, he didn't protest. With a nod, he gave the men their room and floor numbers.

"And!" he called to our retreating backs. "The human stays on her leash any time she leaves her room. We don't want her making a mess."

Before I could stab my knife through his neck, Bash pulled me into the stairwell.

"Cool it, Z," he hissed.

"You cool it," I retorted oh so wisely.

We didn't run into any nightmares or humans on the way we to our room on the second floor. Devlin had rented out two rooms to be split between my princes and me. Axel and the king appointed servants were staying in a room at the other end of the hall.

"How mad is she?" Devlin asked as soon as we stepped into the first room. He sat on the edge of the bed, methodically pulling off each sock and folding them. The man was anal about his clothing, that was for damn sure.

"*She* is fucking furious," I quipped, ripping the collar off my neck and tossing it at Lupe. "How could you guys do this to me?"

"We did what we needed to do to protect you," Lupe argued patiently, as if he were explaining a difficult math equation to a petulant child.

Angry tears burned my eyes, but I refused to let them fall. Absolutely refused. Despite my resolve, one traitorous tear escaped unbidden, trailing down my cheek.

"That was humiliating," I spat, wrapping my arms around my waist. "The way he looked at me..."

"I wanted to rip his eyes out of his skull," Lupe said darkly. His muscles flexed as anger darkened his eyes.

"He'll discover a very nasty surprise in his bed when we leave," Bash drawled.

"We're sorry we had to do that to you," Devlin added, rising from the bed and stepping in front of me. He placed his hands on my shoulders until I finally looked up at him. His violet eyes glimmered in the dim lighting, flecks of gold appearing. "I can't promise that it won't happen again, since we'll do what we need to in order to protect you. I can promise you that not one of us— including Bash—sees you as a slave or servant or anything less than the goddess you are."

Some of the anger melted out of me at the sincerity in his tone. I knew the guys didn't see me the way the rest of the population saw humans, but the pain and humiliation from earlier didn't entirely abate.

"I want to be alone," I admitted softly, stepping away.

Devlin hesitated, only briefly, before he nodded tersely. "Of course. We need to prepare dinner for tonight, and I need to check in on Killian. We'll be just next door, okay?"

I waved his words away dismissively. "Don't worry about me. I'll be fine."

All of my men hesitated in the doorway before one by one, they left me alone. There was no satisfaction when the door closed that final time. If anything, loneliness speared my chest. I wasn't truly mad at the guys, not really. I was more mad at the situation.

Why did we have to live in such a fucked-up world? And, more importantly, how could we fix it?

A single king-sized bed sat in the center of the room, flanked by two nightstands, and I moved to perch at the end. I kicked my shoes off before shimmying out of my pants. Then, with a wicked smirk, I bent down, revealing my panty-clad ass.

Ryland inhaled sharply, and my smile grew.

Pretending I didn't notice him lurking in the corner, I slid my shirt over my head and unhooked my bra. I allowed the bra straps to slide down my arms, but I didn't remove the garment all the way.

"So are you a voyeur only with me or with all the ladies?" I teased, glancing over my shoulder at the silhouette. "I don't know if that's romantic or creepy."

"Romantic," he purred, stalking closer. "Definitely romantic. And you should know by now, my precious Z, that everything revolves around you."

"Why are you still here, Ryland?" I asked, spinning to face him completely. I used one hand to hold up my bra while I placed the other on my hip, cocking it to the side.

"Because I know you," he said smoothly. "You're upset and embarrassed, but you don't want to be alone with your own thoughts."

I snorted. "You act like you know me, but how could you? I don't even know myself."

"Because I do," he insisted, gliding closer. His warm breath wafted across my cheek. "I'm a shadow, Z. I live my life hiding in the darkness and watching. Always watching." His hand cupped my cheek, stroking the skin tenderly. "But if you want me to leave, I will. I'll do anything you ask, Z, except put your life at risk."

I considered the man before me. With the shadows misting around him, I couldn't see his face. It was ironic, in a way, that he demanded complete and absolute truth from me, yet he still hid. The shadows were his armor, and no number of weapons could penetrate it.

"Fine, you can stay. On one condition." I leaned even closer. "You let me see you."

If he was going to see me, all of me, the good and the bad, then it was only fair.

Ryland hesitated before he took a deep breath, dropping the shadows that always seemed to accompany him.

His white scars stood out on his onyx skin, curving his lips downwards and slicing through one of his eyes.

Still, he was beautiful. Ruggedly handsome and sexy, with broad shoulders leading down to a tapered waist.

"Why do you hate it?" I whispered, cupping his scarred cheek. He flinched at the contact, eyelids closing, before he reopened them.

"Because I'm hideous." He covered my hand with his own.

"It's you." There were no other words to describe it.

His body shuddered at my words, and he took a step closer until his forehead could rest against my own.

"I'm sorry about what happened earlier," he said, his icy blue eyes searching mine. The last wisps of my rage dissipated as I sagged against him.

"I know," I whispered, kissing his wrist.

A smirk pulled up his lips. "The only time I'll ever tie you up is in the bedroom."

Yup. I was pretty sure my panties just soaked through.

"Huh?"

Smart, Z. Smart.

"Tell me, Z, have you ever been tied up before?" he questioned as my heart volleyed around in my chest.

"Is that something you...like?" I asked curiously. With Devlin, I was always in charge. He liked it when I dominated him, and I liked it when he submitted. The sex with S had been strictly vanilla. What would it be like with Ryland? To give him complete and utter control of my mind and body? Ironically enough, I'd been pissed only minutes before because of a damn collar and leash. Now, I was intrigued. I'd been ordered around once before by Killian, but I wasn't sure if the incubus had even realized what he was doing.

But Ryland?

He definitely knew what he was doing.

The backs of my knees hit the bed as Ryland took a step closer. "Is it something you want to try?"

Fucking hell. I was a puddle of goo for this man. Heat sizzled through my veins, settling directly in my core.

"What else do you like to do?" I murmured, and his smile only grew, white teeth blinding against his dark skin.

"Get on your knees on the bed," he instructed, "and I'll show you."

Heart hammering, I did as he asked, my bra sliding the rest of the way down my arms in the process. My pussy was already wet for him, greedy for him.

Instead of giving me what I desired—namely, his cock —he paced behind me. I could feel his eyes caressing my skin, looking but not touching.

I moaned something inarticulate, and his hand slapped down on my ass. The brief stab of pain made me jump, and I released a gasp of pleasure. Who would've thought I'd like something like that?

"Don't move," he snapped. "Don't make a noise until you have permission. Is that understood?"

When I remained silent, unsure of what he wanted, he spanked my ass again. "I asked you a question."

"Yes," I gasped out. My ass cheek was still tingling, but his methodical strokes helped ease the ache.

"Yes...?"

"Yes, sir?" It came out more as a question.

When he kissed my spine, I knew I'd gotten it right. I'd never been a sub before, so this was new territory. And...

And I liked it.

"Since this is your first time doing something like this, I'll ease you into it, understand?"

"Yes, sir," I replied with growing confidence.

"Good girl." He bit down on my ass, his mouth wetting the thin material of my panties. "Now, we need a safe word."

"Safe word?" I asked, glancing at him over my shoulder. He'd removed his shirt, revealing his dark skin covered in crisscrossing scars.

Fortunately, or perhaps unfortunately, he didn't punish me for speaking and moving out of turn. Instead, his hands kneaded my fleshy globes, eliciting wave after wave of pleasure.

"You say the word, and I'll stop no matter what. No matter what we're doing or how we're doing it. Understand? Tell me you understand, little dove."

"Pancake," I blurted, cheeks flaming when I realized what I'd said. Still, I wasn't going to back down now. "My safe word will be pancake." He chuckled darkly, but he didn't comment, thank fuck. I probably would've died of embarrassment.

Obviously, Ryland had done this before. Probably dozens of times. I didn't know how to be submissive, but for him, I was willing to try. I knew that if I didn't like it, he wouldn't be upset. However, I wanted to do this for him. For us.

"Pancake it is," he whispered, kissing up my ass and

to my spine. He continued planting tantalizingly light kisses until he reached my neck. Brushing away my hair, he pressed his lips to my neck and then my ear. "But I'm not gonna fuck you today."

"What?" I whimpered pathetically, arching my hips. He slapped first one ass cheek and then the other, tsking in disapproval.

"You accept what I give you." He wrapped my hair around his fist, the way Bash had held my leash, and lifted my head until my entire back was pressed to his chest. With his other hand, he squeezed my breasts, twisting and plucking at my sensitive nipples. I thought I was going to die if he didn't touch me between my legs.

Before I could beg, he released me and stepped away from the bed. My body immediately cried out, but I kept my mouth shut. I could be quiet if orgasms were the reward. As silent as a mime.

A moment later, Ryland returned to the bed with the leash.

"Are you okay with this, little dove?" he asked, dangling it in front of my face. I murmured an inarticulate affirmative. "I need words."

"Yes...yes, sir," I managed to squeak out. He spun me around so I was now on my back, his knees on either side of my waist. He glanced at my bare breasts before focusing on my hands. With practiced efficiency, he gripped my wrists and held them above my head. Quickly, he tied my hands together with the leash and then tied them both to the headboard. The position caused my back to arch, my tits brushing against his naked chest.

"Is it too tight?" he asked, trailing his fingers back down my arms and to my neck.

"No, sir," I replied. Fuck, I needed him. I needed... something. Was that how I was going to die? Spontaneous combustion because my damn mate didn't pleasure me in time? Wouldn't that be a kick to the nuts? Survived the Damning but died because I didn't get an orgasm. I would be so pissed. The least the world could do was lube me before it fucked me in the ass.

He focused on each of my breasts, giving them equal attention, before licking down my stomach. His scarred skin was rough against my own, but it only amplified the pleasure.

With a mischievous smile befitting my playful mate, he caught the hemline of my panties with his teeth and slowly began to pull them down.

I was a writhing mess beneath him, desperate for his lips, his cock, his fingers, anything, to enter my slick channel. I needed him with an intensity that frightened me.

"Do you want me, little dove?"

"Yes!" He swatted at my tits, watching them sway. Fuck, that was sexy.

"Yes, what?"

"Yes, sir."

With another grin, he placed his dark, calloused hands on either of my thighs, prying them apart. "I'm going to enjoy eating you out," he murmured, planting kisses on my skin. "You're going to scream my name before I even enter you."

"Fuck, yes," I groaned. Immediately, he dropped his face between my legs and devoured me like a starving man. He alternated between teasing flicks of his tongue and the grazing of his teeth against my sensitive nub. I was nearly mindless with pleasure, the leash around my wrists only adding to the stimulation. "Ryland!" I cried.

"Come for me," he whispered against my mound, his teeth tugging on my clit.

I exploded. Wave after wave of pleasure cascaded through me as I let out a wordless cry. The orgasm positively destroyed me, wrecked me, in the best possible way.

"Fuck, fuck, fuck, fuck!" I screamed, arching my back as I crested over the edge.

The door to the hotel room was abruptly pushed open, and Bash, Lupe, and Devlin rushed inside. Lupe was carrying an axe, and Devlin had magic crackling in his palms.

"What's going on? Are you okay?" Bash demanded, but he, along with the others, paused when he caught sight of me. The hunger and wanton need in his eyes were impossible to miss. "Oh, fuck."

BASH

Did I feel like an asshole dragging my mate through the hotel lobby on a leash? Hell yes.

Did I get turned on when she punched me in the face? Hell to the fucking yes.

And did my cock turn into a motherfucking rock when I entered the room to see her naked and tied up? No comment.

My eyes greedily moved over her exposed flesh. Perfect tits. Nipples beaded to nubs. A perfect pink pussy slick with arousal. Golden hair disheveled giving her a *just fucked* appearance.

Yup, I would be sporting a boner for days now, thank you very much. My hand and I would become very close acquaintances. Mr. Hand, meet the python. Python, meet Mr. Hand. Heaven knew I wouldn't get any loving from Z.

The girl hated me, not that I blamed her. I was, admittedly, a jerk to her. I didn't believe in mating bonds and fate and all that shit. Who was the universe to decide who my perfect girl was? But then...Z arrived in my life with a nasty right hook and a body that put others to shame, and I was instantly smitten.

Not that I would tell her.

Fuck, I really was an asshole, wasn't I?

Unwilling to torture myself a moment longer with things I could never have, I spun on my heel and exited the room.

Fuck, fuckity fuck. Even the hallway reeked of sweat and sex. The enticing aroma did funny things to my cock. Okay, maybe not so funny. You try walking with an elephant trunk protruding from your nether region.

Grimacing, I made my way into the second room and then ran to the bathroom. I needed a cold shower, stat.

I gripped the edge of the sink, lungs burning and heart racing. What did this girl do to me? She unraveled me, that was what she did. She took what little control I had and smashed it into thousands of pieces.

I'd had my fair share of girls before, but none like Z. None that made me want to go back a second, third, or fourth time. None that made me want to write fucking sonnets and learn to play the guitar.

We were two peas in a pod, her and I, but this pod was laden with explosives.

I made quick work of removing my clothes and stepping beneath the freezing spray of water. It pelted my skin, each drop the equivalent of a hundred tiny knives.

All I could picture was Z. She had been glorious post orgasm, her pouty lips opened in a scream and her face flushed. Those eyes, those damn eyes, had emanated nothing but love and lust, enough to drive any warm-blooded man insane.

I wanted her. No, I didn't just want her. I needed her. She was as essential to my well-being as breathing or eating. She was the air I inhaled, the blood pumping through my heart.

And...

I was officially a sappy romantic. Fuck. Me.

I wrapped my hand around the base of my cock, tugging once. Instead of my hand, I visualized her bright red lips wrapped around it, her eyes staring up at me through her fringe of ebony lashes.

Before I'd even met her, I'd had dreams about her and me. Laughing, cuddling, talking. From the first moment I saw her, I knew she would change my life irrevocably. I just hadn't realized how much.

I began to stroke myself faster and faster, my other hand fondling my balls. I was seconds from exploding, seconds from squirting my cum on the shower walls. Just one more...

"Bash!" Killian raced into the bathroom just as I reached that cliff and tumbled over the edge.

What. The. Fuck?

The incubus's eyes widened in shock and horror just before he turned on his heel, facing the wall opposite the shower.

"What the hell are you doing, Kill?" I griped. If there was one thing that could kill a boner, it was having your brother walk into the bathroom mid masturbation. Well, maybe not mid. I *did* finish.

"You didn't have a sock," he stammered, his stutter more pronounced with his unease.

"A sock?" I sometimes wanted to slug him across the face. With an axe.

"You're supposed to have a sock on the doorknob when you're, um, going to pound town," he continued, his tattooed neck turning bright red the longer he talked.

First, 'pound town' implied that my cock was actually entering a pussy. Which, unfortunately, it wasn't.

Second...

"Killian, Killian, Killian." I flipped the shower off and grabbed a fluffy white towel off the rack. Wrapping it around my waist, and my now flaccid dick, I pushed past Killian and entered the sparsely furnished room. "When a man is in the shower, you don't fucking enter."

Yup. I was pretty sure he was still confused.

"I've seen you naked hundreds of times," Killian pointed out as I slipped on a pair of shorts and a shirt. When he realized how his words could be construed, he turned crimson, scratching at the back of his neck. "That sounded really, really creepy."

"You don't say?" I taunted dryly, collapsing on one of the queen-sized beds. We were going to have to double up, and I was under no disillusion that Z would want me in her bed, in the next room over. Nope, your man Bash was going to be spooning one of his brothers while his mate fucked a different guy.

Deciding to end this painfully awkward conversation, I asked, "Did you message Dair?"

Killian blew out a breath, relieved at the subject change. "I did. He hasn't responded back, but he's probably still sleeping." His face tightened with pain and something akin to anger. Well, at least as much anger as someone like Killian was capable of having. "I can't believe his dad did that. Why didn't he tell us?"

I'd wondered that too, numerous times. We were his brothers, closer than blood, yet he never admitted that his father continually grew his legs back only to cut them off. Again and again and again. If we would've known, we would've...

Would've what?

The seven of us were strong, sure, and it was rumored we'd grow even stronger, but we were no match for our fathers. Maybe if it was only the fourteen of us, but the kings had something we didn't—armies and leverage. They dangled our loved ones over our heads like tasty morsels we were tempted to bite down on.

"He's gonna be pissed," I pointed out matter-of-factly.

"He's going to be furious," Kill corrected. He suddenly sighed, forking his fingers through his tangled red hair. "What about Z? How mad is she?"

"On a scale of one to ten, I'll say she's a solid one thousand. I'm pretty sure she'd skin me alive if she had the chance."

Killian winced, eyeing me reproachfully. Out of all of us, he'd been the only one against leashing Z like a fucking dog. He understood why we had to, but he didn't like it. Not one bit. It was for that reason alone that Devlin instructed him to reach out to Dair and Atta.

He was too soft, too compassionate, to do what needed to be done.

"She seems to have forgiven Ryland," Killian pointed out, nodding towards the wall separating us from them. "I can feel the lust in the air. She...she did the sex with him, didn't she?"

My cock instantly went rock hard as I recalled the scene I'd walked in on. I would give my right nut to be in his position. Okay, maybe not my right one. That was personally my favorite—if a dude could have a favorite ball. But my left one? That was gone.

Wait...

'The sex'?

No, Killian. Just no.

"We need to discuss the plan," I pointed out.

Killian noticeably blanched. "She's not going to like it."

"I don't give a fuck what she likes," I snapped. Not true. I cared too damn much. "We need to keep her safe, regardless of her personal preference. The vamps would eat her alive if she challenged them."

Kill pursed his lips but didn't bother to correct me. Good. I wasn't in the mood to get into an argument with my best friend. Instead, I was content to fall into a deep sleep and dream of Z's pussy clenched around my cock.

The others could bear the brunt of her anger. This mage? He was done for tonight. And tomorrow. And maybe the next day.

I didn't think I'd survive another episode of Z's rage. I might just come in my pants if she punched me again. Messed up? Probably. But also very, very true.

Z

"Absolutely fucking not." I crossed my arms over my chest, body thrumming with a sizzling heat. I'd grabbed a robe from the bathroom, and now I stood in front of my mates with narrowed eyes.

"Baby, don't be like this," Devlin pleaded. His olive-toned skin was paler than I remembered it being, almost like he was afraid of me. Or afraid of my reaction to his words. Smart man.

"It's for your own protection," Lupe added gruffly. He crossed his muscular arms, mimicking my own pose, as my eyes narrowed further.

"Tying me up and treating me like a dog is for my own protection?" I snapped. An elemental fury was brewing just beneath the surface like a kettle over a fire. Any second now, it was going to explode. *I* was going to explode.

"We don't want to do it," Devlin argued in irritation. "But when we're in public—"

"Which we will be the majority of the time," I pointed out.

"—you'll have to act like our human servant."

I clenched my jaw so tightly, I was pretty sure a bone or two broke. Did he even hear himself?

The Alphabet Resistance was formed to protect humans from this exact thing. To rescue those who were used and sold like cattle. This was going against everything I believed, everything I stood for. I knew, logically, that it was nothing more than an act, but the prospect of being paraded around like prized stock fractured that tremulous hold I had on my sanity. What about those humans who didn't go home to loving mates every night? Whose entire existence wasn't based on an act?

Shouldn't we be taking a stand against this bigotry instead of playing right into it?

Arguing would get us nowhere, and frankly, I was too damn tired to mount another protest. I cared about these ridiculous men, more than I even wanted to admit, but that didn't mean I agreed with them.

"Look, I'm tired and I don't want to argue. We can talk in the morning, okay?" I scrubbed a hand down my face. "And this time, I mean it when I say I want to be alone." I gave Ryland a pointed stare. Already, he'd retreated to the shadows, his striking features obscured by a dark mist. It pained me that he once again felt the need to hide, but I couldn't judge him. I hid every damn day of my life. Behind Z, the assassin. Behind Zara, the assistant. Behind Susan, the poor, defenseless human. I wore so many faces that I struggled to recognize my real one.

Silence engulfed us for a long, tense moment. I could tell none of them wanted to leave while we were in the midst of an argument, but at the same time, what could they do? This wasn't something they were willing to compromise on.

And I wasn't willing to forgo my own morals in exchange for my safety.

"Fine," Devlin agreed. When he made a move to kiss me, I ducked my head. His kisses were worse than crack. I was utterly addicted to them. I knew that if I let him, he would make me forget all of my anger and hurt. However, I needed to hold on to them. I needed to remember who I was and what I was fighting for.

He blew out a breath, face twisting, before he pecked me on the forehead. "I love you," he whispered sincerely. "More than anything."

And that was what scared me.

THIS WAS the first night in weeks I'd slept alone.

The bed felt even bigger without a warm body engulfing mine.

Sleep evaded me. I tossed and turned, unable to get comfortable in a bed that wasn't my own.

Was I behaving ridiculously? I didn't know for sure. All I knew was that my people were being suppressed while the nightmares flourished. I supposed I'd just thought...

I'd just assumed...

I'd thought my mates were better than that.

After another fitful attempt at sleep, I pushed back the blankets and climbed out of bed. The room was kept painfully cold, forcing me to wrap a quilt around my shoulders.

I had the irresistible desire to punch something, to find a semi healthy outlet for all of my pent-up anger. I knew I couldn't leave the inn, but I could do what I wanted in the safety of my room.

My decision made, I changed out of my nightgown and into shorts and a revealing sports bra. I made quick work of moving the furniture to the perimeter of the room until there was an immense circle directly in the center.

B, the leader of the Alphabet Resistance, had drilled into my head how important stretching was before any strenuous exercise. Now, the languid stretches were second nature to me.

Placing my hands on the ground, I arched my back until my ass was straight up in the air. Of course, that position made me think about Ryland's hand spanking said ass, and heat flooded my system. I hadn't thought I would've liked something like that, but what the hell did I know? There was a fine line between pleasure and pain, and I was balancing precariously on it.

Fuck, if I wasn't livid with him and the others, I would've invited them all back and alternated between them in bed. Yes, even Bash. I was an equal opportunity lover.

My smirk faded when knuckles rapped on my door. Frowning, I straightened, pushing back a strand of my golden blonde hair.

"Who is it?" I snapped. I wasn't stupid. I knew that

this kingdom wasn't safe for humans like me, and the last thing I was going to do was let a stranger in.

"It's me," a familiar voice announced. And then, sounding flustered, he added, "Killian."

Smiling widely, I lunged towards the door and wrenched it open. Sure enough, my incubus stood in the doorway, his red hair tousled and his delicious tattoos on display. He wore only a pair of low-slung sweatpants, and damn, the man was a work of art. A vine swirled up his chest and over his left pectoral, dozens of roses extending from it. There appeared to be a pocket watch on his opposite side, the golden color a startling contrast to his lightly tanned skin. More tattoos lined his muscular forearms and bulging biceps—a snake, a fractured heart, and a face that looked eerily similar to my own.

"I wanted to check in on you," he admitted, running his fingers through his hair. Halfway through, they got stuck in a tangle, and he made a face as he pulled at the garnet strands. Finally, he freed his fingers and awkwardly shuffled from foot to foot. "How are you? I mean, you're obviously not fine. If it makes you feel better, Devlin, Lupe, and Ryland are all sleeping on the floor in the room next door. Bash and I claimed the two beds." His lips twisted upwards in amusement before straightening once more. "They're truly sorry. You know that they care about you. Just to let you know, I've been against this plan from the start."

I breached the remaining distance between us and wrapped my arms around his waist. He hesitated, only briefly, before returning my embrace.

"That does make me feel better," I admitted.

"The way some people treat humans is awful," Killian continued, lowering his cheek to my head. "I wish I could change it."

"But you can, Kill." I pulled back to look at him directly in the eyes. "You're going to be king soon. You and the rest of them."

"That's assuming the old bastards ever die," he pointed out with a sardonic twist to his lips.

My muscles locked together at the underlying threat in his voice. The spell the kings put on me, the spell making me the official assassin, didn't allow me to harm them. Hell, it didn't even allow me to talk about harming them. I would be forced to fight against anyone, including my mates, who dared to even attempt it.

"Let's not talk about that," I murmured, rubbing a hand up and down his back. His skin was warm beneath my palm, an inferno, and that heat migrated straight to my core.

"I don't want you to think—" Killian's words cut off with an enraged snarl, unlike anything I'd ever heard before. His eyes widened with horror as he stumbled forward, blood coating his lips.

"Kill!" I screamed, eyes flickering from his pale face to the scaly tail protruding from his back. As I watched, horrified, the tail left his body and wrapped around its owner.

"Hello, Z," a sly voice said. He was unlike anything I'd ever seen before. It looked like a humanoid snake, green and black scales covering his cheeks and slithering body. Those eyes, though, carried an intelligence and coherence that contrasted with his snake body. His tail was the width of a small car and seemed to be hewn from pure muscle.

When we were researching extinct supernatural creatures, descended from lesser sins, we'd stumbled across this exact monster. A snake-like creature with a poison so deadly, it could kill the most powerful nightmare in seconds.

A basilisk.

THIRTEEN

Z

Rocking on the balls of my feet, I allowed my gaze to momentarily rest on Killian. Fuck, his skin was pale and clammy, a fine layer of sweat coating his ruddy cheeks. Blood seeped through the wound on his back, staining the floor red.

"What did you do to him?" I whispered darkly. If this asshole thought he could get away with hurting my mate, he had another thing coming. My fist, for one. Probably up his anus.

"My tail, sweetheart." His forked tongue slithered out of his mouth, wetting his scaly lips. The man—creature—was grotesque. Hideous. He was the thing nightmares were made of. "It's poisonous...as is my blood."

Picture the largest, slimiest snake you could think of. Now picture that snake with a decidedly male head. He made the gorgon from before look like a sex goddess. Hell, even Slippy was prettier, and krakens were ugly as sin.

The door to the next room burst open, and the rest of

my mates emerged in the hall. They took one look at the basilisk before breaking into action.

Lupe charged forward first, shedding his human skin and rising up on his furry hind legs. His bear was larger, nearly the size of the basilisk, and had beady black eyes that seemed to swirl like twin abysses. He swatted a paw at the basilisk, releasing a thundering roar.

"Careful," I screamed, stepping over Killian to reach for my dagger. "His tail is poisonous." I glanced help-lessly at my mate, horror consuming me. Before I allowed it to grow and fester, I smothered it beneath an ironclad wall. I would save Killian...after I killed the monster.

Bash pushed through the others, hands cupped as a ball of flame appeared between them. It grew and grew until it was an inferno of molten red interwoven with streaks of orange and yellow. It blasted through the air, hitting the creature on the side of its scaly head. The basilisk hissed, fangs piercing his distorted lower lip, but he didn't back down.

"I'll let your men live if you come with me," he murmured silkily. It was a voice designed to seduce and entice, though why anyone would be attracted to a hideous lizard man was beyond me. "I'll even provide a cure for the incubus."

"A cure?" I asked, pausing with the dagger raised. Behind me, Bash faltered slightly, the fireball dissipating as quickly as it arrived. Killian was his best friend, his brother. If this monster knew how to cure him, then his death would have to wait.

The basilisk smirked and extended his hand in offer-ing. "Come with me, and your mate will live."

"No way in hell!" Devlin snapped, lunging forward and wrapping his arms around the creature's neck. At least I was assuming it was his neck. The basilisk struggled, his tail rising from the floor and sharpening dangerously until it resembled a spear. When it was seconds from piercing Devlin's back, I jumped forward, blade raised. I slashed down on the basilisk's tail, guts and other unsavory substances erupting from his punctured skin.

I turned my face before any of the goo could touch my skin, but a dollop of green liquid landed on my cheek. Immediately, blistering pain erupted on the tiny swath of exposed skin. It felt like acid was corroding away my muscles and bones, as if every one of my nerve cells were alive and singing.

Crying out, I fell backwards and landed on the floor beside Killian. He turned his head to stare at me, and in his gaze, I saw nothing but agony. The pain emanated from his mossy gaze like proverbial fireworks.

Adrenaline shot through my veins as I forced myself back on my feet. If I had to, I would torture the information out of this fucker.

"How do you get rid of the poison?" I snapped, wobbling on my feet. My heart thundered in my ears.

I always knew Killian was too sweet, too pure, for this world. I just never expected that I would be the cause of his death.

The basilisk laughed, his throaty voice grating on my nerves. My entire body ached fiercely, but still, I pressed on. Was that love? Putting someone else before yourself?

"Tell me!" I screamed, spit flying.

He opened his distorted mouth, eyes glimmering

with mirth, when he suddenly lurched forward. Shock crossed his disgusting face as blood formed at the edges of his scaly mouth. With one last wide-eyed glance at me, he collapsed, black ichor pooling around him. Before my very eyes, his tail seemed to shrivel up, the green and gold scales transforming into hideous shades of black and brown.

Behind him, holding what appeared to be an elephant's tusk, was Axel, the former assassin. The lines on his face were hard and unforgiving as he glanced from the fallen monster to me.

"A basilisk can only be killed by an elephant's tusk dipped in unicorn blood," he admitted nonchalantly, removing the weapon from the creature's body. He wiped the black blood on the hem of his shirt before finally meeting my eyes. "Now, are you going to grab his scales before they completely decompose, or do I have to do that too?"

"What?" Now that the adrenaline had worn off, I collapsed back to my knees. Devlin was there in a second, one arm wrapped around my waist, while his hand hovered anxiously over my body as he helped me lie down on the ground.

Axel sighed heavily as if I were purposely being dense.

"A scale," he repeated, rolling his dark eyes. "It's the only known cure for the poison."

"How the fuck do you know that?" Bash demanded, moving to stand in front of both Killian and me. Lupe remained in his bear form, growling threateningly. I knew he was only seconds away from slicing open Axel's throat with his paw.

When I tried to confront Axel, blood erupted from my mouth.

Was I dying?

Fuck, I wasn't ready to die. Not yet. I hadn't reached my orgasm quota yet.

"Does it matter?" Devlin hissed, but his voice was muffled as if I were hearing it through earplugs. My genie stomped forward, magic crackling around his skin in a purple mist, and removed a dagger from his waistband. "This better fucking work!"

"It will," Axel replied lazily as Devlin sliced at the basilisk's scales.

"No, Killian..." I murmured as Devlin knelt before me. Killian first. Killian. First.

But the pain was excruciating, sweeping over my body like lightning, and I was barely holding on to consciousness. I dragged in a lungful of air and pushed myself onto my hands and knees. I'd been broken and reborn in pain my entire life. I knew it as intimately as an old friend. Pain? We went way back. Exchanged Christmas cards and everything.

Devlin gently but forcefully opened my mouth and shoved the scale inside. I only had a second to pray that it had been motherfucking sanitized before darkness consumed me.

I WAS BACK inside the grimy cell, heart thundering as I took in my surroundings.

Like before, there was only a single candle illuminating the gray walls and compressed dirt floor. This time, however, Jax wasn't hunched over in the corner of the room.

Instead, he hung suspended from the wall. His arms and legs were tied to wooden posts in an uncomfortable X position. Blood coated his chest and arms like a second skin, the wound I'd noticed before haphazardly bandaged. His head lolled against his chest as he released crazed spurts of laughter.

"Come back for more, bitch?" he hissed, fangs poking his bottom lip.

On closer inspection, I saw that he was naked, and horror filled me at the sight. What had been done to him? I wanted to murder everyone who'd played a hand in his torture. No, not just murder. Maim. I wanted to fucking maim them all.

"Jax," I cried in horror, immediately running to him. His wrists and ankles were tied with rope, but my knife did quick work on releasing him. "Who the hell did this to you? Do you know where you are? We're coming for you."

He scoffed, collapsing to the ground when the final rope was cut. "Do you expect me to believe you, Z?" He said my name as if he didn't believe it, as if it were a dirty curse word. "Your illusions don't work on me."

"What illusions?" I begged, dropping to my knees before him. He continued to eye me with obvious aversion and fear. Panic flitted through me at the thought that my mate didn't recognize me. "I'm Z, and you're Jax. You're

my mate." Hesitantly, I reached forward to place my hand on his chest, just above his heart. He flinched at the contact but didn't immediately pull away. Good. That was good. "You can feel me, can't you?" I grabbed his bloody hand and placed it over my own chest.

Silence engulfed us as our hearts beat as one.

His lower lip began to tremble as tears filled his eyes. Wonder and awe brightened his haggard features. His hand shook as he moved it up my chest and to my cheek. His palm was calloused and rough as he stroked patterns. Heat exploded from where he touched me, traveling to the tips of my fingers and the soles of my feet.

"Z?" he whispered. "Is that really you?"

I covered his hand with my own. "Of course, vamp," I said with a wobbly smile. "And I'm going to bust you out of here."

"You shouldn't be here," Jax continued. "It's not safe."

"Don't worry about me," I whispered, stroking his light brown hair with my free hand. "I'm safe."

He released a choked sob, body shaking, as he crawled onto my lap. I was stunned into silence as he cuddled against me, his body shockingly cold against my overheated one.

"Please don't leave me," he sobbed, clutching at my shirt. I stroked a hand down his bare back, being extra careful not to touch the lacerations zigzagging across his skin. Acid formed in my throat as I thought about all he'd endured and all he would continue to endure.

I had to get to him. Now.

There was no other alternative.

"I won't leave you," I vowed, kissing his forehead.

But karma was a twisted bitch who liked to fuck me in the asshole with no lube.

Just as the promise left my lips, the cell around me began to dematerialize. My surroundings became fuzzy and warped as if I were seeing them through modified glasses.

The last thing I saw was Jax's horrified, betrayed face and his lips opened in an anguished cry.

I tried to run back to him, tried to hold him, but soon, he disappeared from view too.

The last thing I heard was his agonized scream.

FOURTEEN

DEVLIN

Z shifted in the plush bed, allaying some of my worries and fears. I'd been restless the past hour, unable to sleep, eat, or even function until I knew she was all right. Axel had assured me that the scale would work, but I needed to see it for myself before I could believe it.

Fuck, I'd almost lost her. *We* had almost lost her.

My eyes drifted to Killian lying beside her, his face serene in sleep. My heart splintered down the center. Fissures cracked the organ open until it was almost unrecognizable.

We'd almost lost him too.

His face had been nearly gray before we'd fed him the scale, but he still managed to murmur Z's name like a prayer.

"Thank you," Lupe murmured softly behind me, extending a large hand to the assassin. Axel eyed it cautiously, almost curiously, before accepting it. The man didn't smile. He didn't even blink. His eyes were apathetic, hard chips of stone.

"They'll be unconscious for the next hour or two," he stated gruffly. He folded his arms over his chest, turning away from the shifter. His penetrating gaze landed on Z, but I wasn't able to read the expression in his eyes. He was a blank fucking book, which only made me more uneasy. "We leave in the morning." With that declaration, he stomped out of the room.

"Did you hear the prick?" Bash snarled. He sat beside the bed, idly playing with Z's limp fingers. "He's not the fucking boss."

"I don't trust him," I said immediately, swallowing around the walnut-sized lump in my throat.

"Me neither," Lupe added. He moved to stand directly beside me, scrubbing at his face. To Bash, he asked, "Can you do anything to speed up the healing?"

Bash's lips pushed out as an unreadable emotion flitted across his face. His hand tightened over Z's, veins popping, before he slowly relaxed.

"Did you know that I'm able to see an entire human body when I heal someone?" Bash queried, almost conversationally. Despite his nonchalant tone, I could hear an undercurrent of...of something. I couldn't put my finger on what.

"Huh?" Lupe asked, quirking a brow.

"I can see their organs, their blood. If they have a heart murmur, I can sense that. If they have elevated white blood cells, I can sense that. If they've been poisoned, I can sense that..." Bash trailed off, scrubbing his hand through his blond hair. "Fuck, don't listen to an old man's—err...young man's ramblings. I'm just stressed."

I stared at my brother curiously but didn't press. We all handled our emotions differently. I bottled them in, sealed them, protected them from the world. Bash, on the other hand, allowed them to run rampant, each word a dagger hurling towards its target. Before Z, he would often hide his pain behind booze and girls. Now, his pain, anger, and fear emerged as verbal assaults.

"I'm going to look over the map," I murmured, unable to sit here and do nothing. Fuck, I needed my girl and my brother to open their damn eyes before I lost my mind.

Knowing that Lupe and Bash would look after them, I moved briskly to the adjacent room. The door was still open from when we'd all raced out.

I froze, staring at the hallway with unseeing eyes. My mind was elsewhere, an hour back in time, when we'd first stumbled onto the scene. That...that creature had been threatening my mate, our mate. He would've killed Killian and taken Z.

My mind swarmed with everything I knew about Aaliyah. Which was, admittedly, nothing at all.

I knew that she was after my mate for reasons unknown. I knew that she had an army at her disposal, tattoos etched on their shoulder blades designating them as loyal followers.

But why? None of it made sense. Z worked for the Alphabet Resistance, sure, but so did hundreds of other people. What made her the target?

I hadn't told Z my theory—that Aaliyah was somehow behind Jax's disappearance. It was too much of a coincidence for me to think otherwise. Jax disappeared...at the same time Z was being attacked by extinct supernatural creatures. First the fae, then the revenant, then the gorgon, then the kraken, and now the basilisk.

When will it end?

I moved into my room on quiet feet, eyes immediately fixating on my golden lamp peeking through my backpack.

Lamps were the symbols of all genies. As a descendant of Greed, we relied religiously on deals and contracts. A person had three wishes...but there was always a cost.

Usually, your soul.

A lamp was, essentially, a cage for trapped souls.

My own lamp was a color that was somewhere between yellow and gold. Amber, almost, with a black bottom. Unlike a lot of other genies, I had no jewels encrusted on the sides. Instead, I kept it plain and simple.

The lamp wasn't something I was proud of.

I'd made a deal with a fellow genie, Laurel, in exchange for my previously missing lamp. A deal I still had yet to pay. If I failed to uphold my end of the bargain, she would own my soul.

But, fuck, how could I do what she asked of me?

My heart hammered in my chest as I stared at the lamp. Despite being tucked away in my pack, it seemed to glimmer with its own personal sheen.

Before I could change my mind, I grabbed the lamp and held it tenderly to my chest.

As I did every day, I rubbed my hand down the side of it. I'd only collected one soul in all my years of life.

One soul trapped in a cage for all of eternity. One soul who'd failed to uphold his end of the bargain. I hadn't had a choice.

I didn't make the contract, and I consciously didn't enforce it.

I scrubbed the sides erratically, but I knew no soul would make an appearance. When Laurel gave me my lamp, she'd failed to retrieve the soul inside of it. Or—and this was the most likely scenario—someone had stolen the soul.

I didn't know how it could be done—hell, I didn't think it had ever been done before—but that was the only explanation I could come up with. What else could explain the mysterious disappearance of first, my lamp, and then the soul inside of it?

Someone wanted what was mine.

"You need to tell her."

Ryland's voice caused me to jump a foot in the air.

"Dammit, Ry, wear a bell or something," I snapped, immediately shoving the lamp behind my back. The shadow was always eerily quiet, gliding across the room with inaudible footsteps. Normally, I didn't mind his voyeuristic tendencies, but I didn't want him to see what I was doing.

However, I should've known not to underestimate Ryland. He always knew more than the average person. Maybe because he saw everyone while no one saw him.

"You need to tell her," he repeated, the shadows curling around his body. Despite the darkness obscuring his scarred features, I knew he would be staring pointedly at the lamp.

"I...I don't know what you mean," I lied, tone scathing, as I bent down and shoved the lamp back into my backpack.

Ryland continued to watch me, a silent, unwavering presence, and I didn't know if I wanted to punch him or...

Really, the only option was to punch him.

"You need to tell her," he said one last time before he turned on his heel, disappearing into the room next door.

I waited until he was completely gone before opening my mouth and refilling my air supply. Fuck. Fuck. Fuck. Ryland knew.

But how could I tell Z?

How could I tell my mate, the love of my life, that I'd had the soul of her ex-lover, S? That I'd had him...and then lost him?

JAX

She left me. Again. After she promised she wouldn't. There was a fissure in my heart that was steadily growing and growing until it encompassed an entire ocean. Pain obliterated my defenses until I was nothing but a crying, weak man.

She.

Left.

Me.

Alone.

So alone.

Always alone.

My mind conjured up images of Sasha.

She was twelve when I last saw her, a lanky human with a sheet of long hair and thick, hipster glasses. I remembered that day almost vividly. That dreadful, horrible day...

"Truth or dare, Lupe," Maggie giggled, grabbing her cup of blood and taking a long sip. She was a vampire, like myself, with brunette ringlets and a pretty smile.

I had a little crush on her, though I would never admit that to my brothers. Besides, Maggie had a crush on Lupe, and I'd heard rumors he was planning on giving her a box of chocolates. Damn him.

Lupe, even at ten, was a large boy. Looking at him, you knew he was going to grow to be a real beast of a man. Heck, even his muscles had muscles. Jealousy momentarily speared me at the smitten look Maggie was giving him.

"Dare," Lupe answered, flexing his muscles. Maggie chortled once more, tapping her chin contemplatively.

"I dare you to..." She glanced around the circle with growing amusement. There were a few other girls in attendance, along with the rest of my brothers. The oldest was Sasha at twelve, and the youngest was Atta. "Kiss Killian."

The entire circle broke into giggles as my shifter brother glanced at the incubus. Killian had yet to grow into his powers. He was the smallest of all of us with long limbs, tangled red hair, and glasses that continually slipped off his nose.

"Ew, no," Lupe grumbled as Killian gave him a wide-eyed stare.

"Are you scared?" Maggie taunted wickedly.

"He's practically my brother," Lupe said with a huff.

Maggie frowned, lips pursing delicately, before she crossed her small arms over her chest. "Fine. Be lame. Hmmm. I dare you to interrupt the kings' meeting."

At this, all of us froze. I exchanged an anxious look with Bash, who was sitting directly beside me, before focusing on Lupe. The boy was pathetic, especially when it came to females. He probably thought Maggie would hold his hand if he agreed to her dare.

"Fine," he snapped, getting to his feet and brushing dirt off his slacks. "Before I leave, Jax, truth or dare?"

"Do you even have to ask?" I questioned, lips curling upwards. I'd always been the daredevil of my brothers. It was why Ryland and I were thick as thieves.

"Fine, I dare you to drink Sasha's blood. Directly from the neck."

A series of "ooohs" and "ahhhs" erupted from the assembled group. Sasha ducked her head sheepishly, a tiny smile playing at her lips. I knew she had a crush on me, and though I would've preferred Maggie as my girlfriend, Sasha was a solid second choice. She always carried home-made cookies.

"Fine," I agreed as Lupe released a whoop, running in the direction of the capital building.

The sun was bright today, illuminating the carefully planted perennials and roses lining the garden's walkway. The sky was a canvas of brilliant light blue speckled inter-mittently with swaths of gold. One would think that the sky would've been black with heavy storm clouds. It was only fitting—the worst day of my life deserved fucking storm clouds.

Smirking, I rolled up my shirtsleeves and crawled over to Sasha.

"Are you okay with this?" I questioned, tilting my head to the side. I hadn't ever drunk directly from the source before. My dad had been trying to convince me, but I'd always refused.

Sasha smiled again, nodding her head. "Yeah. I've

never been bitten by a vampire before." She tilted her head to the side, revealing her milky white neck.

"It shouldn't hurt," I murmured, eyeing the throbbing vein with a wanton need.

"Just do it already!" another girl, Talia or something, screamed before breaking into giggles.

My fangs extended as Sasha's pulse thumped wildly beneath her skin. I was so, so thirsty...

Without giving myself a second chance to think, to change my mind, I bit down. Blood immediately filled my mouth as I sucked deeply. Our venom was designed to ensure our victims felt no pain. No fear. When we were older, I heard we could release endorphins—whatever that meant—into the person's bloodstream.

Sasha released a gasp as I fed off of her. She tasted so damn good, her blood significantly sweeter than the blood I got from bags and animals. It was almost syrupy in texture, warm and inviting and soothing my throat. All of my pain diminished, replaced by this insatiable need to consume, consume, consume.

I wanted more.

I was dimly aware of someone screaming my name and telling me to stop. My brothers, more than likely. Atta was crying. A fireball from Bash penetrated my skin, but still, I drank. The blood refueled my depleted reserves. I didn't feel pain with her sweet, sweet blood coursing through my system.

I was positively gluttonous.

Someone grabbed my shoulder and attempted to pull me off of her, but I shoved them away with an enraged *snarl, momentarily taking my lips off her neck. But no, that wouldn't do. I was still hungry.*

I dropped my face back to her bloody neck and resumed with renewed vigor.

So, so thirsty.

More bodies joined the first, pulling me away from my meal. I snarled and thrashed, a wild animal unleashed, before noticing the vacant-eyed body staring up at the sky.

Her neck had been ripped out, blood staining her clothes and the pebble walkway. Her mouth was slightly open, as if she had been in the midst of a scream before death claimed her with the finality it did everything.

No. No. No. No.

I killed her. I killed her. I killed her.

As I watched, horrified, her face began to change and contort. Auburn hair turned into golden locks. Her freckles disappeared until her face was smooth and unblemished.

Now, it was Z looking up at the cloudless sky. Dead.

Because of me.

Because of me.

Because of me.

I vowed to myself, right then and there, that I would never have blood again. Madness was the least I deserved after what I'd done to an innocent.

I was pulled out of the memory by someone slapping me across the face.

"How the hell did you get down?" Aaliyah questioned curiously as she glanced from the chains on the wooden X to my crumbled form. She shook her head once before kneeling down before me. "No matter." Her hand touched my naked stomach, and I winced away from her. I didn't want her touch. No, no, no. Her touch didn't make my blood sing like my mate's. And I needed my blood to sing.

Sing. Sing. Sing.

Her smile grew at my instinctive retreat, but she removed her hand. "I see that you're healing...but you're still refusing blood. Why?"

Blood. Blood cascading down the walls. Staining my hands.

So much blood.

"I can change that, you know," she added almost conversationally. She snapped her fingers, and my cell door was pushed open. An unfamiliar man was dragged inside. He was covered in dirt and soot with dark hair that hung to his shoulders. He trembled, staring wide-eyed at the two men who held each of his arms. "I have...a special power, I suppose you could say." Aaliyah giggled, the sound deceptively childlike. "I was trying to give you time to join me on your own, but..." She shook her head forlornly. "You're stubborn, Jax. I'll give you that."

She leaned over me, teeth glimmering in the flick-ering candlelight. Her eyes ensnared mine, white wisps of smoking encircling my body like chains. I could feel her presence prodding at my mind, demanding entrance. I had to resist, I had to be stronger, I had to—

"Give in," she whispered, her smile growing. "Give in to your sin. Be gluttonous."

Something...cracked inside of me. That was the only word I could think of to use. The last shred of my humanity flitted away, carried by a gust of wind. I was a shell of the man I remembered.

Be.

Gluttonous.

Need roared within me as I focused on the new man's throat.

So, so thirsty.

No! Don't! Stop! Don't do this, Jax.

"Give in!" Aaliyah roared, clawing at my fragile mind.

The next thing I knew, I was lunging forward and tearing out the man's throat.

SIXTEEN

Z

I sat straight up with a gasp, heart splintering as I rapidly inventoried the room. Killian was directly beside me, eyes closed and breathing even. He looked different in sleep. Younger, almost, and softer. His red hair, interwoven with darker garnet streaks, fluttered around his sharp cheekbones.

"He's going to be okay," a soft voice whispered. I spun, heart lodged in my throat, only to relax when I spotted Bash sitting rigidly on the chair beside me. "Lupe went to get some food for you guys for whenever you woke up," he continued in that same calming voice. "Devlin is in his room, and Ryland is...somewhere." He gestured vaguely around the room as if the shadow could be hiding underneath the bed. Honestly? I wouldn't be surprised.

"Bash—"

Placing his hands on his knees, Bash pushed himself up. His sculpted body flexed and bunched as he stretched his arms above his head. I was momentarily struck dumb. Bash was...sexy. All my mates were, honestly, but Bash embodied the boy next door stereotype wrapped in a deliciously dark package. With his blond hair rumpled and shirt creased with wrinkles, he looked nothing like the guy I first met.

The guy who was—snort—in the midst of an orgy with a flaccid dick. Long story.

"I'll leave," he murmured, averting his eyes. I reached for him immediately, my fingers grazing his shirt sleeve.

"Stay." Did I plead? Fuck, I never pleaded. But the thought of Bash leaving, of him walking out that door, was a physical pain. It felt like dozens of tiny knives jabbing at my heart, bleeding the organ dry.

Bash hesitated, only briefly, before sitting once more in the plush armchair. He still looked tense, his muscles locked and rigid. He was like a loaded gun seconds from going off.

And I just happened to be in the pathway of the bullet.

"I assumed you would want me to leave," he said, tone deceptively light and casual. His fingers thrummed on the armrest as he stared intently at a hole in the chair, the sheet on the bed, anywhere besides my probing eyes. I half wondered if he was a coward...or the smartest man alive.

"Why?" I sat up slightly, testing my sore muscles. I felt drained and tired, but other than that, I was perfectly fine. I wondered if this was what Sleeping Beauty felt like when she woke up.

On second thought, ew. The original story had the

princess waking up after being raped and her twin babies kicking in her stomach.

Ignoring my question, Bash released a heavy breath. It wasn't technically a sigh, it was almost as if he needed to make a conscious effort to breathe.

"I checked you over extensively. You'll be sore, but..." He scrubbed a hand down his haggard face.

"Sore but fine?" I finished for him, and his eyes snapped up to me. Bright and wide and *knowing*. I had the distinct feeling he saw me more clearly than I'd ever seen myself. "Bash?"

His jaw clenched as he ripped his gaze away from me, focusing instead on his shortened nails.

"You don't like me very much, do you?" he pointed out grimly. At my stunned silence, he released another pent-up breath. "I don't blame you. I was a bit of an asshole."

"A bit?" I interrupted, snorting. His lips twitched slightly in amusement.

"Anyway, if you don't want me as your mate, I'll go. I'll leave. Just say the fucking word, and I'm gone."

My breath caught as I stared at the man before me. The broken man. God, why hadn't I noticed how badly he was hurting? Why hadn't I seen his pain?

Was that why he pushed me away?

"I don't want you to go," I answered vehemently. And I didn't. Bash might've annoyed the shit out of me, he might've been a condescending asshole, but he was still my mate.

And for better or worse, I cared about him.

Bash's eyes tightened briefly with emotion—raw,

undiluted emotion—before his face turned serious. He leaned forward until his lips were a hair's breadth away from mine.

"I know," he whispered, voice cold. Apathetic.

I veered back as if I'd been slapped. "What?"

"I know about the poison."

I imagined his words were similar to sticking your finger into an electrical socket. Or hell, even a blazing inferno.

My mouth slackened in shock as panic coursed through my veins. I stared at him numbly, and he stared back, neither of us giving anything away. His eyes were icy, lips pursed, but I could see a multitude of emotions hovering just beneath the surface.

"I—" My feeble excuse was gratefully staved off by a muffled groan from beside me. I spun towards my incubus mate as he lifted himself onto his elbows, his blankets pooling around him.

"Z? What's going on?" he murmured drowsily. "Bash, what the turd nugget are you doing in our room?"

Turd nugget?

Before I could comment on his questionable choice of curse words, Killian wrapped an arm around my stomach and cuddled me against his muscular, tattooed chest.

"My girl and I are sleeping. Go away," he murmured. Bash snorted, getting to his feet once more and crossing to the opposite side of the bed. With a malicious smile dancing on his lips, he grabbed a glass of water off the bedside table. Then he poured the water onto Killian's head.

"What the hell, man?" Killian sputtered, wiping at the water droplets cascading down his cheeks. The cold water finally seemed to penetrate his sleepy brain. He glanced at me, then at Bash, and then back at me. "What... w-what-t-t ha-happ-pen-ed?" His stutter made another appearance as he finally seemed to realize the magnitude of the situation. He scrubbed at his smooth-shaven chin absentmindedly. "I remember going to check on Z..."

"We were attacked," I filled in, smoothing down his disheveled red hair. "A basilisk. He poisoned you, and I accidentally got some of the poison on me as well."

Killian's eyes widened in remembrance—hell, it might've been plain old constipation—before he pulled me into his arms.

"Are you okay? Are you hurt? You don't feel light-headed, do you?"

I stroked his bare back soothingly. The old me would've laughed at his overprotectiveness. The new me simply wanted to bask in it.

"I'm fine. It's you I'm worried about. You were fucking stabbed, Kill." I pulled away to stare at him, lowering my gaze to his chest and stomach. His skin had been cleaned of blood, and when I touched his back, I felt nothing but a puckered scar. I knew that it, too, would disappear with time. It was a part of an incubus's allure—physical blemishes never lasted long.

"Bash must've saved my ass again," Killian said fondly, throwing a smile at his brother. The mage's face was unreadable, hewn from stone, but he managed a brisk nod.

"Of course," he murmured. His eyes pierced me, bled me, and then haphazardly stitched me up.

I couldn't get over the fact that Bash knew—he knew my dirty little secret. Had he told the others? Would he? There was a reason I'd been keeping it quiet. I knew my mates would be devastated if they knew the truth.

Life was fleeting. There and gone in seconds. It was a corn stalk sitting in an empty field, the wind rippling through the open expanse. One strong gust could completely blow it away.

I'd known my entire life that I was going to die young. Knew and even accepted it. How could I not? I saw people die every damn day in my line of duty. Friends, family members, acquaintances. My own parents were murdered before my very eyes. As was S, one of my first loves. Something fundamental inside of me died with them—a piece of me I knew I would never get back.

I didn't want my mates to experience the same pain that I had. I didn't want them to fret over the inevitable. Was it selfish? Maybe.

I just knew a part of me would die if they ever learned the truth. At least, die before my expiration date.

Killian intertwined his fingers with mine and offered me a shy smile. "I'm really glad you're okay," he whispered, low enough so the words stayed between the two of us. I gave his hand a squeeze in response.

"And I'm really glad you're okay."

Because a world without Killian wasn't one I wanted to live in.

The door to my room was pushed open, and the first

thing I saw was a chiseled ass. And yes, I was openly ogling said ass. No, I wasn't going to apologize.

Using his ass to push open the door, Lupe wheeled in a cart of delicious smelling food. I spotted glazed strawberries, chicken fillets, and even a bowl of ice cream. The large man looked positively domestic.

My body filled with warmth as he spun around, finally noticing me and Killian sitting up in bed.

"You're awake!" he exclaimed, running forward. He looked as if he was seconds from tackling me, but he managed to stop himself just before he touched me. Instead, his hands hovered over my arms and shoulders as if he was desperate to hold me but didn't dare. "I was so fucking worried." His voice lowered to a primal growl. "Don't do that to me again."

"I'll try not to get poisoned, don't worry," I drawled sarcastically, but inside, I was floating. Yeah, these men were starting to wear me down. Chipping away the hard exterior to reveal the malleable, gooey center. If B could see me now...

My good mood rapidly faded, as it always did when I thought about the leader of the Alphabet Resistance. According to HH and T, the compound that housed over one hundred members had been emptied. No one knew where they went.

Or if they were even alive.

I shook my head to clear my cluttered thoughts, smiling up at the massive man above me. He didn't have his glasses on, so his face looked even more masculine. With his brown scruff, piercing eyes, and slightly crooked nose, he was beautiful. Sexy.

Almost hesitantly, I reached up to touch his face. Yeah, he was my mate and I knew he cared about me—shower sexy times, anyone? —but I was still unsure of how to act around him. Around any of them, actually.

"I'm okay," I whispered, leaning forward to kiss first one cheek and then the other. Lupe's eyes flared with heat and something else, something I didn't want to name. Changing the subject, I asked, "What's the plan? For tomorrow, I mean. We know where Jax is, at least according to the map, but do we know yet what building he's in? Do we need to do recon?"

The mention of Jax brought up blurry images of the handsome vampire tied to wooden posts. And then...

I shook my head, the memory slipping through my fingers. Was it even a memory? A nightmare? Or was I losing my mind?

"We'll scope out the place tomorrow morning," Bash murmured tiredly. "But, Z, you're going to have to be on the leash again when we're in public."

At my enraged noise of protest, Bash held up his hands placatingly. "I know, I know. You want to cut off my balls and feed them to me on a fucking silver plate. But the vampires here see humans as food and toys, nothing more. It doesn't matter to them that you're the kingdom's assassin. You're a female human. I can't even imagine the atrocious things..." He trailed off, face creasing in pain.

I sighed, the fight leaving me. He was right, I knew he was right, but I didn't have to like it.

"Fine. Whatever. Tie me up, you kinky shit."

Bash's lips twitched, but he didn't allow himself to smile.

"There's one more thing we need to talk to you about," Lupe broke in, staring intently at his fingers now holding mine. "I was going to tell you earlier, but I knew the car was bugged. And then the whole attack happened…"

"What's going on?" I questioned, instantly alert. Was it one of my mates? Did I have to tit punch a bitch?

Lupe exchanged an uneasy glance with Bash. Only Killian appeared confused, just as much in the dark as I was.

"Come on. I need to show you." Lupe extended a hand and helped me to my feet. He held me for a second longer, steadying me when I began to wobble, before leading me out of the room. "How are you feeling?" he asked as we moved down the hall.

"Tired. A little sore." I shrugged. "Not horrible."

Lupe nodded, but his gaze seemed almost absent. Distant.

Finally, he stopped in front of a room I knew belonged to Axel and the servants. He rapped his knuckles against the wooden door, and a moment later, it swung open.

Axel stood in the doorframe, eyes heavy and expression almost lazy. He was shirtless, scarred chest on display, and wore nothing but a pair of low-slung sleep shorts.

"What do you want?" he murmured, yawning. He gazed at us with obvious disinterest before sighing, opening the door wider. "Do you want to come in?"

"We need to speak to one of our slaves," Lupe demanded darkly.

Slaves? What the hell was he going on about?

Axel's face tightened, but he nodded once. "Which one?"

"The newest."

The ex-assassin stepped back inside and spoke quietly to someone before a new man returned in his place.

"What the hell do you want?" a familiar voice asked venomously.

My heart froze. All of the blood drained from my face.

The man standing before me had a face distorted with bruises and gashes. Both of his eyes were swollen completely shut. Bandages wrapped around his neck and arms, already stained with drying blood. He wore a simple white tunic, covered in dirt and soot, and two magic manacles were wrapped around his wrists.

"T," I whispered in horror as his face twisted in shock. Spinning on my heel, I jabbed an accusatory finger at Lupe's chest. "What did you do?"

SEVENTEEN

Z

"Not here." Lupe grabbed my hand gently and pulled me down the hall. T trailed a respectful distance behind us, lips pursed with disgust and his swollen eyes twitching.

Killian and Bash stood in the doorway of my room. Killian appeared shocked, face pale, but Bash was utterly impassive.

Giving the mage and incubus a pointed look, Lupe pushed past them and led me farther into the room.

I was...shaking. Fucking shaking. My lungs felt like they were being shredded by razor blades. Anger, hurt, betrayal...they all battled for dominance. One wasn't more prominent than the others. How could Lupe keep this from me?

Fuck, how could he do this in the first place? T was one of my closest friends, practically my brother, and Lupe was treating him like scum.

Fury pulsated through me, white-hot, and

temporarily blinded me. My ears roared like the ocean cresting against the shoreline.

"I can explain," Lupe pleaded when he took in my expression. Killian and Bash had left, leaving me alone with my shifter mate and my human best friend.

"What? Fucking tell me what there is to explain!" I threw my hands out, a hysterical laugh escaping unbidden.

T remained silent, stony, his arms crossed over his chest. I was horrified to see more scars lining his muscular forearms. What the hell had been done to him?

"Apparently, your big, growly mate has a fetish for beating up humans," T drawled, leaning against the wall.

My hands fisted, seconds from pummeling Lupe's face in. I'd thought he was different from his family. I'd thought—

"I see your mind racing," Lupe whispered softly. His eyes implored my own to listen, to understand. "I did what I had to do in order to save his life."

"Save his life?" I gasped, breath stuttering to an abrupt halt. "He looks as if he's been through a fucking meat grinder. Did you do that to him?"

I tried to picture my gentle giant hurting anyone, let alone someone I cared about deeply, but the image eluded me. Lupe wasn't capable of hurting a fly, let alone a human.

At least I hadn't thought so before now.

"My father would've killed him," Lupe snapped. Anger briefly burned in his gaze, a banked fire, before he took a deep, calming breath. "My father would've killed him if I hadn't stepped in. I told the bastard we needed a new servant. Slave. Whatever the hell you want to call it." He desperately reached for me, but I stepped away.

I...I couldn't. Not yet. Not with the anger too raw and bloody, like a wound that hadn't scabbed over.

"Just go, Lupe." I was suddenly exhausted. Why did this shit have to happen to me? Why did I take five humongous steps forward only to be pushed back by an oncoming train? "If we continue to talk, we're only going to fight, and I don't want that. I'm mad at you, furious even, but I care about you too damn much to continue this conversation. So, please. Just go." I pointed in the general direction of the door, but I didn't dare lift my eyes from his chest. I didn't want to see his gaze anymore. Didn't want to feel his eyes as a burning caress on my forehead.

The damn man had imprinted himself on my soul, my very genetic makeup, and it was impossible to stay mad.

But fuck, I was determined to try.

Just like yesterday, Lupe left without any protest. I had just a moment to see his eyes glassy with tears—tears he wouldn't shed—before he shut the door, leaving me alone with T.

"Fuck, I don't want to say this," T immediately said on a moan once Lupe was gone. "But the man loves the shit out of you. And he's right—he did save my life. The shifter king would've killed me if he hadn't stepped in. Lupe took control of my...my torture, but he also saved my life. I was the dumbass who got caught in the first place." He scrubbed a hand through his tangled hair, slightly longer on the top than the sides. He even had a beard.

"What happened?" I asked, moving to stand beside him. My eyes catalogued his extensive injuries, but I was grateful to see there was nothing life-threatening. Thank fuck.

"I was at the safe house waiting for HH. He'd gotten a lead about the disappearance of the others," he recollected, voice distant as he were transported back in time. "I got worried when he didn't check in, so I went looking for him. Stumbled upon a shifter asshole raping a human girl. Killed him." He released a harsh, bitter laugh. "Didn't realize he was the shifter king's fucking guard. The next thing I knew, I was being dragged into the dungeons and tortured by the sadistic bastard himself."

"And Lupe...tortured you as well?" I felt sick to my stomach. Fuck, I was seconds from vomiting.

T's expression twisted and tightened, before becoming unreadable in a matter of seconds. "He did, yes." He pointed to a tiny scar on his upper arm. "But every wound he inflicted was precise. He never intended to scar me or kill me like the king had. He did what he had to, Z. He didn't have a choice. If he refused, his bastard father would've killed me...and probably him."

"He didn't have to do anything," I snapped, but I didn't know if I actually believed that. Wasn't there always another option? Weren't there two sides to every coin? T's assurance didn't negate the pain running rampant through me.

T offered me a wobbly smile, leaning forward to press a chaste kiss on my forehead.

"I know, sweetie. I know."

THE NEXT MORNING, I woke up bright and early to prepare myself for the day ahead. After completing an extensive workout in my room, I showered and dressed in stretchy pants and a black tank top. I twisted my golden hair into a messy braid over my right shoulder.

"You can do this," I told my reflection in the inn's mirror. "You can save your mate."

Taking a solidifying breath, I strode out of my room and to the one adjacent. I knocked twice, shifting from foot to foot as I waited patiently.

When they didn't answer after the fifth knock, I pushed open the door and stepped inside.

Their luggage was strewn over the beds and dressers, but the room itself was empty of any of my mates.

What the hell?

They were too protective of me to leave me alone for an extended period of time. Hell, I'd half expected to see Lupe asleep in the hall outside of my door.

Last night, after saying goodbye to T, I allowed myself to rationally think about Lupe and the decisions he'd made. And I realized...I forgave him. I would've done the exact same thing if the shifter king had confronted me. A little pain was worth sparing T's life.

Fuck, I needed to apologize, and soon. I wouldn't be able to forgive myself if something happened while we were fighting.

I quickly moved down the hall to Axel's room and

knocked on that door as well. Like before, there was no answer.

My irritation shifted into concern as I ran through the possibilities. They could be downstairs, getting food.

Or they could be dead.

In a ditch.

Tone down the macabre thoughts, Z, I scolded myself.

Heart racing, I rushed down the rickety staircase and into the lobby, scanning the array of faces present.

None of them were my mates.

Fuck.

"Where's your handler, human?" a voice sneered from behind me. The vampire was tall and lanky, with greasy blond hair and a shark-like smile.

"Fuck off," I snapped, turning away from him. No one, absolutely no one, was allowed to talk to me like that. Unless they wanted to see the inside of a body bag.

Teeth gnashing together, I turned back towards the staircase. Before I could take a step, the vampire reached for my arm and tugged me backwards.

"Where are you going, human slut?"

That was it. The final fucking straw.

Before I could reconsider my life choices, I placed my free hand on his shoulder and lifted my knee to his nuts. He released a pained wheeze, but his smile only grew.

"I like my bitches with a little fight in them," he purred, eyes flashing red. I grabbed his hair and pulled his face to me.

"Do you know who I am?" I asked darkly, carefully. I leaned closer until my lips were directly beside his ear.

"I'm the kingdom's fucking assassin, asshole. I won the Damning, and I won't hesitate to skin you alive."

With that threat, I shoved him away. He released me, eyes wide with horror, before scuttling away like a fucking dog with his tail between his legs.

Even here, in a kingdom that saw humans as parasites, my reputation preceded me.

"Damn," Ryland murmured from directly behind me. "That was sexy."

I spun towards the shadow standing in the corner, silhouetted arms crossed over his chest. "Shit, Ry, I thought you were gone."

"Did you really think we would leave you alone?" he asked lightly.

"Where are the others?" I queried suspiciously. If they left without me…

"Calm down, little dove. They're getting supplies for the journey."

"Oh." I physically deflated with relief. "Sorry, I'm just…"

"Stressed? Tired of us wrapping you in bubble wrap?" Ryland guessed wryly.

I snorted. "Yup. That's exactly it." A potent pause stretched out between us. "But, Ryland, you have to remember that I was alone for years until I met you guys. And I survived it. I'll continue to survive it. You can't protect me from the world when I've already faced it head-on."

For a brief moment, the shadows around Ryland parted. His smile was timid, almost unsure, but his eyes were bright with emotion. "You don't have to be alone anymore, Z. You have us."

"Yeah, I do. I just—"

My words were interrupted by a deafening blast. A second later, the world around me began to tremble and shake. I only had a second to stare wide-eyed at the flaming walls of the inn before the building crumbled around us.

EIGHTEEN

KILLIAN

I trailed my fingers over the assortment of necklaces draping over the sides of the display case. Some were silver, embedded with rubies, while others were gold with emeralds. The filigrees surrounding the gemstones were intricately designed, depicting everything from vines to angel wings.

Angel wings. Fitting for my angel.

Smiling contentedly, I grabbed the closest necklace and tested the weight in my palm. I didn't understand the primal urge that coursed through me at the concept of Z wearing a gift from me, something that declared her as mine. But it was there, prowling beneath the surface like a savage beast just waiting to be unleashed.

Devlin stood a few feet away from me, surveying an extensive collection of kitchen knives.

"We already have weapons," Bash drawled sarcastically, his arms full of red fabrics. To blend in with the citizens of the Vampire Kingdom, we had to look the part.

And all vampires wore bright red colors.

"I know," Devlin snapped, forking his fingers through his curly brown hair. Since the attack, he'd been more tense than usual. His body was constantly taut with agitation, seconds from springing forward and attacking. Currently, his olive-toned face was colored with anxiety for Z. He hadn't liked leaving her behind, even with Ryland watching over her.

As Bash and Devlin began to bicker amongst themselves, I turned away from the jewelry, still holding the necklace I'd selected, and spotted Lupe talking to the vampire behind the store's counter. His massive frame looked awkward hunched over such a small, rickety surface. The distressed wood appeared seconds from crumbling under his form. A moment later, the storekeeper nodded once and disappeared into the storeroom. He reappeared with long fabric draped over his arm.

Before I could see what my brother was up to, someone tapped me on the shoulder. I turned, fully expecting it to be Bash or Devlin, only to freeze when I spotted an unfamiliar female. My blood froze before turning to sludge, unable to effectively run through my veins.

Since Z, I'd made tremendous steps in talking to strangers. However, fear still strangled me in an unrelenting chokehold. All I could see was my father's cruel, haughty smirk as he raped my nanny, my surrogate mother, and killed her. Since that day, I'd only ever talked to my brothers, and now Z. Strangers? Hated them.

Still, I managed a timid smile. I could totally be polite.

When she smiled, revealing lengthened fangs, I

deduced she was a vampire like everyone else in this kingdom.

"What's a strapping young incubus like yourself doing here?" she asked, twirling a piece of red hair around her finger.

Errr...was this a trick question?

Was she a spy?

Eyeing her warily, I answered, "I'm here with my brothers." I swept a hand out towards where Bash and Devlin had been a moment earlier, only to notice they'd left.

"Well, I charge only a few coins," she purred, winking.

Charge for what? Was she a sales lady?

"Umm...?" I shrugged helplessly, unwilling to say more than one word at a time. I knew my stutter would become more pronounced with my anxiety.

"I'll let you lick my cream," she continued, and understanding dawned on me.

Ahhh. She was a door-to-door saleswoman. Probably selling some type of sweet cream for coffee. I wondered if I should placate her and buy a bottle as a gift for Z. Maybe that would get her to leave me alone.

"Only a few coins, you say?" I reached into my pocket and grabbed a handful of golden coins. They were the official currency of all the kingdoms, though some had a separate currency as well.

"For you, handsome boy, I'll give it to you for free."

Oh, that was awfully nice. My smile turned genuine. Hopefully, Z liked her gift.

"Do you have the product here?" I questioned, raising

a brow. Her face creased with confusion before it settled into a...hungry look. What the fudge pop?

Before I could comment, she dropped to her knees before me.

"We can do it here if you want, big boy." Her hands moved to touch my legs, but I sidestepped her easily.

"Um..."

I really, really didn't understand what was going on.

"Killian!" Bash wrapped his arm around my shoulders, yanking me back. "What the hell are you doing?"

"This woman was selling me her homemade cream," I supplied. "I was going to buy a bottle for Z."

The woman's lips popped open, confusion filling her heavily accentuated features, and Bash's arm tightened around me.

"Can I talk to you for a moment, Kill?" he hissed, excusing us without another word. Before I could reprimand him on his rude behavior, Bash spun me towards him, lips pressed into a tight line. His left eye was practically twitching. "My god, brother, either you're the stupidest person known to mankind or you're a manipulative asshole."

Umm...okay? No comment.

Bash scrubbed a hand down his face in annoyance. "She's not selling you a product, dumbass. She's selling you a service." At my confused expression, he elaborated somewhat reluctantly. "She's a prostitute. You know, sells her—"

"I know what a prostitute is!" I snapped, terror engulfing me. Holy crap. Did I just...? My horror filled eyes met Bash's amused ones. "Do you think Z will forgive me?"

His smile fled. "Why would she be mad?"

"Because I conversed with a prostitute!" I hissed, working to moderate my volume. I knew I shouldn't have talked to the woman. I knew I should've walked away…

"Fuck, man." Bash pinched the bridge of his nose. "She's not going to be mad that you talked to that woman. She would've been mad, however, if you'd fucked her."

My horror increased tenfold. "Why would I ever fuck another woman?"

The mere concept was almost laughable. Z was my entire world. My sun, my moon, and my stars. She was a radiant splash of light breaking apart the cloudy skies of my life. For one, the prospect of touching another woman made me want to vomit. For two, I had too much respect and love for Z to ever betray or hurt her that way. I was almost angry at Bash for suggesting as much.

"You wouldn't fuck another woman," Bash continued, irritated. "None of us would. That's what I'm trying to say."

I glanced over my shoulder towards the lady, who was still on her knees, and gave her a wave goodbye.

"I'll have to refuse your cream," I called to her, garnering the attention of Lupe, who was still at the counter. "Sorry."

Bash growled, rolling his eyes, and the woman appeared appropriately confused. Ignoring them both, I stalked to where Lupe was standing, the red garment still tossed over his arms.

"What was that…?"

"Apparently, she's a prostitute," I filled in seriously. "So don't go accepting any cream from her, okay?"

The large man blinked at me once, shook his head, and then dropped his gaze to the red fabric.

"What's that?" I asked, dipping my chin. His lips twitched slightly as he stroked it.

"It's a present for Z. An apology." His shirt strained against his broad shoulders as he shrugged. "I know she isn't like normal girls. I know that she doesn't care about materialistic things, but..." Once more, he shrugged sheepishly, his cheeks tinting the color of the dress.

I clapped him on the shoulder. "She'll forgive you, brother. She'll forgive us all."

"How can you be so sure?"

"Because she loves us." The answer was obvious. As an incubi, I had the capacity to sense heightened emotions including lust, infatuation, and love. Each one had a unique scent, an addicting aroma, that I savored on my tongue. Z, whenever she was near us, exhibited all three.

I just wasn't positive she realized it yet.

Devlin appeared from the backroom, tucking a brand-new dagger into a holster on his thigh.

"Shall we go?"

I just barely resisted the urge to nod eagerly. It had only been a few hours since I'd last seen Z's beautiful face, but it was a few hours too long. I already missed her. Missed her dewy features and sparkling eyes alight with laughter. Missed her laugh, her smile, and the two dimples that always made an appearance on her face. Missed her golden hair that felt like silk to the touch.

Before I left, I paid for the necklace I'd picked out for Z. I couldn't wait to see it nestled between her breasts.

And...

I was hard. Damn my dick. Damn it to the deepest pits of hell. Or Z's vagina. I wouldn't mind my dick being there.

My cheeks turned crimson at the direction of my thoughts.

"You behave," I whispered to my cock. "You'll see her soon. Don't be getting greedy."

As we stepped out of the store and onto the bustling cobblestone street, I glanced wide-eyed at the red-haired prostitute who was currently draped over a vampire's lap. How had I not realized who she was before?

Bash snorted a laugh at my expression. "I can't believe you almost fucking bought an exchange of oral services from her. Z would've murdered you."

I shoved his shoulder in irritation. I may have been the most innocent of my brothers, but I wasn't an idiot. I would've stopped the woman before she ever laid a finger on me.

"It's not funny, dickhead," I murmured.

"It kind of is," he chuckled, and I couldn't help but laugh as well. Because, hell, it was kind of funny.

Note to future self—cream isn't always a liquid you put in coffee.

"Holy fuck!" Devlin cursed suddenly, breaking into a run. I followed the direction of his gaze and felt my own heart lurch in my chest.

It was...smoke. Lots and lots of smoke.

As my feet carried me forward, easily keeping pace

with the others due to my athletic body, my blood turned to ice.

The inn we were staying at was on fire. Heavy flames ate at the wooden walls and roof.

Another blast reverberated, shaking the ground, and the roof caved in on itself as if an immense weight were resting on top.

Horror like no other filled me. Consumed me. I couldn't breathe, couldn't think, couldn't even see.

No. No. No.

"Z!" I screamed, lunging forward. Lupe caught the back of my shirt before I could take more than a step. "Z!"

Before he could say anything, a figure streaked by us —a familiar figure with blond hair and magic dancing at the tips of his fingers.

Bash.

He brought his sleeve to his nose as he ducked beneath a low-hanging pillar, the fire crackling in vicious, unforgiving waves.

The moment he entered the inn, the rest of the roof collapsed in a cloud of gray smoke and orange flames.

A part of me went numb as I fell to the ground, still holding Lupe. My mate, my best friend, Ryland...

I wanted to run in after them. The need was almost a physical force, a voice in my brain demanding I take action. For the first time in forever, I berated myself for being weak and fearful. For jumping at my own shadow.

How could I protect Z when I couldn't even protect myself? When I couldn't protect my brothers?

My thoughts consumed me like a tsunami as I waited

for Bash to exit the flaming building. As I waited for Z to walk out, covered in soot but with a beautiful smile pulling up her lips. As I waited for Ryland to emerge from the shadows like an avenging angel.

But none of them did.

NINETEEN

Z

Smoke.

It engulfed me in a thick, gray sheen, swarming around in my lungs until it felt like I was suffocating.

Licks of fire ate away at the wooden siding of the inn. It was a surprisingly...beautiful sight. Orange bled into red, and yellow specks completed the enticing image.

"Z!" A rough voice penetrated the murkiness residing in my brain. I blinked rapidly, attempting to dislodge the smoke particles caught in my eyelashes. "Z!" Someone shook my shoulder, and I trembled slightly, turning away from the kaleidoscope of red, orange, and yellow.

Ryland's anxious face, devoid of shadows, peered down at me. Smoke curled around his dark features until only the whites of his eyes were visible.

When I stared at him blankly, unable to articulate a response, he grabbed my arm and wrenched me to my feet. Half dragging and half carrying me, he led us beneath a flaming archway.

Finally, *finally*, I regained my senses, propelling myself forward.

Someone had attacked the inn. Either this person had bombed us, or he'd hired a skilled mage.

Fuck.

Was it Aaliyah? The kings? A new threat entirely?

We seemed to have entered a hallway that wasn't permeated by smoke. The air wasn't fresh, but it no longer choked me.

"Are you okay?" Ryland demanded, pulling me forward. I wasn't surprised that my shadow mate had memorized the layout of the inn. No doubt, he knew every nook and cranny.

"I'm fine. You?" My heart thumped erratically in my chest. The others...

They're fine, I scolded myself instantly. *They weren't at the inn during the explosion. They're fine.*

I repeated those two words until I began to believe them. I couldn't handle any other alternative.

Ignoring the nerves roiling in my stomach, I followed directly behind Ryland as he pushed open a backdoor. Immediately, sunlight sliced through the thick, cloudy air. The heat dulled significantly as we stepped outside, away from the burning building.

"What the fuck happened?" I demanded, coughing harshly. My lungs were protesting all of the smoke they had inhaled.

"I don't—" Whatever Ryland was going to say was interrupted by something heavy hitting him over the back of the head. I released a startled yelp, my initial fear resurfacing, as his eyes rolled to the back of his head. He collapsed against the asphalt with an audible thump, blood pooling from a wound on his head.

Immediately, I slid my favorite dagger out of its sheath and raised it, narrowing my eyes at the figures surrounding us. Terror thumped through me, a palpable entity that perfumed the air in a sickly sweet scent.

I counted at least a dozen men standing in a semi-circle around me and my fallen mate. They all wore variations of red, identifying them as vampires, and had masks covering their faces. They almost appeared to be... baby doll masks, decidedly cherubic in appearance. Rosy cheeks, thick painted on lashes over empty eyes, and perfectly plush red lips. The vampires were different genders, if their heights and builds were any indication.

The only person not wearing a mask was the man directly in the center. His aristocratic features—sharp nose and jaw—gave him almost a haughty look. His honey blond hair was swept away from his face. When he stared at me, it made the wrong type of butterflies flutter around in my chest like they were trying to escape. Trying to warn *me* to escape.

"Who the fuck are you?" I hissed.

Aaliyah really needed to stop fucking with me and my men.

"Don't worry," the handsome vampire drawled, a slight lilt to his voice. "We won't kill the prince."

"Do you know who I am?" I demanded, casting furtive glances at the men and women surrounding me—the term "asshole" didn't discriminate by gender.

I hoped to scare these people the same way I'd terrified the man in the inn's lobby. If they didn't work for

Aaliyah, I might be able to convince them to leave me the fuck alone.

But when Vampire Buttlicker's smile only grew, I knew I was shit out of luck.

"You're Z, the kingdom's assassin. And the mate to all seven of the princes."

Horror and shock rammed into me like a one-thousand-pound truck. That shock momentarily stole my capability of speech. All I could do was gape at him as my arm lowered marginally.

"How do you...?" I managed to stutter out. To my knowledge, only a few of the kings, if not all, knew about my mating bond to the princes. The mermaid king had practically confirmed it.

But this random stranger? In the middle of the Vampire Kingdom?

There was no possible way he could've known about it.

Unless...

Before my thoughts could formulate into something coherent, I felt something prick my neck. The world around me began to sway as my eyes desperately latched on to Ryland's still form.

No, stay awake, Z. Stay the fuck awake!

But I was fighting a losing battle. With great reluctance, I surrendered myself to the storm and was promptly swept away by a pitch-black wave.

WE WERE NO LONGER in the grimy cell with stale air and menial light.

Instead, the room was bright and cheery with a plush white bed, three-tiered chandelier, and dark carpeting that provided the room with a masculine flair.

Lying on the bed, a satisfied smile on his face, was Jax. His pasty skin was smeared with fresh blood that dripped from his fangs and onto his bare chest.

As I stepped farther into the room, his head snapped up, baring his teeth. There was something almost animal-istic in his gaze. Something primal and hungry, as if I were a deer and he the lion.

But beneath the savage exterior, there was also some-thing I would almost describe as...clarity. Coherence.

As if he was no longer driven by the madness that had once consumed him.

I knew that when vampires went too long without blood they became crazed. And for as long as I'd known the eccentric vampire, he'd refused to drink any. But what changed? Why now?

Horror filled his eyes as he dropped the bag of blood I'd hadn't realized he'd been holding. At some point, he must've shaved his beard. His jawline was now smooth-shaven, emphasizing his chiseled features.

"Z," he murmured, lurching to his feet. Instinctively, I backed away. It was what I always did when I came face to face with a predator. And that was what he was, now that he'd given in to his thirst—a dangerous predator. "Z." His voice was a low murmur, and his face was drawn and haggard. Despite the clarity emitting from his eyes, he'd never seemed more upset. "I will never hurt you."

"What the fuck?" I finally managed to stutter out, volleying my gaze around the elegantly furnished room. "What happened?"

This room was one thousand times better than the piss-smelling cell, but my heart still lurched unevenly in my chest. Why was Jax here? What had happened? Question after question ran unattended, rampant, in my head. Fear coiled in my stomach like a slithering snake.

"I'm so thirsty," Jax whispered brokenly. As if he couldn't help himself, he grabbed the blood bag once more and began to drink in earnest. It cascaded in red rivulets down his neck and chest, hitting the waistband of his pants. "I'm sorry, Z, but I can't stop."

I took a hesitant step closer, staring at the man as if he were a cornered, feral animal.

"It's okay, Jax." I kept my voice low and soothing, attempting to reach a part of him I knew was buried deep down. Whatever this Aaliyah bitch did to him...it wasn't entirely her fault. I'd always known there was something lurking just beneath Jax's eccentric surface. It was only a matter of time before it sprang free. She'd cultivated and encouraged the creation of a...of a nightmare.

It was only as I took a second step closer that I noticed the body leaning against the wall.

A dead body.

His hair was greasy and disheveled as if he hadn't showered in weeks, and his body was frail. I could see each individual bone through his yellow skin. His throat had been ripped out, now dried blood staining his neck and chest.

And...

And I recognized him.

His name was DDD, and he was a member of the Alphabet Resistance. I hadn't known him too well, but he'd been a skilled sharpshooter.

My horrified gaze flickered from the dead body to Jax and then back to the dead body.

No. No. No.

"I didn't kill him," Jax pleaded, tears filling his eyes. "I promise. At least I don't think I did. I don't..." He shook his head rapidly. "I was so thirsty."

My forward momentum turned into hurried steps backwards.

He was my mate...but I didn't recognize him. The Jax I knew would never hurt, let alone kill, an innocent man. Not Jax. Not my mate. Not the man who cuddled next to me in bed, stroking my hair and whispering sweet nothings in my ear.

"I didn't kill him," he insisted again, lunging forward. "She did. She did. She did." For a moment, some of his original lunacy returned as he repeated those two words over and over again. His face was pale, stark white, and not even the blood could obscure the plea etched into his features.

Slowly, cautiously, I wrapped my arms around his shoulders. Holding him to me? Holding him together? I didn't know for certain.

Incrementally, like ice melting on a hot summer day, the stress tightening the muscles of his body loosened. He hugged me as fiercely and desperately as I hugged him.

"She thinks I'm lost to my bloodlust. She thinks she

has me under her control," he murmured into my hair. "But she's wrong."

"Jax..." My eyes continued to flick over his broad shoulders and towards my fallen comrade.

"I'm going to get out of here," he vowed. When I pulled away, I saw his lips pressed into a stubborn line. "And then I'm coming for you and the others."

Before I could respond, before I could beg him to be careful, I felt a tug in the center of my chest. My surroundings began to blur and distort like a window that hadn't been washed. Jax's features twisted at our inevitable goodbye, his hands lifting as if to reach for me. I desperately lunged forward, towards him, but the pull was too strong.

The last thing I saw was Jax's pain stricken face as darkness once more consumed the entirety of my vision.

TWENTY

BASH

I used to sit underwater in the bathtub and hold my breath.

One second.

Two seconds.

Two minutes.

There was something soothing about the water caressing my naked skin. In that brief moment, as my head ducked beneath the surface, I heard and felt nothing. The world was utterly silent.

My surroundings themselves were immensely blurry and distorted. From my vantage point, all I could see was the cracked ceiling with zigzagging water stains.

Oddly enough, that memory reverberated through my head now as I brought my arm over my nose. Flames and smoke were everywhere, creating impenetrable barriers I had to stumble through in order to move forward. Screams bounced off the walls, seeming to come from all directions. I couldn't discern where one scream ended and another began.

Z. I needed to find Z.

With that thought driving me, I held my breath and continued to race through the burning, collapsing inn. The smoke was getting thicker and thicker the farther I went, clogging my airways.

Fuck, how long could she last? How long could Ryland last? I had no doubt that my brother would do everything in his power to get our mate to safety.

But...

But it might not have been enough.

Refusing to allow that thought to solidify, I kicked open a door that led to a smoke congested kitchen. Empty. Of fucking course.

My lungs were protesting, demanding I inhale, but I stubbornly held my breath.

Was she still in her room? Had she already left?

My thoughts raced in a circle as I dived forward, just barely missing a falling wall decoration. Stumbling back to my feet, I forced myself forward, the flames eating away the walls on either side of me.

Fuck. Fuck. Fuck. Fuck.

Up ahead, I could see a sliver of sunlight piercing through the monotony of gray smoke. My cautious pace broke into a run at the prospect of getting fresh air.

With a loud cough, I exited the inn, just as another log of wood sparked and hissed, collapsing directly behind me.

I dropped to my knees beside the familiar figure lying unconscious on the pavement.

"Ryland," I gasped, shaking his shoulder. Was it the smoke? Had he passed out?

And where the fuck was Z?

I knew he would never leave without her, which meant she must've left to look for help. She would probably appear any fucking moment now.

Any.

Fucking.

Moment.

"Ryland!" I slapped his cheek softly, and his eyelids fluttered open.

"What?" he murmured groggily. Soot covered his face and clothes, and I noticed a section of his shirt had been burnt off. "Z!" He sat up abruptly, head swiveling from side to side.

"What the...?" I attempted to place my hands on his shoulders to calm him. "You're okay. You're safe."

"And Z?" he asked desperately, clenching my sleeves.

A lump the size of an acorn took up residence in my throat. If he didn't know where she was...

"Didn't she leave with you?" I asked, already preparing to run back into the burning building.

"She did," he agreed, and I exhaled in relief. His next words, however, were a proverbial kick to the nuts. "Someone attacked us."

"Someone?" I asked darkly. Red coated my vision at the thought of anyone, absolutely anyone, hurting my mate. Yeah. Yeah. Yeah. Hypocritical, considering how much of an ass I was to her? Maybe. But also very true. "Aaliyah?"

"I don't know." Ryland jumped to his feet, wobbling slightly before he steadied himself. "We need to fucking find her."

"We will," I assured him, already planning a tracking spell. Like with Jax, we needed an object from the person she loved the most and a strand of her hair. No matter what it took, we would get our girl back. But... "Jax." I stopped abruptly, and Ryland turned to stare at me, for once forgoing his usual shadows.

"What about him? We'll look for him as soon as we get Z back. It's what he would want."

I knew Ryland was right, but he was forgetting one important bit of information. "If we don't get him back soon, Z's life will be forfeit."

Fuck. Fuck. Fuck. My insides tangled into dozens of tight knots.

Ryland's face turned grave, seemingly carved from stone. "We need to split up."

I nodded sharply. "We need to get our girl and our brother back."

Or else we'd lose them both.

DAIR

tta ducked behind one of the ornately carved thrones, her bright red hair disappearing from view. I just barely resisted the urge to roll my eyes as I wheeled myself forward, the marble floors allowing my chair to glide smoothly.

"What are you doing, you dork?" I questioned, eyeing the strange girl.

Her freckled face popped over the gilded edge of the chair as she flashed me a smile.

"Being badass, of course," she answered matter-of-factly. This time, I *did* roll my eyes at her antics.

Atta had come to the conclusion that the mage king kept the tiny green portal tablets in a secret compartment under his throne. How she'd deduced this, I had no idea. Honestly? I didn't want to know.

The throne room was eerily silent, almost unnaturally so, like the quiet before a lion pounced. Most of the kings had retired to their respective kingdoms for the time being. Only the vampire king remained.

"We're a prince and princess, Atta," I stated. "We're allowed to be here."

Actually, our parents expected us to be. Some of us, like Bash and Devlin, were born with silver spoons in their mouths. They practically embodied royalty and privilege, capable of charming a crowd and bringing that same crowd to their knees. We were born to be our parents' perfect replacements.

Cold, vindictive, cunning.

I pictured my dad's malevolent expression as he cut through the tendons and bones of my legs. The glee emanating from his blue gaze. The curve of his lips in a sadistic smile.

The last thing I ever wanted to be was like them—the seven kings who ruled this empire, and their children, with iron fists.

Shuddering slightly, I focused back on Atta. Currently, she was on her hands and knees as she dug through the threading of the throne where she'd slit a barely perceptible hole. I wasn't surprised in the slightest to see a handful of magical pills, potions, and hex bags. The mage king might've been a lazy son of a bitch, but he still exuded power. If I had to guess, I would've said half of those spells were used for protection against assassination attempts.

The kings liked to believe they were untouchable, but that couldn't be further from the truth. I knew for a fact that there had been over twenty assassination attempts in the last six months alone.

"There!" Atta exclaimed triumphantly, holding up a tiny pill. She quickly shoved the rest of the supplies back into the throne's lining. "This right here will transport you to your heart's home. Cheesy? Fuck yes. Effective? Also fuck yes." She flashed me a smile, skipping forward until she was able to deposit the tablet in my hand.

"Thank you, Atta," I said sincerely, capturing her hand in mine and giving it a squeeze. "I know it hasn't been easy for you..."

Briefly, her bright eyes flashed with pain. I couldn't imagine what she must've been feeling, what she must've been going through. I would lose my fucking mind if I lost Z. To lose your other half...

No words could encapsulate it.

"I'm surviving," she murmured softly. Those large, haunted eyes turned away from me suddenly, as if my sympathy was too much for her to bear.

Before I could respond, the throne room doors were pushed open and a familiar man stepped in.

His light brown hair was slicked back from his arresting, chiseled face, and his eyes were two shades darker than his son's. Still, Jax's father, the vampire king, would've been recognizable anywhere. He moved with a purposeful, brisk gait, as if he didn't even notice the two of us hovering nearby like imbeciles. No surprise. He was entirely enraptured by the bag of blood he was drinking. That was his sin, after all.

Once you had a sip, you always craved more.

Finally, he halted, his head doing a comedic double take when he spotted us.

"What the blazes are you two doing here?" he demanded. His voice wasn't cruel like my father's or the shifter king's. It wasn't even indolent like Bash's dad. Instead, I would almost describe it as curious.

Yes, that was it. He was genuinely curious about why we were here.

But curiosity from the kings was very, very dangerous.

We survived by remaining under their radar, not at the forefront of it.

"We wanted to see you," Atta chirped, infusing false sincerity into her voice.

The vampire king, Dominic, appeared shocked. He blinked his long lashes at her in confusion.

"Yes," I agreed, hands tightening on the wheels of my chair. "We wanted to see how you were doing."

"Yes!" Atta nodded her head, face twisting. "It must be awful losing your son. Have you heard from him? Do you have any idea where he is?"

Dominic still appeared bemused, the wrinkles around his eyes becoming more pronounced, as he considered the two of us. It was almost as if he'd completely forgotten about Jax and was only now remembering that his sole heir and only son was missing.

Anger thrummed through me, the emotion momentarily blinding. Jax didn't deserve this piece of shit as a father. None of us fucking did.

"Oh, yes. Tragic," he drawled, already bored with this conversation.

"Let's hope Z is able to bring him back," I said through clenched teeth, seething.

Stay calm, Dair, I scolded myself. I couldn't afford to react to every minuscule thing the dumbass kings said. If they knew how much their words impacted me, it would only fuel the fire.

"Yes, yes." Dominic waved a hand dismissively, gliding past us to his throne. I sometimes wondered if the kings sat on them in empty rooms just to make themselves feel more powerful.

If Dominic was any indication, the answer to that question was a resounding *yes*.

"I'm sure it's imperative that you get him back," Atta insisted as I began to wheel myself out of the room, still gripping the tiny pill.

The vampire king regarded her lazily, almost impassively, as he reclined in his high-back throne. With his red cloak cascading around his slender frame and golden crown, he looked regal and powerful.

Terrifying.

"We have contingencies," Dominic stated, rolling his eyes.

"What do you mean?" Atta pressed, ignoring my warning look. She was always too curious for her own good. "Isn't Jax slated to take the throne when you retire? Or when you die?"

Fucking hell, Atta.

Dominic's grin grew, splitting his face in two. Twin fangs bit into his lower lip, making his smile appear even more terrifying. It was a face that evoked nightmares— bone-chilling nightmares. He'd never been the star of mine, though. That spot was reserved for a different king.

"*If* I die, my dear," he corrected, eyes glinting.

"Everyone dies," Atta prodded, crossing her arms over her chest.

He winked once before settling back in his throne, arms crossed and eyes closing. It was a dismissal if I'd ever seen one. Even Atta retreated, stepping up behind me to wheel me out of the room.

His following words trailed after us like a bitter wind slicing skin.

"Not the people who make a deal with the devil."

Z

The room smelled like death.

It had a distinct, pungent scent—oily almost, with undercurrents of copper and sweat. Words failed to truly encapsulate the atrocious smell that barraged my senses.

Wrinkling my nose, I forced my eyes to remain closed as I studied my surroundings. Someone was crying a little bit away from me, the sound grating at my eardrums. I could hear flesh hitting flesh, followed closely by a masculine scream. And someone else laughed raucously.

Where the fuck was I?

Surprisingly enough, I didn't appear to be tied up. My muscles flexed intermittently, the movements barely perceptible. First, my fingers wiggled, and then my toes. I shook my hands out, then my feet. Slowly, ever so slowly, I regained control of my numb body.

The ground was rough and cold beneath my cheek. Cement, more than likely.

Was this Aaliyah? Had she finally accomplished what she'd always wanted?

Me.

And where was Ryland?

Panic pulsed through me at the thought of my shadow mate. Was he here with me, or had he been left behind at the burning inn?

Oh, fuck. Phantom remnants of smoke clogged my airways as I thought of him. I prayed to whoever was listening that he was okay, that he was safe. I didn't want to consider the alternatives.

Cautiously, I popped open one eye to inventory my surroundings.

I appeared to be in a large cell, easily capable of housing at least twenty people. Bright fluorescent lights hung from the ceiling, illuminating the haggard faces of a dozen other humans.

What the actual fuck?

"Get the fuck up, bitch!" A kick was aimed at my unprotected middle. Before the foot could connect, I snapped my hand out and caught his ankle. He grunted, stumbling under my sudden assault, and I took his lapse in concentration to jump to my feet.

"Who do you work for?" I demanded, volleying my gaze from the man to the frightened humans. They were a variety of ages and races. The youngest appeared to be maybe fifteen, and the oldest was well into his eighties. Each of them had greasy, unruly hair and dirt stained cheeks. They looked...starved. Hollowed almost, as if they hadn't been fed a decent meal in weeks.

I counted at least ten assailants in the room with us,

all broad-shouldered and terrifying vampires. Their thin white shirts molded to their chests and biceps, and I noticed a strange symbol etched across the fabric, just over their hearts. It almost appeared to be a logo of some sort.

What the fuck?

"This one's feisty," the vampire before me sneered. "Where did you find her?"

A second man joined him, and my eyes narrowed into slits.

"You," I accused, glaring daggers at the arresting man from the inn. The one who'd kidnapped me.

His smile grew, childish dimples appearing in his cheeks, as he stepped forward.

"She won't bite, Bert," he soothed the other man, attention still locked on me. "She's only human, just like the others. Nothing special. Besides..." In a span of seconds, he was across the room with his hand around the fifteen-year-old boy's throat. "There's an easy way to subdue her."

"Don't!" I pleaded, instantly relaxing my defensive posture. The kid's wide eyes stared at me, begging me to do something, to save him. He looked at me as if I were supposed to be the hero of this story. The savior.

Didn't he know I was only a monster? I couldn't even save myself.

My body sagged in resignation as the guard, Bert, stepped in front of me and secured cuffs to my wrists. Fucking cuffs. When this was over, I was melting all of them.

Well, except for the ones Ryland wanted to use.

A thick chain was clasped from my handcuffs to the cuffs of the man in front of me, effectively holding all of us humans in a line. The boy was placed directly behind me, body trembling with terror.

"It'll be okay," I assured him meekly. But fuck "it." I didn't even know what "it" was. How could I promise it would be okay?

For some unidentifiable reason, this didn't feel like Aaliyah. I didn't know how I knew, only that I did.

So if it wasn't her, then who?

As one of the vampires checked my restraints, I peeked at his crisp white shirt and the strange image I'd noted earlier. On closer inspection, it appeared to be a pair of black fangs dripping with blood. That blood cascaded downwards to spell out "Bloody Carnival."

That didn't sound good.

We were led through what appeared to be an industrial warehouse. A draft made the air bitter and chilly, slicing at my exposed skin.

A woman near the front of the line began to cry, and one of the vampires hit her over the head. I bared my teeth but remained stubbornly silent. As soon as I was free...

And then what, Z? I asked myself dryly. *Could you really take on ten vampires? While simultaneously protecting the humans?*

Have you ever had an *oh, fuck* moment? Well, this was mine. Sometimes, I liked the word fuck, especially when it concerned my mates. But this type of fuck? It was a *fuck me in the asshole without any lube* sort of deal.

Basically, it was a fuck times ten.

The vampire who'd kidnapped me paused suddenly, standing at the front of the group with his hands clasped behind his back.

"When you are placed with the other cattle, you will remain silent. No speaking. No crying. No fighting. If you do any of that, we will kill you." He nodded towards the other guards to indicate whom, exactly, he meant. My pulse skyrocketed at his crude words.

Cattle?

"Stay in a single file line as we lead you to the bullpen," he instructed. With that ominous statement, he heaved open a heavy metal door.

Immediately, sounds assaulted me—laughs, screams, cries, and conversations. Intermingled with all of that was thumping music, the bass reverberating through my body.

As we stepped through the door, my eyes practically bugged out of my head. It appeared to be a tent, pillars erected around the sides and in the center. At first glance, it looked like a circus of some sort. The red fabric of the tent and bright artificial lights provided the area with an eerie feel.

Horror filled me, consumed me, gripped my throat in an iron vise and refused to let go. What I was seeing...

It was beyond wrong, beyond depraved. My stomach twisted and tightened, seconds from expelling the contents from last night's dinner. I'd known the Shifter and Mermaid Kingdoms were fucked up and twisted, but this was an entirely separate level.

Bloody Carnival catered to vampires, which was no surprise, given the name. Near the front entrance of the tent, two female vampires were selling tickets to nightmares of all species. The majority were vamps, but I spotted a few of the others as well.

A stage was assembled near the back of the room, where humans were being sold off. At least that was what I assumed the purpose was. A stout auctioneer stood behind a podium, gesticulating wildly with his gavel. In the center of the stage, a thirty-year-old woman stood naked under the blinding lights. She was sobbing, attempting futilely to cover her body from the prying, hungry eyes.

Against the opposite wall, numerous benches were positioned for vampires to feed from humans. All of the humans were shackled and screaming as the nightmares tore at their flesh. More than one dead body littered the ground.

In the center of the tent, numerous stalls were set up, each detailing a morbid game. One appeared to be pin the tail on the human. A lone human male stood in the center of the stall, crying, as vampires jabbed him with daggers and swords. Next to that stall was an ancient guillotine and a bucket full of severed heads. I spotted what appeared to be gallows a little ways down, each holding a wiggling, thrashing human.

The bastards weren't just selling humans.

They were torturing and killing them.

As I watched, horrified, the woman on the stage was gripped by two smirking vampires. She screamed as they dragged her down the steps and straight to a forest just outside of the tent. The wooden sign overhead labeled it as "The Maze."

Fuck. Fuck. Fuck.

My hands trembled as we were paraded forward. Vampires leered at us, flashing fangs.

How could this type of institution exist?

Did the princes know about this?

I wanted desperately to believe that they didn't, but I remembered Bash mentioning human carnivals.

We stopped in front of a large, wooden pen that sat adjacent to the stage. Over fifty humans were huddled together in the cramped space. Before we entered, one of the carnival's employees unhooked us from each other and removed the handcuffs from everyone *except* for me. Asshole. The guard then slid open a padlocked door and pushed us inside, slamming it behind us.

From this position, we were on display for the malicious vampires to see. More than one stuck their faces to the fence and hurled insults and derogatory phrases at us.

How am I going to get out of this? How am I going to save all these people?

I didn't want to admit it, but I wasn't sure it would be possible.

Somebody appeared behind me and stuck a key into my cuffs. They clattered to the floor with an audible clank.

I turned, instantly on alert, only to freeze when I noticed who'd joined me in the bullpen.

"Axel?"

TWENTY-THREE

Z

I said his name again, half wondering if he was a mirage that would disappear when my sanity returned. But why I would imagine Axel, of all people, remained a mystery.

He placed a single finger to his lips before disappearing from view, blending into the shadows so seamlessly, I couldn't differentiate where he ended and they began.

My head was left spinning as I stared at the spot he'd disappeared from.

Was he a part of this?

Question after question clamored for my undivided attention. Instead of focusing on any of them, I spun in a wild circle.

The younger boy from earlier huddled near me, as if he sensed the predator lurking just beneath my angelic exterior.

"What's your name?" I whispered to him, my voice

overshadowed by the desperate cries and screams of the other prisoners.

"Miles," he responded. His hand instinctively hooked under the hem of my shirt, holding on for dear life. When he realized what he was doing, he released me instantly and straightened his spine. He attempted to appear nonchalant, unfazed by what we were enduring, but his hands trembled by his sides. His face turned ashen as he stared through the throng of humans, wincing as he looked towards the stage.

"I'm Z. It's nice to meet you, Miles. How old are you?"

"Fourteen," he answered immediately.

"What happened?" I questioned, carefully observing my surroundings with an almost clinical detachment. One of the humans, a burly male, lunged towards the fence, pounding his fists against the distressed wood. Two guards stepped forward instantly, sticking a cattle prod through the gap. The human fell backwards with an enraged snarl before blissfully drifting into uncon-sciousness.

"I live with my sister near the border of the Vampire Kingdom," he began doggedly. A lump in his throat moved as he swallowed. "I was gathering supplies at the marketplace when a trader captured me."

I stared at the kid, truly looked at him, for the first time. His honey blond hair was curled around his ears, accentuating the golden flecks in his spring green eyes. His face was slim and lean, his cheekbones prominent. Despite his disheveled appearance, there was an iron glint in his eyes that made me think this kid had been through hell. Been through hell...and survived. Maybe not unscathed, but then again, none of us were.

We all wore scars from our battles, not all of them visible.

"Where are your parents?" I queried.

"Dead," he said bluntly, not an ounce of inflection in his voice. His features were just as cold and impassive.

"And your sister? Where is she?"

His mask cracked briefly as raw pain flitted across his face.

"She should be fine..." He scrubbed a hand through his curls. "She's smart, smarter than most kids her age..."

"How old is she?" I questioned, dreading the answer.

"She turned eight last month."

"Fuck," I cursed. An eight-year-old kid? Alone? In this world?

"We live over in RoseGrove," he muttered, another stab of pain appearing in his eyes. "By the watermill. The property has been abandoned for years. She loves it. Says it reminds her of those adventure novels Mom used to read us."

From the way he talked about her, I could tell he loved her immensely. His eyes warmed significantly, like a piece of ice being held over a flame. A wistful smile anointed his face as he talked about her.

"You're going to get back to her," I vowed. A tiny sliver of steel surrounding my heart withered and died. "I promise."

He appeared unconvinced, but nodded once.

That was fine. He didn't have to believe me for me to follow through on my promise.

The lock clicked open, and the long-haired man from before sauntered in, a wicked gleam in his eyes. Ignoring me completely, he grabbed a fistful of a woman's hair and dragged her towards the stage. Two more guards closed and locked the door behind them.

"Who is that?" I asked, lips curling away from my teeth as I stared at my kidnapper.

"Hans," Miles replied, voice curt. "He runs the Bloody Carnival."

I watched Hans parade the woman to the center of the stage, where the auctioneer leered at her. In one swoop, the girl's dirty dress dropped to the ground and she stood naked before the assembled vampires.

"One female human, aged thirty-seven. Found near the Shifter Kingdom. Bidding will start at one hundred coins. Do I hear one hundred? One hundred to the gentleman in the back. How about one-fifty. Do I hear a one-fifty? One-fifty to Cindy Mason! How about two hundred?"

The voices of the crowd blurred together as the bidding total increased. Males and females alike raised their paddles in the air, demanding the auctioneer's attention. At one thousand two hundred coins, the woman was sold to a slimy vampire who wasted no time collecting his purchase and dragging her towards a series of secluded rooms.

I didn't even want to think about what went down there.

"I'm scared," Miles whispered, interlocking his fingers with mine. I gave his hand a reassuring squeeze, attempting to soothe the terrified boy.

What if I couldn't get us out of this mess?

What if I could...but at the exchange of all these other people's lives? Would I be able to live with myself?

It was important to accept the girl staring back at you in the mirror. But my reflection was riddled with scars and bruises, each one depicting a new horror. My experiences had shaped me and molded me into the assassin you saw today. I relied extensively on my own morality, my ability to detect right from wrong. Without that, I had...nothing. I would be no better than the nightmares I'd been tasked to kill.

The door to the bullpen opened again, and this time, Hans made a beeline directly towards me. No, not me.

Miles.

The boy attempted to hide behind me, fear dancing in his eyes, and I moved to stand protectively in front of him.

"Don't you fucking dare," I hissed through clenched teeth.

Hans's smile only grew. "Z...Z...Z..." He shook his head slowly. "Why do you feel the need to protect the boy?"

I didn't answer, staring at him with narrowed, penetrating eyes. I hoped he felt my rage on his skin like a physical burn.

I hoped he bled.

"Don't touch him," I said darkly. My daggers had been confiscated when I'd been knocked unconscious, but I was still capable of fighting with my fists.

"I won't touch the little boy," Hans drawled, a

sardonic twist to his plush lips. "But you, on the other hand…"

I didn't fight him, or the five other guards, that grabbed me and pulled me out of the bullpen. I should've been flattered that they thought I required additional men to secure me.

Behind me, Miles screamed, the sound eerily similar to that of my own voice so many years ago. When I saw my parents killed by shifters.

Hans laughed, the sound borderline manic, as he dragged me up the stairs of the stage.

The lights were so bright, it was impossible to decipher any faces in the crowd. I didn't know if it made this situation more or less daunting.

More. Definitely more.

When Hans made a move to rip off my clothes, I growled at him. Actually fucking growled, as if I had the slightest chance in hell of being the predator here. His eyes glimmered with mirth, but he held his hands up placatingly, backing up a step.

Keeping his eyes trained on me, Hans stalked to the podium and grabbed the gavel out of the auctioneer's hand.

"We have here a lovely specimen, straight from the capital itself!" he declared to the enthusiastic cheers from the crowd. "Z here is the winner of the Damning and the kingdoms' assassin!"

This time, the cheers were nearly deafening. More and more people were congregating at the front of the stage, staring up at me in rapt fascination. Though their features were blurry, indistinct, I knew their eyes would be trained on me.

"Isn't she beautiful?" Hans slapped my ass, and it took every ounce of willpower not to grab his wrist, crack all of the bones, and then shove each individual finger up his nose. Or butt. I might have an unhealthy fascination with anal play. "Starting bid is two thousand gold coins."

There was a flurry of movement down below, almost as if every nightmare was taking a collective breath, before the shouting began. My heart pounded in tandem to each new number being hurled at Hans. Two thousand. Three thousand. Four thousand. More and more voices were screaming over each other as they attempted to buy me.

Buy me.

Two words I'd never thought would be used in the same sentence.

A strange sort of calmness cascaded over me, leaving me oddly bereft, as if I were missing a crucial piece of myself. Was this how I was going to die? By asshole vampires attempting to sell me off?

How did Hans even know I'd be at the inn when I was? How did he know the truth about my mating bonds to the princes? Those were questions I wasn't sure I'd ever get the answers to.

And, oddly enough, I didn't care. Sure, I cared that I was dying—there was still a lot I needed to do, a lot I needed to say—but the why didn't matter. Only the how.

My eyes flickered towards the cage still housing the other humans. Miles had his face pressed to the wooden bars, staring at me as intently as I was him. He was a stranger, but I felt an odd pang in my chest at the thought of never saying goodbye to him.

Fuck, my mates were turning me soft. But then again, I'd always had a spot in my heart reserved for kids in need. Maybe because I'd once been that kid desperate for someone to save me, to love me, to protect me from this strange, cruel world with monsters lurking behind every corner.

Hans's voice filtered back to me, snapping me out of my reverie. "Going once, going twice, sold! To the gentleman in the back for twenty thousand two hundred and seventy-five gold coins."

The crowd began to grumble as one of the guards pushed me forward, towards the stairs leading down the stage.

"I can walk, asshole!" I snapped at the man holding my arm. My eyes were narrowed into slits as I descended with as much poise and dignity as I was capable of having in a time like this. These horrid men and women could do whatever they wanted with me, but they wouldn't break me. They *couldn't*, not after what I'd endured. My heart had been broken and trampled on, but I was still standing, still fighting.

And I would continue to do so.

With an imperious set to my chin, I stared down my nose at the approaching figure. I half expected it to be Axel. Maybe it was wishful thinking, but a part of me deflated when the assassin didn't saunter up with a cocky grin on his face.

Instead, the vampire was unfamiliar, with carrot

orange hair, bright blue eyes, and a pudgy belly. I could feel my heart shrinking, shriveling into a ball, at the sight.

"Hello, Z," he hissed, baring his fangs.

I didn't know what was going to happen, but I had a feeling I would be irrevocably changed.

TWENTY-FOUR

LUPE

My body thrummed with unrestrained energy and agitation as the car glided down the backroads. Killian sat in the passenger seat, while Devlin drove.

Bash had performed a spell to discover Z's location—a secluded forest on the outskirts of the Vampire Kingdom. We didn't know for sure what we would face, but we were prepared for anything and everything.

He hadn't told us which object he'd used, which person he believed she loved the most, and we hadn't pressed. At least not at that moment. I would hound my brother for information as soon as we got our mate back. Killian had claimed he saw Bash with an object from each of us, though, which abated my possessive jealousy.

Fuck, we needed to get Z back.

I wasn't a violent person by nature. I much preferred to settle arguments and disagreements with my words instead of my fists. Did it make me a horrible person that I was contemplating violence and murder in order to rescue my mate? Maybe. But I would do what needed to be done in order to ensure her safety.

My hands fisted on my thighs, sharp claws protruding from my fingers and digging into the fabric of my pants.

As a direct descendant of Wrath, shifters were known for being volatile. Quick to anger and slow to forgive. I'd always considered myself better than my brethren. But now? I was filled with an insatiable rage that demanded release, demanded an outlet.

If Z was hurt...

Red consumed my vision at the thought of anyone harming my mate.

I'd screwed up with T. I knew that. Z knew that. T knew that.

But what the hell was I supposed to do? There were no right answers. Either I allowed my father to inflict unspeakable horrors on the human...or I did it myself.

At least with me, I could ensure that the man didn't die.

I scrubbed a large hand down my face as pain speared me, a physical entity that drew blood. It felt like I was in one of those coffins with nails protruding from every wall. No matter where I stepped or how I moved, the nails dug into my skin.

"Take a left up here," Killian murmured quietly, attention fixated on the map. Bash and Ryland had gone the opposite way to retrieve Jax, while we went to find Z. Was it stupid to separate? Absolutely. Did we have a choice? No way in hell.

Z had five days to find and bring Jax back to the capital, where the vampire king was awaiting us. One day had already passed, and this day was rapidly drawing to a close.

Fuck! I pounded my fist against the back of the seat, and Killian jumped, spinning towards me with wide eyes. I knew all of my brothers were scared that I would give in to my inevitable rage, like all of the other shifters in my family line did before me. Each new event was a block being balanced precariously on an already toppling building. How long until it fell over?

As the sun dipped beneath the boughs of trees, casting the road in shades of gray and black, a snarl escaped my lips.

I needed to get Z back.

It wasn't long until we entered what appeared to be a warehouse district. I counted at least twenty warehouses sprouting from the ground, like gray cement prisons. My eyes latched onto the farthest building, adjacent to the forest. Connected to the corrugated, iron warehouse was a red tent, easily the size of three modern houses. Swaths of orange and yellow dipped down from the pillar holding it up in the center. Raucous laughter drifted through the air, easily audible through the opened windows of the car. Vampires were both spilling out of the tent and entering it.

Women were dressed in long, elegant gowns, while the men wore impeccably-tailored suits. Some carried machetes and swords and wore masks that obscured their features.

What the fucking hell was this?

"What?" Killian muttered, echoing my own thoughts.

His face had gone a deadly shade of white. Devlin's hands were clenched on the steering wheel.

"I've heard rumors about places like this," the genie said, tone dark and deadly.

"What are you talking about?" The words were practically a growl ripped from my throat. I could feel my teeth elongating into sharp canines, seconds from tearing into flesh. And fuck, I wanted to. I wanted this entire goddamn world to burn if that was what it took to find and save Z.

"A human carnival," Devlin whispered.

I was out the door before the car even came to a complete stop, stalking across the lawn. The tent loomed before me ominously, lights emanating from the fabric. Two female vampires manned what appeared to be a ticket booth, and they both perked up when they caught sight of me.

"Are there humans in here?" I growled. My clawed hands dug into the gilded wood of the booth.

"Duh," one woman replied, cocking her head to the side. She nodded at the logo hanging above her head.

Bloody Carnival.

The second girl's eyes flickered towards the warehouse, where I saw a truck marked "Trader" idling near the entrance. The back door was open, revealing a collection of chains, ropes, and handcuffs.

Anger thrummed through me at the thought of any human enduring such treatment. No doubt, these traders collected humans, brought them to the warehouse, and then transferred them to the carnival.

It was a human-trafficking ring.

Footsteps echoed behind me, and I stepped out of the way just as two vampires walked up. A couple, if their interlocked hands were any indication. They were smiling, laughing, as if they were visiting family friends and not a fucked-up version of hell.

"Do you see all this?" Devlin asked, sidling up behind me. Killian stood directly beside him, arms crossed over his chest and eyes anxious.

"I see it," I replied through gritted teeth. I nodded towards the warehouse. "You guys go look in there for Z. Free any humans you find. I'll go to the carnival."

I didn't wait for them to protest, marching towards the ticket booth and dropping a handful of gold coins onto the counter.

The woman slid a golden ticket through a gap in the screen, a sultry smirk playing on her lips.

"Anything else I can give you, big guy?" she purred. Without bothering to respond, I stalked through the tent curtain.

It was...awful. Absolutely fucking awful. My eyes latched first on the stage, where an older man was being bid on by vampires and other nightmares. Various stalls lined the perimeter of the tent, all popular carnival games but with a macabre twist.

It was crowded, almost unbearably so, as I shouldered my way through the throng of eager participants. How could people go along with this?

I watched as a blindfolded human was spun wildly in a circle, stumbling over his two feet. When the vampires finally released him, he was forced to run as they fired arrows at him. One caught him in the back of the shoulder blade, and he fell to the ground with an audible thump. The vampires didn't waste a second before pouncing, eating him alive to the sound of his agonized screams.

Oh, God. I'm going to be sick.

A group of incubi stepped past me, all bedecked in masks. I wondered, briefly, if these were the same men and women who'd kidnapped Z. An instinctive growl emitted from my throat before I could contain it.

"Ah, who do we have here?" A vampire stealthily glided forward, and the crowd parted like Moses parting the Red Sea. "The shifter prince?" His eyes widened comically as he stopped directly in front of me, surveying me with a critical, penetrating gaze.

"Who the fuck are you?" I growled out, flexing my muscles. I had a precarious hold on my bear, who was currently roaming and prowling just beneath the surface of my human skin. Focusing on my enhanced sense of smell, I inhaled deeply.

And growled vehemently at the scent of Z wafting off of him.

"Where the fuck is my mate?" I hissed, wrapping my meaty hand around his throat. One snap, and this man would cease to exist. One fucking snap...

The psychopath laughed jovially, as if I weren't threatening him but instead inviting him over for dinner.

"I wouldn't do that if I were you," he gasped, face turning red. Some of the bystanders fled at my aggressive act. There was nothing more terrifying than a shifter overtaken by wrath. Guards in white shirts with the demented black logo circled me, raising tranquilizer guns.

"Where is she?" My words were guttural, nearly unrecognizable, as I peered into his bright eyes. Maybe if I squeezed hard enough, they would pop out of his head.

The thought filled me with grim amusement.

But any good will fled as I considered the slowly circling employees of Bloody Carnival.

We were going to play a new game.

Me—attack.

Them—die.

With a feral roar, I shifted into my bear and lunged.

TWENTY-FIVE

Z

The vampire led me down a long hallway and into a derelict room at the very end. Moans, cries, and screams emitted from the surrounding rooms, each new noise sending pinpricks of terror skating down my spine.

The room we entered had a musty, stained couch positioned against the far wall of the room. Opposite, there was what appeared to be a box of chains, whips, and other grisly instruments. I gagged over the noxious smell that barraged me as soon as I entered—piss, tobacco, coppery blood, and something that was almost akin to shit. Cobwebs hung from each corner of the room, and for the first time in my life, I felt more like the helpless fly trapped in the spider's bindings than the predator itself.

But even spiders could be squashed.

I repeated that in my head as anger rampaged through me.

This man, this nightmare, would pay for what he'd done.

My feet landed in a puddle, and I prayed to whoever was listening that it was only water, not piss or blood.

"Get down, bitch," the vampire snapped, shoving me onto the lumpy-looking couch. The stench was more pungent with my face against the cushion, my nose wrinkling in disgust at the myriad of putrid smells. "I'm going to fuck your pussy so fucking hard. Then I'm going to cut you open and drink you dry. Don't worry. I'll fuck your dead body too, just as I did with the other women before you. Though…" His hand moved to my ankle, trailing up my calf and to my thigh. "They weren't as pretty as you."

There was chafing at my wrists from the handcuffs this man had placed on me, but I ignored the sudden stab of pain as I lifted my head and leveled a glare at him.

"You're going to pay for this," I hissed as he placed his hand on the nape of my neck, traveling down my spine. When he reached the hem of my shirt, he paused, fingers gliding across the exposed skin. I couldn't help but tremble in revulsion.

Spewing vitriol from my eyes, I flipped onto my back and glared up at him with elemental fury.

"Is this the only way you can get laid?" I mocked. "Buying women and bringing them here? Pathetic."

My head jerked back as his fist connected with my cheek. His lips curled in a hideous sneer.

"Shut your mouth, bitch!" he hissed through clenched teeth.

"Bitch? Seriously? What type of misogynistic shit is

that?" I said with a scoff, enjoying the way his face turned red with rage. I could handle his ire, his anger, his fury.

I couldn't handle his lust.

He wrapped his meaty hands around my throat, squeezing tightly, but my smile only grew.

Fury pummeled me from all sides, demanding an outlet.

Still smirking, I lifted my legs up, my hands firmly secured behind my back with the handcuffs, and wrapped them around his neck. His eyes widened comically as he released me, scratching at my face, but I only tightened my ankles around him.

With a twist of my legs, I flipped him onto his back on the ground, falling on top of him. The position caused an intense ache to reverberate through my arms.

Fuck, I needed to get these handcuffs off.

I scrambled to my feet, glaring down at the disgusting excuse for a man, and stomped on his nuts. His enraged roar was music to my fucking ears. To make sure he stayed down, I kicked them a few more times until he was crying helplessly, cupping his cock.

After he'd secured the handcuffs on me, given to him by the employees of the carnival, I'd watched him slip the key into his jacket pocket. I wasted no time squatting down and grabbing them behind my back.

It took me a few tries to unhook the cuffs, fumbling with the key behind my back, but after the sixth attempt, the cuffs clattered to the ground. I clenched and unclenched my hands, staring at the bloody skin on both my wrists, before focusing my attention on the vampire still moaning in pain.

"Fucking asshole," I murmured, straddling his waist and raining down punches. They weren't just for me, not really. They were for the countless other women who'd come before me. The women who couldn't fight back. The women who'd endured god only knew what because of this man.

Everyone in this carnival would fucking pay.

His mottled face contorted in pain as I grabbed his neck and twisted once. I took great satisfaction in staring at his bruised, disfigured face. Both of his eyes were swollen shut, and his skin was a combination of blue and green.

I hoped he felt fear before he died. Pain.

I hoped he regretted all of his life decisions.

Breathing heavily, I climbed off of his chest and spat on his face. Fucking asshole.

"Wow," a sly voice said from the shadows. I spun, heart hammering a mile a minute, only to relax marginally when I spotted Axel. A grin played on his lips as he stared between me and the dead body. "I came here to save the day, and lo and behold, you've already killed the man."

"He's scum," I snapped, anger thrumming through me. "Not a man."

"True." Axel shrugged once before stepping up to the body and unzipping his pants. I quickly turned away before I could see his penis.

Because, ew.

"What the hell are you doing?" I squeaked. If Axel was into necrophilia, I might kill him. Again, ew.

I heard what sounded like splattering liquid and realized the crazy assassin was peeing on the vampire's dead body.

"Just giving the rapist a present," Axel murmured conversationally.

"You're fucking psycho." Rolling my eyes, I took one last glance around the room, my eyes zeroing in on a puddle of blood pooling across the disgusting green carpeting. My heart ached for the men and women who perished every damn day because of this event. "We need to stop this," I said at last, turning to Axel, just as he zipped up his pants. "We need to end this once and for all."

His growing smile terrified me. Like, if I were a lesser human, I would have shit in my pants right at that moment.

"One step ahead of you, little one." With an elaborate flourish, he pulled open his coat so I could see the detonator hidden under the flaps. "We get the humans out... and then this building goes boom. Then we'll find and rescue your vampire lover."

Was it fucked up that my smile grew exponentially? Probably.

But I rather liked his exploding building plan.

"I might not hate you, Axel," I mused, accepting the knife he offered.

He flashed his blindingly white teeth. "You definitely should hate me. But how about a truce for today?"

"A killing truce?" I asked with a snort.

"It's my favorite kind."

Z

"You take left, and I take right?" Axel suggested, raising one dark brow.

"No hurting innocents," I warned.

He grinned devilishly. "Person with the most kills wins?"

"You're on."

Without another word, we separated, my borrowed knife raised. In the distance, I could hear enraged growls and screams. It almost sounded as if...as if a shifter was attacking. What the hell?

Pocketing that snippet of information away for later, I focused on the bullpen. I counted five guards, all vampires, standing sentry in front of the entrance.

Five against one? I liked those odds.

With a beguiling smile, I raced through the teeming throng of nightmares. A few of them screamed as I roughly shoved them aside, but no one tried to stop me. They may have been monsters, but at the end of the day, they were nothing but cowards first and foremost.

I slid my dagger into the first guard's head, stealthily pulling it out and aiming it towards the second man. He lunged at me, fangs extended, but I ducked before he could initiate contact. Sliding my leg out, I caught him on the back of his knees, forcing him to the ground. Before I could shove my dagger into his eyes, a third vampire grabbed my arm and wrenched it back.

I cried out at the initial stab of pain as he roughly pried my fingers open, forcing me to drop my dagger. With a ferocious snarl, I threw my head back, listening to the satisfying crack of bones breaking as it connected with his nose.

"You little—" Before he could finish his sentence, I dropped to the ground, grabbed my dagger, and sliced it across his heels. He fell to the floor with a pained cry.

Without preamble, I sliced a line from ear to ear.

The vampire I hadn't been able to kill lunged at me, but I easily turned my blade upwards so it landed in his chest. His eyes glazed over before he collapsed beside his buddy.

The remaining two vampires, farthest away from the bullpen's entrance, rushed forward at the same time, one from each side. The fastest one reached for me, but I agilely flipped over his head, landing on my feet behind him. The second one wasn't able to slow down his forward momentum, and I moved away, just as he collided with Baddie One.

A bright burst of purple erupted around me like a violet mist permeating the air. I squeezed my eyes shut, turning my face away from the eerie light. When I reopened them, all of the vampires had disappeared from sight. All that remained were piles of ash.

Devlin and Killian stood before me, radiating energy and raw power. Purple light emanated from Devlin's body, and his dark curls were swaying in an invisible breeze. Killian held Devlin's lamp.

I watched as my genie's eyes slowly focused on me, the power diminishing, almost as if it was being sucked back into his body. Before I could make a noise, Killian raced forward and took me into his arms.

"You're okay," he breathed, burying his face in my tangled hair.

"I'm okay," I agreed as Devlin joined the huddle. He wrapped me in his arms from behind, body shaking, and whispered inarticulate words into my hair. I wanted to remain in their embraces forever, but I couldn't. Not with the guards running towards us. Not with the participants of the carnival screaming and fleeing the scene. Not with the humans staring at me with wide-eyed wonder. "But we need to stop this."

Pulling away, I focused on the bullpen's padlock. Maybe one of the guards had a key…

"I got this," Killian said determinedly, stalking forward with Devlin's lamp. He held it up to his lips and whispered, "I wish for this door to be opened."

"Your wish is my command." The purple mist once more surrounded Devlin like a plum-colored sheen. Power emitted from him in palpable waves as he focused on the padlock.

It dropped to the ground instantly, and the door swung open.

The humans rushed forward in a flurry, thanking me and sobbing. It was heartening to see people helping people. Women and men alike were huddling protectively around the younger children and older women.

"Miles?" I called as the last of the humans disappeared from the bullpen. "Miles?"

I couldn't see the young boy.

"Z, wait!" Devlin called as I broke into a run, racing opposite the stampede of people.

"Miles!" My voice was hoarse from screaming as I looked in each direction. "Miles!"

Near the entrance of the tent, I spotted a large bear fighting off at least twenty guards. He broke through the ranks ruthlessly, viciously, blood coating his teeth and matted fur.

Lupe, I thought dizzily, watching the bear shifter bite the head off a vampire.

I didn't see Hans among the bodies, and my stomach tightened painfully at the reminder that the ringleader was still out there.

"Miles?" I spun in a circle, blinking to stop the onslaught of tears, when I finally spotted the honey blond mound of hair. I raced towards what appeared to be a shooting range, though all of the nightmares had long since evacuated. Lying on the ground, in a pool of blood, was the young boy.

I dropped to my knees as a sob was wrenched from my throat.

No. No. No. No.

I reached a hand out to touch him, only to immediately pull it back. Something as pure and as bright as him shouldn't be tainted by my darkness.

You failed him.

An enraged cry left my lips as I stumbled to my feet. Away. Away. Away.

I needed to get away.

"My God," Killian breathed, materializing directly behind me. When he placed a hand on my shoulder, I exploded like a dam bursting. I couldn't handle the pain. I didn't *want* to handle it.

I turned in the incubus' arms, shoving my face into his neck as I sobbed.

"I'm so fucking sorry, Z," Devlin whispered from behind me.

"I want them all to pay," I rasped out, pushing away from Killian and brushing at my eyes. Miles' face was going to haunt me for years to come.

"They will," Killian promised, brushing at my hair. His eyes ensnared mine, and I was the helpless prey caught in his trap.

"Baby," a guttural, husky voice said from behind me. When I turned, I saw Lupe standing amidst a sea of bodies, naked and drenched in blood. His eyes glimmered as he struggled to control his bear. When he caught sight of my stricken expression, he roared, his face contorting slightly. Fur sprouted on his cheeks and neck before he pushed his animal further down.

"Go," Killian whispered. "He needs you."

I stumbled forward, my legs failing me, and Lupe breached the remaining distance between us. His hard, sculpted body molded to mine as I clung to him.

"He's dead," I murmured into his salty skin. "He's dead."

"I'm so sorry, baby. I'm sorry I couldn't get here sooner." Lupe's protective embrace was comforting and soothing, abating the tension thrumming through me.

"I didn't even know the kid," I whimpered. "But he's..." I trailed off. They all could see what, exactly, had happened. "I want them all to pay," I repeated.

"Well, I can't make them all pay," Axel murmured from in front of us. Lupe growled sharply, angling his body so it was in front of mine protectively, but I peered at the assassin grimly, eyeing the body he held like it was a demented offering.

Unlike my mates and me, he wasn't covered in blood. There wasn't a hair out of place, but the manic gleam in his dark eyes hinted that he hadn't stayed away from the fight.

Axel dropped Hans in front of me.

"I'll allow this kill to belong to you," the assassin purred with a wink.

Lupe growled threateningly but didn't stop me from stepping forward with my blood covered blade extended.

"You hurt a lot of people," I whispered darkly to the vampire at my feet. Funnily enough, he didn't look so scary in my shadow. He appeared weak. Vulnerable. The hint of fear in his eyes only emphasized that.

Still, he laughed maniacally, throwing back his head and clutching his stomach.

"I'm sorry about your little friend," Hans said cheerfully, nodding towards Miles.

Rage momentarily blinded me. It ate away at my soul,

gnawing at a precious, diminutive piece of me. Only Killian's hand on my shoulder stopped me from running forward and jabbing my dagger into his heart.

"How many of these…these *torture houses* do you run?" I asked, upper lip curling in disgust.

"Bite me, bitch." Hans spat at my feet, and Lupe lunged forward, a roar emerging from his throat. He punched Hans lightning fast in the face, and the vampire's head jerked back. Blood coated his lips and cheeks, but he still offered a feeble smile. "I'm not telling you anything."

"No?" I asked darkly, kneeling before him. I grabbed his right hand and splayed his fingers out. Maintaining eye contact, I placed the tip of my blade below his thumbnail. "Are you sure about that?"

Like before, genuine fear flickered in his bright gaze, but he tamped it down before it could completely manifest.

"Positive," he stated, smirking. I hesitated, only briefly, before glancing over my shoulder at Killian.

"You can leave," I told my gentle incubus quietly. I didn't want him to see me like this. I would die inside, shatter irreparably, if he looked at me any differently. Killian had always been the one to see the good in me, the light. He made me want to be gentler and kinder.

He made me want to be a better person.

Devlin had seen my darkness, my hostility and anger. He knew my demons intimately. Even Lupe, as gentle as he was, understood my vengeance better than anyone else. He dealt with his own wrath every day of his life.

Killian's jaw clenched stubbornly as his hands balled into fists. "I'm staying."

"You sure, brother?" Devlin queried, placing a hand on his shoulder. "No one will think less of you if you choose to leave."

Killian's face paled slightly, but he held his chin up with grim determination. "Positive."

"He's the weak one, isn't he?" Hans snarked, seemingly unconcerned that my blade was underneath his nail. Either he didn't see me as a threat or he was an idiot.

"He's one of the strongest men I know," I said resolutely, dropping my knife and unbuttoning Hans's pants in quick movements. His eyes flared with lust and banked heat, but that expression quickly turned into horror when I dropped my knife to his cock. "Now, tell me what I want to know." I grabbed his balls with my other hand, holding them out so my blade could touch the sliver of skin connecting them to his dick. "I'll cut off your balls first before moving to your penis. Don't test me."

Horror filled his expression, and it was fucking orgasmic to see.

"Tell the lady," Axel said cheerfully. I smirked, pressing hard enough with the blade to draw blood.

"Yes, tell the lady," I mocked, smiling wickedly. "Or don't." I shrugged nonchalantly. "I'm always looking for an excuse to cut off dicks." Leaning forward until my face was a hairsbreadth away from his, I added, "Tell me fucking *everything*."

"Who sent you after Z?" Devlin threw in from behind me. He sounded begrudgingly impressed at my methods of torture, and when I glanced over my shoulder at him, his eyes flickered with pride. I'd always known Lin had a dark side to him.

When Hans remained stubbornly silent, I pressed down with my blade. He attempted to move away, but Axel was quick to press down on his shoulders, stilling him.

"Fuck!" the vampire cried, throwing his head back.

"Was it Aaliyah?" Killian questioned. "The kings?"

"No, no, no!" Hans adamantly shook his head. "It was a male. I didn't recognize him. We made a deal."

"What was the deal?" I demanded.

Tears sprang to the vampire's eyes, but if he thought they would deter me, he was sorely mistaken. This monster didn't deserve my sympathy or pity.

"He gave me your location in exchange for a soul," he cried, thrashing.

I exchanged an uneasy look with Devlin. "A soul?"

"Yes." Hans was sobbing now, fat, ugly tears cascading down his disgusting face. "Our carnival came into contact with a soul a few years ago. This man wanted it."

"What's his name?" Lupe growled out, hands bunching into fists. I didn't know if he was planning on punching Hans or the unnamed traitor, but I couldn't fault him on either.

I was also feeling quite punchy.

Someone had betrayed us. Someone who knew about our mating bonds had sold us out to the lowest of scum.

"I don't know his name. I never saw him. He always wore a mask."

"How many more of these carnivals do you have?"

Axel leaned down so he was at face level with the sobbing man. "And don't you dare fucking lie to us."

"Only this one," Hans cried. "I swear to you. Please, just let me go. I won't do this again. I promise. I swear on my life."

"But what about the lives of all the humans you killed?" I moved my blade from his dick to his throat, staring into his soulless eyes. Had he been born this evil? Or had life made him like this? I knew that there wasn't just one thing that shaped and contorted people. If B hadn't taken me in, if I had been left to stew in the aftermath of my parents' untimely death, I might've ended up just like Hans.

A slave to my rage.

"I'm sorry," Hans blubbered, his words nearly inarticulate as snot dripped down his face. "I'm so sorry."

"Sorry isn't good enough," I whispered, flicking one last glance at Miles's still form. Sorry was a word you used when you ran out of things to say. It didn't comfort, and it sure as fuck didn't bring back the dead. Apologies were only as sincere as the person who spoke them.

With my face devoid of any emotion, I cut Hans's neck.

But just like apologies, vengeance couldn't fix what had already been broken.

TWENTY-SEVEN

RYLAND

I stared through the thicket of trees at the small house nestled snugly between two large oaks. Smoke wafted from a chimney on the shingled roof, and freshly planted perennials dotted the driveway. It appeared...cozy. Domestic.

Not a building that held my kidnapped brother.

"This doesn't seem right," Bash murmured, echoing my own thoughts. He was perched rigidly on a low-hanging branch, his face taut with tension. Dusk was settling, painting everything in shades of gray and metallic violet. We would have to wait until nightfall to make our move.

"I keep expecting my grandma to exit with a tray of cookies," I replied dryly, narrowing my eyes.

What the fuck was Jax doing there?

A horrible thought occurred to me like a physical blow to my chest. Maybe we had been going about this the wrong way.

Maybe Jax hadn't been kidnapped. Maybe he'd chosen to leave willingly.

Even as the thought formed, I shook my head vehemently. There was no way in hell Jax would leave Z and the rest of us. This cozy house with the opened windows, freshly trimmed shrubbery, and welcome mat on the front porch was nothing but an illusion. Something pretty designed to hide a prickly interior.

"I want to do some recon," I decided, stepping forward. Bash immediately grabbed my arm, pulling me to a stop. When I swiveled my head to glare at him, his eyes were brimming with grim determination.

"Not on your own. I'm already worried sick about Z and the others. I don't want to be worried about your ugly ass too." He ground his jaw, a brief flicker of vulnerability appearing in his eyes before he shut that shit down. Bash didn't do emotions, but it was easy to see how frightened he was for Z and the others.

Aw. The mage actually had a heart.

I, on the other hand, trusted that our girl would escape whatever hell she'd found herself in unscathed. She was a fighter, a brawler, and she wouldn't hesitate to kill every one of those assholes who'd kidnapped her. Z would come home to me, to us.

I had to believe that.

I shoved my worry behind a steel box and focused on the mission before us. Find and save Jax.

Before time ran out.

My heart lurched in my chest, each consecutive thump more deafening than the last, but I kept my face blank when I turned back to Bash.

"I'll be fine," I said roughly, pulling the shadows away from my face to meet his eyes. "Stand guard. I'll be back in a bit."

Before he could mount another protest, I stealthily jumped higher up the tree until I was dangling above the flat roof. With the shadows concealing me, I jumped down, silently rolling until I came to a complete stop.

Sliding onto my stomach, I reached downwards until my fingers brushed the window pane. It took only a second for me to slide it open and flip inside, the shadows my only shield. One of my hands held a double-edged blade, while the other had a smaller dagger. Both weapons, when wielded by me, could be fatal.

It was...not what I was expecting.

Multicolored couches were scattered around, taking the cold edge off the wood-paneled room. Two brown, battered armchairs were placed in opposite corners of the room, and a large fireplace was embedded into the wooden logs. A myriad of paintings dotted the wall, though I couldn't decipher what they were supposed to represent.

The room appeared cozy, just like the exterior of the house.

I strained my ears for any sound, but when the house remained silent, I crept to the door and pushed it open on silent hinges.

A flurry of shivers skipped through my veins as I surveyed the perfectly mundane hallway. Plush, red carpeting. Wooden walls. Vases resting on wooden stands.

Something wasn't right.

I easily slipped through rooms unnoticed, my unease growing with each passing second. One of the rooms appeared to be a modest master bedroom with a connecting bathroom and closet. Another was a game room with two antique pool tables on one side and a dusty couch on the other.

There was no sign of Jax or Aaliyah. Actually, there was no sign of anyone at all.

After checking each room twice, I climbed out of the window, shimmied down the side of the roof, and hurried back to a stone-faced Bash. He aimed hard, searching eyes at me as his magic crackled in his palm.

"Anything?" he questioned, and I shook my head mutely, wispy shadows moving in tandem.

"Are you sure this is the right building?" I crouched down behind a thick bush, narrowing my eyes at the cheery house.

"Positive." Bash nodded his head resolutely as he unfolded the yellowing map. "He should be here."

"This must be a trap set up for Z," I declared, and the thought of anyone attacking my girl made my hands clench into fists.

"I detected remnants of magic when we first arrived," Bash admitted, eyes scrunching in concentration. His long lashes flickered over his cheekbones as he took a deep, fortifying breath. "I assumed it was protection wards, but now, I'm not so sure. It's unlike anything I've ever felt before." His eyes snapped open abruptly, piercing me with an unreadable look. "The power this person wields rivals that of all of the kings combined."

Fear slashed across my chest like a clawed hand. I

tightened my grip on my blades as I stared at Bash in growing horror.

"No one is that powerful."

"This person is," Bash argued, voice curt. He closed his eyes once more as his own signature power rippled just beneath his skin, transforming his veins from blue to a luminous green. "Fuck!" He scrubbed at his short blond hair, causing the strands to stick up in all directions.

"What?" I was instantly on alert, seconds from attacking anyone who dared venture too close.

I didn't like this. Not one fucking bit.

"The magic I noticed...it's not a protection ward. It's a fucking illusion spell."

TWENTY-EIGHT

JAX

I drank deeply from the man, licking up the column of his neck to catch any fallen drops.

Fuck, he tasted good. Like sunshine and whiskey bottled together.

My fangs retracted back into my mouth as I dropped his body to the ground. He landed with a thump alongside the dozens of other men and women.

Murderers and rapists, Aaliyah had told me. They didn't deserve to live, and they sure as hell didn't deserve my mercy.

Licking at my bloody lips, I prepared myself for my next meal when a manicured hand landed on my shoulder.

"Now, now, Jax, you need to slow down," Aaliyah purred, smiling in what she probably thought was a seductive manner. She leaned forward until her breasts were practically spilling out of her dress, but I paid her no mind.

She could try to seduce me all she wanted, but she wasn't my mate. No, she was the enemy.

I knew I had to kill her, had to cut open her tiny neck, but I was too driven by bloodlust to think coherently. I was mad when I didn't drink, and I was mad when I did.

Still, I was sane enough not to touch the vile woman with a two-foot pole.

She provided me blood sources, and that was it. I wouldn't fuck her if she were the last woman alive.

I would never, not in a million years, betray Z. My love. My light. My world.

The memory of her momentarily propelled me out of my gluttonous thoughts. I vigorously shook my head, attempting to dispel any and all thoughts of her. Whenever her face made an unwarranted appearance, I forgot myself. I forgot the monster I knew myself to be.

No! I need to drink.

More. More. More. More.

Aaliyah placed another hand on my shoulder, and once more, I shrugged her off. I eyed the pulsing vein in her neck, but she merely laughed giddily.

"It's not me you'll be drinking from," she whispered ominously, brushing at my hair. I snarled at her, but my mind was already elsewhere.

More. More. More. More.

I craved blood more than I craved anything else in my life. I needed it.

Aaliyah stood, swiping a hand down her thick skirt, before nodding towards the dirty man being dragged forward. He was dropped unceremoniously before me, his head lolling to the side.

"He raped and killed two little girls," Aaliyah said, answering my unspoken question. "Drink from him."

Power fizzled in the air as she focused on me. I didn't know how to describe the sudden, intense urge coursing through me. I wanted to—no, I needed to sink my fangs into the bastard's neck. Any neck, really.

"Be gluttonous," Aaliyah continued darkly, and another image assaulted me.

My fangs piercing the neck of a golden-haired angel. Her eyes wide in terror. Her blood cascading down her porcelain skin like a brand.

I could taste it, taste *her*, like my fangs were already embedded in her throat, sucking. It was unlike anything I'd ever drunk before. Decadent, like I was drinking directly from paradise.

No! You can't hurt her! She's your mate!

She's your...

I couldn't formulate the rest of the thought as Aaliyah poked and prodded at my mind.

With a ferocious roar, I lunged at the man and stuck my fangs in his neck. I would drink until he was dry. Until there was nothing left of the pathetic excuse for a human being.

And then I'd find my golden-haired angel and drink her dry too.

TWENTY-NINE

Z

I knew we were on a time crunch, but none of my guys protested when I insisted we bury all of the dead humans. I suspected they could see how close to the edge I was, how perilous my hold on rationality was. Normally, I didn't like it when they treated me like a porcelain doll, but there was no denying that currently, I was a doll.

Miles's death had broken me.

Altogether, there were one hundred and sixty-seven deaths. One hundred and sixty-seven humans who'd been murdered today alone.

My stomach clenched tightly, threatening to expel all of its contents. I pressed my lips together to keep the impending vomit at bay.

As Lupe carried the last body over to the hole my other mates had dug, I placed a hand on his arm to stop him and peered at the dead female. She appeared to be in her mid to late twenties, with dark hair, hazel eyes, and an athletic body. Like with all the humans, I sifted through her pockets until I stumbled across an identification card.

Ali.

"I'm so sorry, Ali," I murmured, closing her eyes. I didn't truly believe that closing the eyes of the dead would bring them any peace. I supposed I did it for myself more than anything. I could at least pretend that they were only sleeping.

A sob got lodged in my throat as Lupe gently set her body in the hole alongside the other deceased humans. Most of the ones I'd rescued had long since fled, but a few remained and helped us bury their fellow humans. I noticed a man drop to his knees as he stared at a vacant-eyed female. He cried for his lover, his wrenching sobs clawing at an already empty spot where my heart should be.

It took hours to bury all of them. Long, grueling hours where more and more of my soul became buried right alongside them. I kept their IDs in my backpack.

When the time was right, I would get into contact with their family members. They deserved to know what happened to their loved ones.

"I am so sorry, Z," Killian whispered brokenly. His glassy eyes stared at the mass graveyard with blatant horror.

"We need to bury Miles," I said with a sniffle, wrenching my gaze away. Killian had always made me feel too much, too quickly. His eyes were capable of stripping away my carefully crafted layers until I was bare before him.

Killian, easily able to read me, nodded once, turning

towards Devlin and Lupe. My two mates were crowded around the young man who'd weaseled his way into my heart. There was no rhyme or reason for it. He'd arrived like a wrecking ball, destroying a crucial piece of myself in the process.

Devlin smoothed back a strand of Miles's honey blond hair, a tender expression on his face. The kid was the only one who would receive a separate burial. Self-ish? Maybe, but it felt unexplainably right.

"Do you have any words you'd like to say?" Lupe asked quietly, his rough voice a balm to my tattered soul.

Ignoring them all, I crawled on the muddy grass until I was able to press my lips to Miles's cold forehead. God, he was so still. A living icicle.

Well, not living anymore.

A choked sob escaped me as I squeezed his fingers with one hand and brushed his hair away with the other.

"I'm so fucking sorry, Miles. I broke my promise. I'm so, so sorry." The tears continued to escape faster and faster, trailing down my cheeks and landing on my lips. To my mates, I said, "He had a sister. A younger sister. We have to find her."

It was the least I could do.

Because I'd failed him. I'd failed this innocent, cherubic boy. He'd placed his trust in me, and I'd shat-tered that gift. Now I was left holding the broken pieces.

"We will," Devlin promised quietly, squeezing my shoulder. With a tenderness that belied the scowl currently contorting his face, he helped me to my feet. I sunk into his embrace, inhaling his scent. "The kings will pay for this," he vowed into my hair.

"Do you think they knew about the carnival?" I whispered against his skin. Devlin took a shuddering breath, not answering, but his silence was confirmation.

"It wouldn't surprise me," Killian stated at last. "They're power-hungry assholes. They'll look for any way to stomp on the humans."

"Then we kill them," one of the men I'd rescued said vehemently, his eyes hurling daggers. "And if you pompous assholes stand in our way—"

"These pompous assholes helped save your life," I roared, pulling away from Devlin to face the crowd of humans. I counted at least thirty, all dirty-faced and frail. More than one hundred must've already fled when I freed them.

"How do we know they're any better than their fathers?" another woman demanded, glaring at my princes. I bristled at her tone, but I knew she had a point. These people had been through hell and back. If I were in their shoes, I would've been cautious and fearful as well. For all they knew, the princes had something much more nefarious planned.

"Because we're sickened by the way humans are treated," Devlin said, stepping forward. "We're disgusted by it. When we take over, we'll work to grant equal rights to all citizens."

"That's all talk!" someone screamed, voice shrill. "Why should we believe you?"

"Because we're in love with a human," Killian answered simply, a hint of his incubus allure unintentionally slipping into his voice. My mouth dropped open at his declaration.

Surely he didn't mean *love* love.

Did he?

I shoved it into a metal box, locked it, and buried it beneath layers and layers of pain. I'd have to dissect his words, and my own feelings, at a later time.

"I want a world where she and my children can live peacefully alongside us," Devlin added, expression turning wistful and almost dreamy. "I want to make this world a better place not just for her, but for all of you. What happened here today should never happen again."

Lupe merely grunted in agreement.

"We were blind before," Killian added, eyes forlorn. "We knew our parents were capable of evil, but we hadn't understood the extent of it. We see it now. And we want to stop it."

I could still see indecision flicker on the humans' faces, so I took a step forward until I was shoulder to shoulder with Devlin.

"I'm the official assassin of the kingdom," I stated, my steely voice ringing out in the electrically charged air. It was unnaturally silent, as if even the birds had stopped chirping to hear my speech. "I won the Damning, and a strong magic was placed on me to protect the kings." Murmuring erupted immediately from the assembled crowd as they sent me scathing, distrustful looks.

I understood their fear and unease. How could you trust the same female whose sole purpose was to protect the kings and kill the dissenters?

Silencing their indignant cries with a sharp look, I continued. "But I never agreed to hurt innocent people. I might not be able to harm the kings, but I can promise you that I will spend my entire life working to break the spell they have on me. In the meantime, I will protect you all. I will be the champion for the human race. I'll be the voice when you feel as if you've been silenced." An awed hush fell over the crowd, and I made sure to meet each and every one of their eyes.

"You're not going to get a princess out of me," I stated calmly. "I'm dirty, messy, and I like blood way too much." A flurry of chuckles erupted from the crowd, disrupting the tension hanging stagnant in the air. When the laughter abated, I stared at them all with steely determination. "But I *will* fight for you. And I always win."

"I'M SO FUCKING proud of you," Devlin whispered as we said goodbye to the last human. I had no idea where they would go, but I prayed they ran as far and as fast as they could. I cautioned them not to mention my involvement, but I did advise them to warn other humans about what had happened.

"We will, Liberator," one of the men declared with a reverent nod of his head.

My stomach fluttered at the nickname, but not in a good way. I didn't feel like a liberator or a hero.

I was the fucking villain in this story.

A kid had died because of me, because I'd failed to save him. Self-loathing gripped my heart in a vise and refused to release it.

"It's all so fucked up, Lin," I whispered.

"But we'll fix it," he assured me, wrapping an arm around my shoulder. "We're next in line for the thrones."

"I don't know if we can wait that long." If my estimation was correct, the kings had twenty, maybe thirty years before they would be too senile to rule their kingdoms. And me? I only had a few months, give or take, with the poison currently running rampant through my system. I had no idea how my mates would react when I was gone. Would they continue fighting? Continue advocating for the oppressed humans? Or would they give in to their primitive instincts and become the puppets the kings had always wanted them to be?

No, they wouldn't do that. They were too good, too kind. They saw the evil in the world, and unlike a lot of others, they sought to fix it. To shine a light on the darkness. I had no doubt they would grieve me, but they would survive and continue fighting.

Devlin kissed my forehead softly. "I know, baby. I know."

"Here!" Killian declared suddenly, materializing behind us. He unhooked Devlin's lamp from his belt loop and handed it to my Genie.

"You don't owe Devlin your soul now, do you?" I queried, only half teasing. I knew that each wish required an extensive contract crafted by the powers that be. Killian had made two wishes inside the carnival, and who knew how many he'd made before that.

"Don't worry," Devlin said, opening up his backpack and sliding the lamp inside. "We made the contract before we even entered the carnival."

"I have three wishes to use before I owe him my

soul," Killian explained, grabbing my hand and playing with my fingers. It was such a mundane gesture that I was struck speechless, staring at where our skin connected. His hand was warm on my own, eliciting full body shivers that danced across my skin.

"He only made two," Devlin added. "As long as he doesn't make another wish..." He trailed off with a pointed look in Killian's direction.

"I won't touch the damn lamp for the rest of my life," Killian promised, not bothering to lift his head from where he stared at our joined hands.

"Good." Devlin folded his muscular arms, peering over my shoulder. "I wouldn't want your ugly soul hogging up space in my lamp anyway."

Killian glared playfully. "We both know that's not true."

Whatever Devlin was going to retort was interrupted by a grinning Axel emerging from the tent. "Would you like to do the honors, little sister?" He removed the detonator from his jacket and held it out to me enticingly.

"Fuck yes."

Devlin and Lupe stood on one side of me, with Killian on the other. Axel remained a short distance away, hands in his pockets and a sardonic grin twisting his lips.

"Fuck this place," I murmured, pressing down on the button.

Immediately, the tent exploded in a kaleidoscope of colors. Smoke permeated the air as sparks hissed and danced in fireworks of red, orange, and yellow.

I held up my middle finger, saluting this shithole the

only way I knew how. Devlin, Lupe, and even Axel were quick to join me.

"Oh, sorry! I didn't realize..." Killian stuttered, staring at our raised fingers. He quickly joined us as we gave the burning carnival the bird.

It was a fitting send-off for such an atrocious place.

THIRTY

Z

It was silent as we drove away from the flaming carnival. The cold wind from the opened window was a balm to my overheated skin.

No one spoke as we crossed flat plains and entered a surrounding forest. By then, the sun had completely fallen and darkness had descended. Stars peppered the velvety sky, bathing everything in hues of gold and white.

At some point, Killian had drifted off to sleep, his head resting on my shoulder. I absently brushed through his gorgeous red locks as my mind wandered.

No matter what I did, what I thought about, Miles's face haunted me. All I could see were his soulful eyes, gazing blindly up at the burning tent. Had he been scared before he died? Had it been a quick death or a long one?

Fuck, I couldn't think about it. I would drive myself insane with the what-ifs.

"It'll be okay," Lupe whispered gruffly from the passenger seat. He'd slid his glasses back on as soon as we entered the car, and they somehow demoted him from intimidating to approachable.

"I don't think it'll ever be okay." My voice was low and distant, heady with pain and self-loathing. Guilt ate away at my insides like a parasite. Could someone die from this—from this gnawing, undefinable bug prowling in your stomach?

"Axel is looking for Miles's sister right now," Lupe continued. "She'll be okay."

"But can we trust Axel?" I questioned, pain splintering just behind my eyes. A part of me *did* trust the eccentric assassin, but a larger part of me was fearful. For five years, he'd been in the kings' back pocket. It was ingrained within him to follow their commands and rules. He was loyal to the kings, first and foremost.

Lupe turned quiet, contemplative, seemingly unable to answer my question any more than I could. He scrubbed at the dusting of hair coating his jaw.

"I think—"

I let out a sudden scream as a body fell on top of me. Killian jerked upright, karate-chopping the air chaotically with an audible "Ahhh!" Devlin cursed, the car screeching to an abrupt stop in the middle of the road, and Lupe growled, jumping into the backseat and holding the intruder in a headlock.

"Nice to see you assholes too," a familiar voice choked out.

"Dair?" I asked in disbelief, slipping my dagger back into its sheath. I blinked rapidly at the golden-haired prince as he smiled back sheepishly.

"The one and only." He flickered his gaze towards

Lupe, still holding his neck, and then back to me. "Errr... can you release me, please? Choking might be your kink, but it's not mine. At least not with your ugly ass doing the choking."

"What the fuck, man?" Devlin exclaimed, swiveling in his seat. His violet eyes flared brightly in the darkness of the cab.

Dair's smile grew on his face as Lupe reluctantly released him.

"A pill," he declared with a smirk. "From the mage king himself. It acts as a portal to send you to your heart's true home." His eyes focused intently on me, and a flush erupted in my chest. I'd used those pills frequently when I worked for the resistance. It had always brought me back to the compound with the other assassins. Now I wondered if my home wasn't truly a place, but a person.

Or people.

"So cheesy," I murmured, attempting to stop the satisfied blush creeping up my neck and to my cheeks. Dair, in answer, merely pecked me on the lips. One touch from him was nuclear.

He froze suddenly, pulling back to survey me with unwavering intensity. His eyes traveled over my dirty clothes and bloodstained skin, darkening infinitesimally when they landed on a gash on my forehead.

"What happened?" he inquired dangerously, his animosity saturating the air.

My lower lip began to tremble, but I stubbornly held my tears at bay.

Later. I would fall apart later.

I would fall apart until there was nothing left of me to

weave back together. It felt as if my heart was ripping open and weeping blood.

"I'm so glad you're all right," I whispered, staring at his handsome, chiseled face. His eyes softened slightly as he cupped my cheek, leaning forward to dot kisses on my nose. The last time I'd seen him, he'd been unconscious in his room—a shell of the man I knew and loved. Something settled inside of me at seeing the vibrant light returning to his sea-blue eyes.

"I'm all right," he agreed, peppering kisses across my lips. "But you're not."

My heart cracked like a stone being dropped as I told him what had transpired. The more I talked, the more I wondered if I would ever be mended. Fixed.

Or if I was always fated to remain broken.

ONCE MORE, I was in the elegantly furnished bedroom.

My vampire mate sat on the bed, sucking the neck of an unconscious female. Horror momentarily stilled me before I forced myself into action.

With lightning fast reflexes, I gripped the girl's arm and dragged her body away from Jax.

"No!" I screamed in horror as her head lolled to the side, giving me an unrestricted view of her lifeless eyes. The gathering darkness I always felt, just lying in wake, exploded out of me like a whirling tornado. "Jax, how could you?"

He growled, the sound more monster than human,

before prowling closer to me. Blood stained his chin and dribbled down his bare chest.

"I'm thirsty!" he roared, his fangs poking his chapped bottom lip.

"This isn't you," I insisted, stumbling back a step. Anger rampaged through me as I stared at the girl's face. Her features twisted and contorted until they took the shape of a young man with honey blond hair and wide, innocent eyes.

Miles.

"How could you?" I whispered hoarsely, dropping to my knees. "I don't even know who you are anymore."

"I'm thirsty!" Jax screamed again, shoving at the nightstand flanking his bed. It fell to the ground, the glass vase on top of it shattering into pieces. I winced at the cacophonous, almost deafening, noise.

This wasn't Jax. Not my sweet vampire. My Jax wouldn't look at me with vitriol spewing from his eyes. Instead of the love and warmth I usually saw, there was nothing but coldness. An icy tundra I didn't dare venture across.

"What happened to you?" I remained kneeling, unable to find the will to climb to my feet. I'd lost Miles, and now, I'd lost Jax. He'd killed someone, and there was no turning back from that.

"She's a murderer," Jax growled out through gritted teeth. "She killed seven innocent children. She didn't deserve to live."

"And that makes you God?" I screamed, my voice infused with so much passion and emotion, I felt like a completely different person. Finally, finally, I stumbled to

my feet, jabbing an accusatory finger into his chest. "That makes you judge, jury, and executioner?"

His face darkened, something unrecognizable flitting across his features.

"And you're one to talk? You're an assassin! You kill people too! Why do you get to judge me?" By the time he'd finished his spiel, he was panting, chest rising and falling with his erratic breaths.

And...

And he was right. Some of my anger diminished as I considered the broken, scared man standing before me. I had no fucking right to judge him when I, too, was a pawn to death. I'd enacted my own form of vengeance daily before the princes had come into my life. I still did. At the carnival, I'd killed Hans because I'd deemed him a horrible man who didn't deserve to live.

Fuck, I was a hypocrite.

"I'm." He stepped even closer until we were nose to nose. "Thirsty."

"This isn't you," I tried again, dropping my hands from his chest and balling them into fists. "Aaliyah did something to you. I don't know what, but I swear to you, Jax, I'll find out."

"You don't know what I am!" he roared. He continued pushing me backwards until I was flush against the wall, my chest heaving. His strong arms blocked me in on either side, caging me against his sculpted frame. His face contorted in mild recognition as he roared out, "I killed before, when I was younger. I killed a human maid's daughter because I was weak."

"Jax..." I whispered, my heart splintering at the raw

emotion in his voice. He sniffed my neck, and dissonance once more clouded his features. His eyes rolled back in his head as my scent curled around him, a soft smile playing on his luscious lips. It was almost as if he were adrift at sea, my presence keeping him tethered to the shore. With each inhale, coherence returned to his face, accompanied by something primal. Feral.

"Mate..." he rumbled, voice almost guttural. Something like wonderment sparked to life in his eyes as he lifted a strand of my hair and sniffed it. "Mate."

"Yes," I whispered, cupping his cheek. I gently wiped the remaining droplets of blood off his lips with the pad of my thumb. "I'm your mate, and you're mine. I'm coming for you, Jax. I'll help you. I promise."

"Mate." His eyes lowered to my lips, and the previous anger and rage I'd noticed before diminished instantly to be replaced by liquid fire. Lust saturated the room like a perfume.

"Mate," I echoed. Before I could think better of it, I pushed myself onto my tiptoes and pressed my lips to his. He held himself rigidly, body taut, before he kissed me back with reckless abandon. His hands fisted in my hair, pulling tightly enough to sting.

"Mate," he growled against my lips. His kisses were feverish, and I rivaled it with my own intensity. When his hands dropped to my ass, I jumped up his muscular body and wrapped my legs around him.

He spun, still carrying me, and lowered us both roughly onto the bed.

"Come back to me, Jax," I pleaded, kissing up his neck. "Please."

My vampire mate released a roar, the sound eerily similar to that of Lupe's bear, before he ripped my shirt straight down the middle. His eyes devoured my revealed skin before he lowered his lips to the valley between my breasts.

His fangs scraped at my skin, but instead of pain, molten lava flooded my veins. I gasped softly as those same fangs pricked my nipple through the thin material of my bra.

"Mate," he whispered against my skin.

"Your mate," I agreed readily.

Using his teeth, he cut through the flimsy fabric of my bra and pulled it off my body. He cupped both of my breasts, tugging on and twisting my beaded nipples.

"So. Beautiful," he murmured dazedly, lowering his lips to my right nipple as his hand continued to knead my left. He traced my areola with his tongue before grazing his fingers over the sensitive nub. I gasped, arching off the bed, as he sucked and licked my aching nipple. He quickly moved his head to my left breast, giving it the same attention as my right.

He was already shirtless, and I took the moment to trace the contours of his beautiful body. He wasn't as muscular as Lupe or even Killian, but he had a defined six-pack and a prominent V.

I twisted his nipples, just as he did mine, and he groaned against my chest.

"Z..." he whispered, and when I guided his face back to mine, there was a flicker of coherence and intelligence in his eyes. It was quickly replaced by primal hunger as he devoured my lips with his own.

We made quick work removing our pants, but before he entered me, he sat back and admired my dripping pussy.

"Jax!" I begged, but he gave me a disapproving look.

"I want to taste you..." he murmured, dropping to his belly on the bed. He gripped my legs and hoisted them on his shoulders. "You smell good."

His tongue flicked at my entrance, and I swore my eyes rolled back in my head. When he began to eat me in earnest, I saw fucking stars.

He demolished my pussy as if he were on death row and this his last meal. His lips sucked on my bundle of nerves as he added first one finger and then a second, scissoring them in and out of my sopping cunt.

"Fuck!" I screamed as my orgasm crashed over me. I was drowning in it, drowning in him, but it was the sweetest death imaginable.

When he leaned forward to kiss me, I tasted myself on him. Somehow, that only heightened my arousal.

"You taste so fucking good," he stated candidly.

"I want you in me," I pleaded, tugging at his cock.

For a brief moment, insecurity flared to life in his eyes as he surveyed my face.

"Are you sure?" he whispered, sounding more like my old Jax than ever before.

"Make love to me."

Maintaining eye contact, he lined himself up with my entrance and slowly pushed himself inside of me. It was a tight fit, since he was bigger than I'd expected, but my pussy clenched around his dick as if it were made for him.

"You're so fucking tight," he murmured, his hips jerking forward.

"Move." I wrapped my legs around his waist once more, digging my feet into his ass.

He was slow at first, careful almost, as if I were glass he was afraid would break. But he couldn't deny his more primitive instincts any more than I could.

He began to fuck me relentlessly, his balls slapping against my ass as the bed shook and rocked. He gripped my breasts punishingly as he mumbled inarticulate praises.

"Fuck, yes!" I moaned as I felt his cock expand inside of me.

"Z!" he screamed, his hips jerking erratically as he came inside of me. When his hand found my clit, pinching tightly, I careened over the edge myself, milking his cock for all it was worth.

He collapsed, sweaty and sated, onto my chest seconds later, his head nestled beneath my chin. His thumb idly stroked my nipple as we held each other.

"I'm scared," Jax whispered after a prolonged moment of silence. He turned his head to press a kiss between my breasts. "I don't know what's wrong with me. I think I'm losing my mind."

"You'll be okay," I assured him, stroking down his back. "We're on our way."

"Please be careful," he said brokenly. I felt something wet cascade down my chest. Tears, I realized blankly. "She has something planned."

"We'll be careful," I promised. "Pinkie promise." He snorted as he eyed my proffered pinkie before intertwining it with his own. "Have you discovered anything?"

Jax stilled for a brief moment before his fingers resumed playing with my breast.

"She has an illusion spell on the house," he stated at last. "I don't know what she is. Not a mage, not a vampire...not anything I've ever seen before."

"Bash and Ryland traveled ahead of us," I whispered, tension radiating through me. "Have you seen them?"

He shook his head. "No. They must not have gotten through the illusion spell."

Immense relief crashed over me like a tidal wave. When Devlin had told me where my other mates were, I damn near lost my mind. I wouldn't be able to handle losing them—any of them.

"Z," Jax began doggedly. He swallowed audibly, his hand once more still. "Aaliyah is obsessed with you. I don't know why. She asks about you all the time, and she warns her...her monsters not to hurt you."

I pondered this newfound information. Why me? What did Aaliyah want with me? Question after question continued to swirl in my head like a hurricane, but conjuring up an answer was like grasping the wind. Utterly impossible.

"You did good, Jax," I praised, brushing back his sweat soaked hair. He preened at the compliment, a dimpled smile appearing on his handsome face. "Just hang in there a little bit longer. We're coming for you."

"She's waiting," he warned, the smile abating as quickly as it had appeared. I kissed his forehead as he cuddled against me.

"I'll be ready."

THIRTY-ONE

JAX

When I woke up a few minutes later, she was gone.

I held on to the memory tightly. Guarding it with every fiber of my being.

Aaliyah would try to make me forget, but I would fight her every step of the way.

Her golden hair splayed across my pillow. Her wet pussy lips. Those beautiful, perky breasts with taut nipples. The spark of fire in her gemstone eyes.

Z.

My mate.

My love.

I repeated those words over and over again, branding them into my brain. I would do better. I *had* to do better.

My gaze lowered to the dead human, and guilt rushed through me. This woman had kidnapped children and murdered them, so I didn't feel bad about killing her. I did, however, regret Z seeing me like that.

I had been so blinded by my bloodlust and rage that

I'd failed to realize I had my own personal angel standing directly in front of me.

Z.

My mate.

My love.

I didn't know how she was able to visit me here, but I wasn't complaining. Perhaps it was a product of the mate bond. Maybe it was something else entirely.

All I knew for certain was that she had saved me.

Smiling softly at the memory of my gorgeous mate writhing underneath me, I hopped out of bed and stepped into my pants. The last thing I wanted was to be naked when Aaliyah came back to check on me and remove the body. She'd made her intentions clear more than once, and though my mind had often been under her thrall, my heart had always belonged to Z.

Still, perhaps I could use this to my advantage.

Aaliyah assumed I was still driven by gluttony—still trapped in a cage of my own making, fortified by her powers. She didn't know that Z had freed me.

I could see and think clearer than I ever had before in my life.

Maybe, just maybe, she would let something slip if I played my cards right.

I waited only an hour before Aaliyah sauntered through the door, her red hair styled high on her head. She wore a fitted green gown that made her look like a fucking Christmas decoration from the before times.

She smiled coyly as she glanced at the dead girl. Her nostrils flared as she sniffed the room, and her grin grew. I realized she could smell the lust and sex still permeating the air.

Fuck.

"Did you fuck the girl before or after you killed her?" Aaliyah asked, sashaying forward. My shoulders instantly sagged in relief.

She thought I'd fucked the dead woman, not my mate.

And though the thought of pretending to touch anyone but Z made bile rise up my throat, I kept my expression impassive as I shrugged. Not confirming or denying.

"I didn't know you were down with playing..." she purred, running a finger down my chest. I caught her hand before it could go any farther. This bitch would never touch me.

Still, I had a persona I had to keep up. For Z.

"I'm thirsty," I rumbled, infusing sincerity and primal hunger into each word.

She continued to smile, locking eyes with me.

"I don't have any more meals for you today," she said, tugging at her hand. I released her quickly and took an instinctive step backwards. "But you can drink from me."

She undid the first few buttons of her dress, revealing a hint of nipple, and canted her head to the side.

Yeah, no.

I would rather stab myself in the eye until I'm shitting out pupils.

I pretended to consider it, leaning forward and sniffing her neck. She smelled like...like darkness. I didn't know how to describe it, only that shivers overtook my body. She was swords clashing against shields and thunder reverberating in the night air. She was the monster that hid beneath miles and miles of murky ocean water. She was darkness personified.

Z, on the other hand, smelled like sunshine and roses, breaking apart the monotony of darkness that had been my one constant for years now.

I scrunched my nose, pulled away from her, and shook my head vigorously.

"I'm. Thirsty." I grunted once. And then again, because that seemed like something a primitive asshole like myself would've done.

Her red lips pursed as she gave me a long once-over, her eyes lingering on my crotch longer than I felt comfortable with.

"Very well." She redid her buttons and pivoted on her heel. "Come."

I prowled behind her as we left my room-slash-prison and entered a dark, gothic hallway. Both the floor and walls were painted various shades of black with numerous candles dotting the wall. The flames danced as we descended a swirling staircase.

When we finally stopped, my stomach bottomed out at the horrendous sight before me.

Humans, men and women alike, were chained to the wall. All of them were naked, their ribs protruding from their papery skin.

"Have at it," Aaliyah said, waving her hand dismissively. "They're all rapists and murderers." For a brief moment, a forlorn, pensive expression flashed across her face. "It hasn't always been like this. Before the demons arrived, the world was…peaceful. Serene." She shook her head vehemently and released a heavy sigh. "I have to meet someone upstairs, but help yourself to any of them. And clean up after yourself."

With that, she turned on her heel and stalked back up the stairs, leaving me alone with the scared humans.

I didn't know if what Aaliyah told me was true, if they truly were murderers and rapists, but I wasn't going to drink from them either way. I knew that if I gave in, the bloodlust would pull me back under kicking and screaming. I would become the ravenous, blood-sucking monster I strived to escape from.

A nightmare.

Instead, I stealthily moved away from the prisoners and climbed up the stairs on silent feet. I had to be careful. If Aaliyah suspected I wasn't under her control, she would be livid.

I pressed my ear to the door, but the wood muffled any sound. Silently cursing, I pushed the door open inch by excruciating inch, willing it to remain silent. I practically sagged in relief when the door was open enough for me to stick my head out.

Clipped voices greeted me from farther down the hall, and I tapped into my enhanced hearing.

"…get it done," Aaliyah said curtly, and I imagined she was folding her arms over her chest. There was a heavy sigh, the sound of crinkled papers, and then silence.

I'd begun to believe that the mysterious visitor had left when I heard a contented moan and a harsh grunt.

Aaliyah.

And a male.

Straining my ears, I heard what sounded like skin hitting skin, and something inside of me died forever.

Yup. I was going to gag on my own vomit.

Their fuckfest went on for what felt like hours, but was probably more like a few minutes, when I heard the sound of a zipper and a deceptively light giggle.

"Don't worry," Aaliyah purred. "I keep my promises."

"You better," a rough voice snapped, and every hair on my body stood on end. Cold fear skated down my spine like an ice cube. My hand tightened on the door-frame until my knuckles turned white.

"We'll see you soon," a third voice declared, sounding bored with the entirety of this conversation.

Aaliyah laughed again, high-pitched and childlike, as the footsteps retreated down an opposite hall. I quickly ducked back into the room, racing down the stairs and sticking my fangs in the neck of the nearest man. I didn't suck and I didn't pierce him enough to draw blood, but the angle from the staircase didn't show that.

Aaliyah bounced back down moments later, significantly more cheerful than before. There was a rosy hue to both her cheeks that had been absent prior, and her red hair was tousled.

"How does he taste?" she asked coyly as I pulled away from the trembling man and pretended to lick him with my venom.

"Sour," I growled, staring at the woman with newfound horror.

I'd recognized the two voices she'd spoken to, and it felt like an iron vise was closing around my heart, drawing blood with each consecutive squeeze. My head buzzed like a hornet's nest had been set loose.

Why the hell were the incubus king and mage king visiting Aaliyah? And how did they even know about her in the first place?

I feared my family and I had found ourselves trapped in the sticky strings of a web, seconds from being devoured. The more we unraveled the secrets plaguing this world, the further trapped we became.

Pulse skittering, I followed Aaliyah back up the staircase.

Please be safe, Z. Please.

THIRTY-TWO

DAIR

My wheelchair didn't come with me.

I only realized it when we pulled to a stop at the side of the road, directly beside a rundown truck. A growl of fury emerged from my throat as I stared down at my stubby legs.

Failure.

Worthless.

Nothing.

Each of those words scraped at my heart like a blunt blade. It didn't quite draw blood, but it was a constant presence that I couldn't escape from.

It was ironic, in a way, the amount of power we gifted physical strength. It was why women were often seen as weaker than men. Why men and women alike with disabilities were frowned upon. I was just beginning to realize that my apparent "inadequacies" weren't inadequacies at all.

But now, watching my mate and brothers strap

weapons onto their bodies, all of those emotions returned with a vengeance.

"I want to come with you," I whispered, drilling a hole into Devlin's head. He spun, brown brows raised as his violet eyes widened.

"You don't have your chair," he stated, already dismissing it. Dismissing *me*. I fucking hated when they did that.

"And it's uphill," Lupe added offhandedly. He eyed a dagger with obvious aversion before slipping it up his sleeve. I didn't think he would even end up using it, but then again, what did I know?

"Then fucking carry me!" I snapped, leaning forward and piercing them with a scathing look. "I'm not leaving my mate."

"Dair..." Z's voice was soft, almost placating, and that pissed me off even more.

"No, Z." I turned towards her and gripped her cheeks fiercely. She was so beautiful, it physically pained me. "I'm your mate. I need to protect you."

A somber smile flirted across her face as she placed her palm over my hand. I couldn't help but note how jagged my nails appeared when compared to her perfectly trimmed ones. It was a product of the damn chair—I constantly tore my nails off when they got stuck in the wheels.

"And *I* need to protect *you*." I opened my mouth to protest, but she cut me off by climbing into my lap. She nestled her head beneath my chin, and I peppered kisses on her hair. She felt warm in my arms, *right*, as if the world was finally beginning to make sense.

"Because I'm weak," I lamented bitterly, tilting her head up to stare deeply into her eyes. Her long lashes fluttered as she met my penetrating gaze with a fierce one of her own.

"Because you're you," she responded matter-of-factly. "You're not weak." She pressed a tantalizingly soft kiss to the corner of my lips. "You're not less of a man. I don't know how many times I have to remind you of that, but I will. I'll remind you every day of my fucking life if that's what it takes."

"I love you so damn much," I whispered, capturing her lips fully with my own. She tasted sweet, decadent, like when you had dessert before dinner. Nirvana and bliss overshadowed the darkness, filling those spaces with light.

"I love you too, my perfect mermaid." She ran her fingers through my hair, and I turned into her touch.

I sometimes really hated my species name. Why couldn't we be called mer*men*? I was anything but a maiden.

"You're perfect," I countered, knowing she would never believe me but also knowing it was true. She possessed this inner spark, this inner light, that made me want to fight the darkness and all of the monsters inside of it.

It might not have necessarily been just her. I knew she fought demons daily, and I knew that she didn't always win. It was *us*—her and me and my brothers. We complemented each other, each providing something crucial that we hadn't even realized we needed.

As expected, Z rolled her eyes, a delicate blush

blooming on her cheeks like a flower unfurling in spring. My cock tented my pants instinctively, and I just barely resisted the urge to scold it as Killian would've done.

"We'll be right back, my love," she whispered, kissing my cheek tenderly. I squeezed her hips tighter, as if that could keep her with me, before reluctantly releasing her.

"Keep her safe," I warned my brothers as Z climbed out of the car.

"With my life," Lupe assured me, removing his glasses and placing them in the glove compartment. I was beginning to believe there were two sides to my shifter brother. One was studious, preferring to spend his days in the library and read about the world in books. The other part of him was ruthless and vicious. Fierce in his need to protect those he deemed as his.

Killian pointed his finger at me and pretended to shoot. When he realized how dorky he looked, he dropped his hand and smiled sheepishly.

"I'll protect her."

"With your fingers?" I asked dryly, and his blush deepened. Smiling, I shoved his shoulder. "Protect our girl, okay?"

Devlin leveled me with an intense stare before dropping the keys into my outstretched hand.

"You're the getaway driver. Be ready. We might have to make a quick escape."

I nodded seriously, knowing it was a job I could handle. A lot of the cars the capital invested in had a button I used for the gas and brake. I had perfected the art of not being able to drive with my legs.

And now, I could use those skills to protect Z and my brothers.

I stared at my reflection in the rearview mirror—mouth set in a grim line, eyes shadowed, and skin pale. I vowed to myself that I would do everything in my power to protect my family.

Whatever it took.

With a skittering pulse and heavy heart, I crawled into the front seat and gripped the wheel until my knuckles turned white.

I would wait.

And if it was required of me, I would fight.

THIRTY-THREE

Z

There was a stillness to the air. A hush, as if we were all holding our breaths. We walked single file through the dense forest, pushing aside branches and twigs with the moonlight as our guide. Lupe led the charge, with Devlin and Killian taking up rank behind me.

None of the guys told me to stay back, and I appreciated it more than they could've possibly known.

I gripped my knife tightly as we exited the forest, stopping in front of a modest home with a flat roof and rows of carefully planted flowers.

"This is…"

"Not what you were expecting?" Ryland finished dryly, materializing from behind a bush.

"You're okay," I said in relief, lunging forward before I could stop myself. Ryland caught me easily, his arms muscular bands around my thin waist. His shadows parted, revealing glimmering blue eyes, as he touched his lips to my own. I kissed him back feverishly, tangling my fingers in his dark hair. I hadn't realized how much I'd missed him, how worried I'd been for him, until that moment.

"Yeah, yeah, yeah. Shadow boy is alive and well," Bash murmured, pushing aside a few buoyant branches.

I reluctantly pulled away from my shadow mate to face Bash fully. His lips were curved downwards, but besides that, there were no outwards signs of his discomfort. Only his eyes gave him away—they were vibrating with jealousy, hurt, and relief. A myriad of emotions I couldn't even begin to understand.

"I'm glad you're okay too, Bash-hole," I said meekly, surveying his body for injuries. His own eyes did the same to me.

"You too, princess."

For a moment, time was suspended as we stared at each other. His mossy green eyes swirled with undefinable emotions. I wanted to run to him as I had with Ryland. Wrap my arms around him and kiss his plush lips.

Yet I knew we weren't there yet. There was still a chasm we had to venture across before we could even consider doing such things. With time, we'd be able to build the bridge that hadn't yet existed. Piece by piece. Day by day.

Love, after all, was nothing but a waiting game.

Before either of us could act on our more primitive instincts, Ryland's voice captured my attention.

"...nothing I could see. Bash claims they're hiding underneath a powerful illusion spell."

Illusion spell? Why did that remind me of something?

It was on the tip of my tongue, resting there and begging me to spit it out. I rubbed my hands against my legging-clad legs as I struggled to grasp the memory that constantly wanted to elude me.

"I think I can undo it," Bash declared, finally wrenching his eyes off of me. "I already started before you guys arrived."

"Where's T and the other guards?" I questioned suddenly. It had only just occurred to me that I hadn't seen them anywhere.

"The kings' asslickers?" Bash raised a sculpted blond brow. "We left them in the city near the inn."

"Good," I murmured, turning back to study the nondescript building. "I don't want him in this mess." Smoke emanated from the chimney, and the air was perfumed with the smell of freshly baked goods. If it was an illusion spell, it was more powerful than any I'd ever experienced before.

"How long is it going to take you to break the spell?" Devlin snapped out, once more reverting to his role as the unofficial leader.

"I'm almost done. Maybe ten more minutes," Bash answered. He took a step towards his brother, a step towards me, and his arm brushed my own. Fire erupted in my veins at the contact.

"Good. Start working on that," Devlin instructed, and Bash nodded once to show him he understood. "The rest of us...be prepared."

Lupe immediately moved to stand directly beside me, a formidable force of nature, even in his human form. My pinkie finger extended to wrap around his own as we stared up at the moonlit house.

I always preferred to do my battles in the dark. Maybe it was because I understood it better.

The darkness? It always won. It was where you could hide, where you could seek solace when the world crumbled around you, piece by piece. The light, on the other hand, spotlighted you. It put you on this unattainable pedestal and displayed you to the world. All of your fears and weaknesses, your insecurities and anger. Everything.

Darkness had always been more powerful.

"Are you ready?" Lupe whispered softly.

"This isn't my first rodeo," I replied, my voice a hushed murmur.

But it's the only one that matters.

Fuck, what if we couldn't save Jax? What if he was already dead?

I took a steadying breath, attempting to calm my racing heart, as I pushed those thoughts to the back of my mind. A part of me *knew* Jax was alive and waiting for me. I didn't know how, only that I did.

You need to get a hold of yourself, Z. You can't go into battle with your emotions on your sleeve.

I mentally inventoried myself, checking to see if there were any chinks in my armor. Finding none, I tightened my grip on Lupe's pinkie.

"I'm ready," I whispered more to myself than the giant man beside me. "I'm ready."

"If ready means you think you're going to pee your pants, then I'm totally ready," Killian muttered from behind me, and a smirk twisted up my lips before I could contain it. Trust Killian to break the tension hanging palpably over all of our heads.

Green mist erupted from Bash's hands suddenly, encompassing the home. As I watched, transfixed and horrified, the diminutive cottage turned into a towering, six-story mansion. There seemed to be no rhyme or reason for the architecture—gables and turrets sprouted from the slanted roof at unnatural angles. The siding was a dark brown, while the trim was black. Row after row of dusty, unwashed windows rose up the side of the house.

"Holy fuck," Killian breathed, craning his neck to look his fill. I spotted two gargoyles perched on a balcony overhead, their wings pressed into their stony spines. I couldn't help but wonder if they were real—new monsters Aaliyah had created or raised to capture me.

"Let's go get our vampire back," I said to the others, venturing a tentative step closer, except...something didn't feel right. I didn't know how to articulate it, only that the hairs on the back of my neck stood on end. Each step forward felt as if I was walking to my execution. "Something doesn't feel right," I said out loud, glancing at my men.

Before they could respond, I heard what sounded like pebbles hitting the ground.

"Oh, fuck," Devlin cursed as two figures stepped forward, silhouetted in the inky darkness.

"Um...let's hope they're not fucking *us*," Killian added, shakily raising his gifted dagger.

The two gargoyles I'd noted earlier now stood before us, tiny rocks cascading down their bodies with each step they took.

Stone faces displayed long fangs, pinprick black eyes, and haphazardly carved noses. Horns sprouted from their heads and curled at the tips. Their bodies were nearly as large as Lupe's, with spindly, bat-like wings protruding from their backs.

They immediately zeroed in on me.

"Give us the girl," they whispered in unison, the noise similar to rocks being rubbed together.

Lupe released an enraged snarl, fur exploding on his body.

"Over my dead body!" Killian piped up with false bravado, stepping closer. The two gargoyles turned towards him with matching sneers.

"That could be arranged," they said, and Killian's face drained of all color.

"Why don't you come out here and fight your own battles?" I screamed, peering around the gargoyles' mammoth bodies. "Aaliyah, get your ass out here right now! Fight me yourself, you coward!"

I didn't expect my taunts to actually work. I honestly didn't.

But a moment later, the door to the mansion opened and a gorgeous woman stepped out. Her alabaster skin glowed in the moonlight, emphasizing the silver flecks in her eyes. Red hair cascaded down her shoulders, held back with a golden barrette.

Jax stepped out directly behind her, face impassive and eyes glinting red.

"You wanted to talk?" Aaliyah asked coyly, focusing on me. "Then we'll talk. Long time no see...*sister*."

THIRTY-FOUR

AXEL

I was once the most feared man in all the kingdoms. My name was said in both reverence and disgust.

Axel the Assassin.

Axel the Butcher.

Blood flooded the streets, intermingling with severed limbs and heads. The world always knew when I found my target, as not even their houses remained by the time I was done with them.

Killing was in my blood, in my bones, in my heart. It was all I was good for, all I knew how to do. I wore the skin of my enemies like a badge of honor, as a way to warn away predators.

No one could stop me. Not even the kings. They'd attempted to put a leash on me, but I'd destroyed it with one eloquent look. Chains couldn't hold a monster like me.

And now, I was nothing but an errand boy. Oh, how the mighty had fallen.

I moved swiftly down the pebbled street, towards a

section of town driven by poverty. The lawns were overrun by knee-high weeds, and most of the buildings were missing windows. Graffiti covered the walls, displaying everything from the kings with nooses around their necks to a golden-haired angel with the word "Liberator" spelled out beneath it, the paint still wet.

Interesting. Very, very interesting.

I made it to the old mill in record time, slowing my pace as I stepped up to a deteriorating wooden building built directly above an ancient-looking wheel. There appeared to be three sections to the house, the middle being twice as tall as the two on either side. The roofs were slanted and cracked from age and weather. The wooden siding of the house seemed to be rotting away, the windows covered in a fine layer of dust. It looked seconds from crumbling into the water roaring below.

Silencing my footsteps, I stepped up the rickety staircase and stared through the closest dirty window.

Despite the atrocious exterior, the interior appeared well-preserved. The floor had been scrubbed so meticulously, it almost appeared to be brand new. Only a few spiderwebs hung in the rafters, and the furniture, though old, was devoid of any dust or dirt.

Miles may have been a kid, but he'd taken great care of his home.

Pain briefly assaulted me as I pictured his cherubic face and innocent eyes. That was one line I'd never crossed—killing kids. The mere prospect of it made bile swim in my throat.

All too often, they were the casualty of a war they couldn't even begin to understand.

Anger and indignation warred for domination inside of me, but shock kept them both adequately subdued. The intensity of my emotions surprised even me.

When did I get so soft? When did I start caring about the humans?

I wasn't one to actively hunt them down, but I sure as fuck didn't go out of my way to rescue them. The human female was getting to me.

Releasing a breath, I dropped the shadows surrounding me and adopted a cheerful smile. I was a master of disguising my emotions. A master of faces and masks.

One moment, I could be charming the pants off of a target, and the next, I'd be stabbing a knife into his or her throat.

All in a day's work, my friends.

Now, I rapped my knuckles against the door and waited.

Silence.

Miles had taught his sister well, though it was making my job slightly more difficult.

Tapping my foot impatiently, I knocked again.

Silence.

Heaving out a breath, I tried the handle, only to discover it was locked.

Fucking hell. I was going to scare the kid before I even had the chance to know her.

Out of options, and too lazy to scale the wall to reach the second-story window, I shoved my weight against the distressed wood. After the second try, the door collapsed, taking me with it. I landed with an *oomph* inside the mill, a sliver of wood catching in my cheek. Grimacing, I plucked the wood out of my skin and tossed it to the side. Blood welled, a brilliant shade of red, but I knew it would heal in time.

Scars and bruises were just a part of my life. I wore them proudly, a reminder of all I'd faced. Of all the people I'd killed.

"Come out, come out, wherever you are!" I called out, and then instantly winced.

Shit, that sounded creepy. Tone it down a notch, Axel.

"I brought candy!" I added helpfully.

When not even a floorboard squeaked, I focused on my senses. What I smelled, what I felt, what I heard, what I saw.

There!

Upstairs, I heard the barely audible patter of footsteps against the wooden floors.

"Just come down, okay?" I demanded, growing impatient. I had places to be, people to kill, and monsters to maim. Grumbling beneath my breath, I ascended the surprisingly steep staircase, keeping one eye peeled for the little girl. "I don't want to hurt you. I'm just here to—"

Something hard hit me straight in the chest. Normally, it wouldn't have done anything but annoy me, but I supposed I was losing my touch. The sheer shock of the assault caused me to lose my balance on the staircase. My arms windmilled as I fell backwards, body flipping and twisting as I thudded down the stairs.

Motherfucker!

When I finally landed, I landed hard. I groaned as pain reverberated up my spine and down my legs.

"Ow," I deadpanned, blinking up at the dusty, three-tiered chandelier.

A tiny face appeared over mine, blocking out the light from the hanging ornament. Her chestnut hair was streaked in hues of gold and red. Large brown eyes framed by thick lashes glared down at me. The little spitfire couldn't have been older than eight.

"You're Miles's sister," I deduced as she pressed a blade to my throat.

"Where's my brother?" she demanded, her voice high-pitched and whimsical. "What did you do to him?"

"Funny story, sweetheart, but—"

A burst of green light appeared in her hands and rammed straight into my chest. I arched my back against the blistering pain coursing through me.

"Motherfucker!" I screamed, staring at her with newfound appreciation. I'd assumed she was human like her brother, but apparently, Spitfire here was a mage.

But wait...

My shadows caressed her cheeks with surprising tenderness, and my confusion grew exponentially.

She was a Mage...but she was also human.

A hybrid.

"Impossible," I whispered, widening my eyes.

"I'll ask you again, mother trucker," she sneered. "Where. Is. My. Brother?"

Z

I remembered the day my parents died vividly.

I didn't *want* to remember, didn't want to be hounded by those memories. For years after their deaths, nightmares pummeled me. I couldn't escape from their threatening, damning blows.

All I could see were the shifters barreling through our front door and gripping my mother's hair. She screamed for me to run, to hide, but I was helpless to do anything but stare up at her.

Dad had run forward, sword raised, but he'd been batted aside as if he were nothing but a pesky bug. When he'd fallen to the ground, two more shifters converged on him, tearing into his flesh.

"Run!" Mother's eyes were shimmering with unshed tears as the shifter on top of her grabbed the waistband of her pants and pulled. "Gabriella, run!"

I learned that day that monsters didn't always come out in the dark. Sometimes, they lurked in broad daylight.

Those memories crashed over me now like a tidal

wave as I stared up at Aaliyah. Her pretty face was juxta-posed by the harsh, manic glint in her eyes. She looked...mad.

And no, not mad as in hostile.

Mad as in crazed. Manic. Unnerved.

Her words echoed in my head like the steady beat of a drum.

Sister. Sister. Sister.

Was it a figure of speech? A way to unsettle me?

Tilting my chin up, I met her eyes. It was strange to know such an angelic female could be so lethal.

Hell, maybe we were sisters. We both had a tendency to kill first and ask questions later.

"I knew you would come for him," Aaliyah said, nodding at Jax. My vampire mate snarled sharply, eyes fixed solely on me. He looked as if he was seconds from jumping down the staircase and devouring me alive.

And not in a good way.

"What did you do to him?" I demanded, eyeing Jax warily. There was no recognition in his gaze. No indication at all that he knew where he was. That he knew who *I* was.

"I simply helped him." Aaliyah shrugged her shoul-ders, moving to stand between the two gargoyles. "I made him...gluttonous." Jax growled again, pupils dilating and turning the irises completely red.

Blood red.

"Fuck," Lupe cursed, stepping forward slightly to shield me. He couldn't help his overprotective tendencies any more than I could.

Devlin, Killian, and Bash also moved in tandem,

forming a line in front of me that Aaliyah would have to break through in order to get to me.

"What do you want with me?" I demanded. It was the easiest question to ask.

Aaliyah's smile grew as she languidly pet the wings of her monsters.

"I can't give away all of my secrets, now can I?" she purred, throwing her head back in laughter. "But I'll give you a hint. The opposite of up is down. The opposite of right is left. The opposite of good is bad."

"What the fuck are you talking about, witch?" Devlin demanded, his power sparking. I didn't know what he would be able to do without someone making a wish, but his show of strength was formidable. He practically exuded raw power.

"Witch?" Aaliyah laughed again. No, not laughed. *Cackled.* Her blood-red lips curved into a malevolent smile. "Try *demon,* boy." Once more, she focused on me, and I felt something shift inside of me at being the sole focus of her gaze. I would've almost described it as... familiarity. It wasn't the same connection I felt with my mates, but it was eerily similar. No, I didn't want to bang the chick suddenly or anything like that, but it was as if something fundamental inside of me changed and contorted. "I don't want your men, Z," she hissed. "They're loyal to a fault." She jabbed a finger at Jax, still snarling behind her. "That one didn't break, no matter what I did."

Red distorted my vision at the thought of her attempting to seduce one of my mates.

Because the bitch, though psycho, was fucking beautiful.

"Just come with me, and this will all be over," she said in irritation.

"Can you tell me *why?*" I pressed, quirking a brow. She rolled her eyes as if I were a petulant child asking repeatedly if we were at our destination yet.

"You're so annoying." She took a step backwards, a wry smile playing on her luscious lips. "Grab her for me, will you?"

Without preamble, the gargoyles leaped into action.

They were strong, but they weren't smart. Immediately, they dove straight towards me, their wings flapping erratically.

Before their stone hands could come into contact with my arms, Lupe lunged forward in his bear form. He bit down on the first gargoyle's arm, shaking his head wildly until it broke free.

Holy shit! My mate was a savage.

The gargoyle didn't even react to his severed limb. Instead, he grabbed at my arm a second time as his shit-head teammate tugged on the opposite one.

Bash and Devlin sprung into action, both lethal despite their slender frames. Bash released a green fireball at first one gargoyle and then the second, cracks appearing across their faces. Devlin parried a blow from the first gargoyle, sweeping his sword out to slice at his legs.

"I got your back, Z!" Killian called, holding up his dagger. "Errr...your front technically."

"Have you ever used that thing?" Bash teased,

ducking before the second gargoyle could land a hit. "I don't want you stabbing yourself or our mate."

"You're so funny," Killian responded dryly, attempting to toss the dagger in the air and catch it. He missed, obviously, and scrambled to pick it back up. "I could totally seduce the gargoyles to stop fighting and masturbate."

"What would they excrete?" Devlin joined the conversation, cutting off one of the gargoyles' hands. "Stones?"

"I can find out."

"Please don't," I pleaded, focusing my attention on Aaliyah. She was standing on the front steps, a tiny smile on her lips as she watched the scene unfold. She didn't seem at all upset that her monsters were getting destroyed mere inches away from her. If anything, she seemed thrilled.

As if she could sense me watching her, she turned towards me completely.

"I always knew you would attract the strongest mates," she mused. "They need someone like you to balance out their darkness."

"What the fuck is that supposed to mean?" I screamed, racing forward. "Don't act like you know me."

"But I do." She tilted her head to the side as she watched me approach. "I know you better than you know yourself."

Cryptic, crazy-ass bitch.

"So what?" I laughed humorlessly. "Are you going to kill me?"

"What made you think I wanted to kill you?" she

asked seriously. "I just—" Her eyes widened marginally as blood drizzled down her chin. Slowly, her head lowered to the knife protruding from her chest, directly through her heart.

Jax stood behind her, panting, the manic look from before nowhere to be found. Incandescent rage darkened his features as he stared at Aaliyah with an all-consuming hatred.

"You foolish, stupid vampire," she gasped, dropping to her knees. When she laughed this time, blood coated her teeth, staining them shades of red and pink. "That's not the way you kill a demon."

With a ferocious roar, she pulled the knife out of her chest and whirled on my vampire mate. Jax's gloating expression turned stricken as he stumbled back a step.

"No!" I cried, racing forward. Behind me, I could hear the sound of metal hitting stone. Stone hitting flesh. Pained grunts and snarls.

"I'm truly sorry, Z," Aaliyah hissed, bearing down on my mate. "He left me with no other choice."

She raised her dagger, and for a brief moment, her form changed. It was almost as if *she* was an illusion, her beauty a mask that hid a truer evil. Her face turned red laced with golden veins visible through her papery skin. Horns rose through her fiery red hair, and leathery wings unfurled from behind her.

She looked...demonic.

"No!" I screamed again as I met Jax's resigned gaze. Tears flooded his eyes as he mouthed three words to me. Three words that cracked open my already broken heart until I was weeping blood. "No!"

Aaliyah stabbed the knife into Jax's heart, and I watched his eyes glaze over. Blood bloomed on his chest as she twisted the copper handle, lodging it even deeper.

Tears of rage and despair trailed down my cheeks as I raised my own dagger, preparing to cut open Aaliyah's chest and bathe in her innards.

No. No. No. No.

I couldn't think of any other word. I didn't *want* to. All I could see was my mate falling, the life draining from his eyes.

The air around Aaliyah began to shimmer as she called upon a portal. Blood still seeped through her emerald dress as glanced at me over her shoulder.

"I'm truly sorry," she whispered as she dove inside the portal. Before I could follow her, it disappeared from view with a bright flash.

Any thoughts of revenge diminished as I fell to my knees beside a gasping Jax.

"No. No. No," I sobbed, putting pressure on the wound. "You're going to be okay. You're going to be fine."

"It's okay," he stuttered out, gasping around the blood in his mouth.

"You're going to be fine," I repeated inarticulately.

Not Jax. Not him. No. No. No.

"It's okay." His bright eyes stared up at me with more coherence and clarity than ever before. I had the distinct feeling that he was *seeing* me, truly seeing me for the first time. "Dying in the arms of the woman I love—"

"You're not dying!" I screamed, pushing down harder on the wound. Blood soaked through my fingers, but I didn't let up.

"I love you so damn much," he whispered. "I'll always be with you."

"Shut your fucking mouth, Jax Vampire. If you die, I'll go into the afterlife, bring you back, and then kill you myself."

He smiled weakly, his face creased with pain, as the light gradually began to leave his eyes. I never knew it was possible to see a soul physically leave a person's body before, but that was what happened. One moment, there was life in his eyes, and the next, there was nothing. They were just...eyes. Opened and blind eyes.

"No," I gasped, shaking his shoulder. "No, no, no." I pounded my fists against the ground on either side of his suddenly still body. "No!"

Something inside of me snapped.

Something inside of me was set loose—a monster I hadn't even realized hid just beneath the surface.

I screamed, infusing all of my anger and rage and heartbreak into that one soul wrenching sound. It felt as if my heart had been dropped and shattered into thousands of unfixable pieces. Pain like I'd never felt before consumed me. Choked me. Killed me.

No!

Blinding light emitted from my hands where they were still pressed against the ground on either side of Jax. I could feel electricity vibrating through my veins as my body shook with raw, unrestrained power. Heat sizzled through my system as I focused on Jax's unmoving body. Fury pummeled me from all sides as the light grew and grew and grew until it encompassed Jax's entire form.

The world around me was still and silent. All I could

hear was my volatile heartbeat as a flurry of shivers skipped through my veins.

Jax.

Jax.

Jax.

Memories bombarded me.

Jax's broken body hanging in a cell. His lips stained red as he fed off the dead human. His ferocious snarl as he stared at me with no sign of recognition. His body moving in tandem to mine as he took us both to the peak of pleasure. His lips a flurry against my own. His warning about Aaliyah.

My dreams hadn't actually been dreams…somehow, someway, I'd been able to see Jax. To visit him. To save him. To bring him back from the cusp of insanity.

My heart splintered down the center, fissures cracking open the entire organ, as I focused the blinding light on Jax. Only Jax.

There was still so much I didn't know about him. So much I hadn't had the chance to learn. For as long as I'd known him, he'd been ruled by madness. I was only just beginning to learn about the man beneath it all.

What made him decide not to feed? What had he endured?

What was his favorite color?

I screamed, pressing my hands to Jax's chest, where the bright light had congregated.

He needs to live. He needs to live.

He needs to live.

Color began to return to his face as his eyes fluttered

slightly. The vibrancy that had been absent only seconds before returned as he smiled up at me.

"Z..." he whispered, his voice clawing at something raw and bleeding in my heart.

"Jax." Before I could say anything else, darkness rushed at me from all sides. It wrapped around me like a tightening leash, and I was utterly helpless to resist its thrall.

I allowed the dark waves to carry me away.

THIRTY-SIX

AALIYAH

I cursed vehemently as I exited the portal, landing in an undignified heap on the cold wood floor.

The asshole vampire had pushed his luck too far. I could only be so forgiving.

Stumbling to my feet, I waited for my flesh to begin stitching itself back together. That hurt more than the actual wound.

I crossed the bamboo floorboards and ducked into my bedroom. The windows had been drawn, just the way I liked them, and candles lined the windowsills. It was my home, my sanctuary, my one escape from this disgusting world and the sheep that resided in it.

Soon, they would all be dead—nightmares and humans alike.

A forlorn feeling, one I wasn't used to, settled in my chest like an uncomfortable weight at the thought of Gabriella. It wasn't unbearable by any means. It just sat there, like a mosquito bite that didn't itch quite enough to scratch.

She'd never forgive me for killing her mate.

Hopefully, she would understand why I did what I did. I refused to accept anything else.

"Can I get you anything, mistress?" one of my servants inquired, bowing her head submissively. Mali, I believed her name was. One of Gabriella's little friends.

To me, she was nothing but a fucking sheep.

I smiled at her, allowing her to see the madness that swirled in the abyss of my eyes. My beautiful face hid something even more beautiful, more enticing.

Darkness.

"I'm fine, my faithful servant," I purred, pulling back my dress to stare at the rapidly healing wound.

Why did Gabriella have to find the most hotheaded mates in the world?

Stupid, stupid girl.

She would come to me eventually, though. It was the only way she'd survive the poison I'd had Zack administer.

When Mali bowed, attempting to make a quick getaway, I threw my power at her with a simple flick of my wrist. Immediately, her back hit the wall, trapped in my carefully crafted web.

"One more thing, dearest," I said softly. When I met her eyes, I was surprised to see absolute hatred reflecting back at me. Maybe she wasn't as much of a sheep as I suspected. Maybe she had the makings to be a lion.

"What?" she snapped, jaw clenching.

"Help me down to my basement." My smile grew as the color drained from her face. She, more than any of my servants, knew what lurked at the bottom of my house. "I need to raise more of my monsters."

Z

"Momma!" I cried, reaching my arms out as if I could grab her and hold her to me. Tears burned my retinas as I witnessed something no child should ever see.

The shifters' faces were etched into the skin behind my eyelids. When I closed them, they were all I could see.

One was burly with midnight black hair, teal-colored eyes, and a tattoo of a dragon climbing up his neck.

Another had blond hair so light, it was almost white. He, too, had a tattoo, but his rested on his muscular forearm. From my position beneath the couch, I couldn't decipher what it was. A tree, perhaps? A garden? It was decidedly plant-like in appearance.

The third was handsome in a traditional, aristocratic type of way. With sharp cheekbones, a strong jawline, and long lashes, he could've been a fairy-tale prince come to life. He didn't participate with the other two. Instead, he was content to lean against the wall and watch, an indolent smirk on his face.

"Momma!" I cried again, my tiny hand stretching forward feebly. The normally vibrant light in her eyes was beginning to dim. A single tear cascaded down her cheek before her body went still. I didn't understand it at that age.

Had she given up? Why wasn't she fighting back? Why wasn't she blinking?

My little brain couldn't comprehend the aspect of death. The finality of it. People left all the time, but they always came back. Always. Just the other day, Daddy left the house to retrieve supplies, but he came back only two days later with my favorite ice cream.

"Mommy?" I whispered, my voice breaking. She stared back at me with vacant, unseeing eyes.

The third shifter kneeled until he was eye level with me, his cheek practically against the ground.

"Little girl, why don't you come out and play with us?"

Behind him, the other two men leered maliciously.

"I just want my mommy and daddy," I sobbed, my heart splintering. It was the first time I'd ever broken. At the time, I hadn't realized that was what the gaping hole in my chest was. I hadn't realized how difficult it would be to sew myself back together, to find the pieces that had been lost that day.

"I'll be your new daddy," he told me. The interest in his eyes turned to avarice. "I'll always find you."

The shifter extended a hand, his smile growing, but before I could accept it, his features twisted, becoming someone else entirely. His chestnut hair turned black, and his smooth face became wrinkled with age. Those hard, cruel eyes shifted from a bright shade of amber to an emerald green. When he smiled, the crinkles around his eyes became more pronounced.

I was no longer underneath the couch. Instead, I was seven years old, hiding in an alleyway behind a bakery as I searched for food.

"You're okay now," he promised, extending a hand. "My name is A, and I'm going to take care of you."

The vision changed abruptly.

Now, I was twelve years old, kneeling on the edge of a roof. A was on one side of me, and B was on the other. Over the years, I'd begun to think of A as my father. He couldn't replace my true dad, but he was slowly refilling the numerous cracks in my heart.

"Steady hand," A instructed as B languidly reclined on the roof next to me.

I lifted my dagger, trying to control the involuntary tremor coursing through me.

"Aim," A continued as B yawned dramatically.

I focused on my target—a thirty-five-year-old genie with greasy brown hair and violet eyes.

"Fire."

Without preamble, I threw the dagger with painstaking accuracy. It landed in the genie's forehead, and he immediately dropped to the ground, dead. The nightmares nearby began to cry and scream, but A was already pulling me back towards the portal B had created.

"You were phenomenal, my daughter," he praised, slapping me on the back.

Together, we stepped through the portal, and the two men dematerialized like clouds of smoke. In their place was S.

"You going to cry over your ex forever?" he teased, knocking me with his shoulder. I rolled my eyes playfully, but my stomach twisted into dozens of knots when I thought about Lin. It was an invisible scar, one only Mali was privy to.

"I don't want to talk about him," I murmured, turning on my heel to smile up at him. "Now are we going to train, or are you going to continue staring at my ass?"

"How can I stare at your ass when I'm facing forward?" he joked. "Wouldn't I be staring at your tits?"

I swatted him with the back of my hand, a laugh escaping unbidden. "You're such a pervert, S."

"And you love it."

Suddenly, we were no longer in the compound I'd come to love. We were at the edge of the woods, a scream lodged in my throat as I watched a shifter tear at S's throat. I screamed in anguish as blood squirted from the gashes on his neck.

No. No. No.

Don't leave me.

Everyone always leaves me.

S stared at me hopelessly, the same glint in his eyes I'd seen in my mother's before she'd died years ago.

I tried to crawl towards him, but my injuries prohibited any and all movement.

"No," I croaked out, grasping at the leaves. Rain pounded down around us, obscuring my vision. "No!"

It was supposed to be a simple mission. Find the shifter responsible for raping and killing two dozen women and kill him. But while we'd been hunting him, he had been hunting us.

The shifter turned towards me, his features as handsome as they were when I was a child. I'd killed the other two, but he...he had always evaded me.

"I told you that I'll always find you," he whispered as he brought his claws to S's throat.

"No!" I screamed as the forest changed to the throne room in the capital. I spun towards the thrones, only to freeze when I noticed the occupants sitting lazily on the huge chairs.

Bash's head lolled to the side as he slept, his breathing even. Killian sat in the throne directly beside him, shirtless with his tattoos on full display. Was that a...?

"When did you get a nipple ring?" I questioned, staring intently at the silver bulb piercing his left nipple. He turned towards me with cold eyes.

"Do I know you?" he asked darkly.

"She's cute enough," Jax drawled, a hint of fang poking his bottom lip. "I'll suck her dry."

"Stop teasing the girl," Ryland snapped as the shadows pressed in on all sides of him, stealing the light from the room.

"But it's fun," Dair threw in. There was something in his smile I'd never seen before. Something...evil. He stared at me as if he couldn't wait to stick a knife into my neck. It went beyond vengeance, beyond anger. It was hatred.

"Enough!" Lupe's strident voice cut through the

mutters like the crack of a whip. He rose to his feet, his lumbering frame making me feel small and dainty. "We don't talk to humans. They're scum. They're nothing."

"I'm your mate," I pleaded, tears blurring my eyes. When all of them began to laugh, I tried again. "You love me."

"Why would we ever love you?" Devlin asked coldly, stroking his lamp. "What makes you so special?"

"I don't feel any lust when I look at you," Killian purred, gripping his crotch in a vulgar manner.

"Nothing to be envious of," Dair added.

"I'm not greedy to have someone like you as a mate," Devlin said harshly.

"I wouldn't be proud to have you on my arm." The shadows tightened around Ryland with each word he spoke.

"Killing you wouldn't make me wrathful," Lupe threw in. "It would make me...glad."

Bash continued to snore away, oblivious to the conversation happening around him.

Jax stood as well, stalking forward until he was directly in front of me. His eyes were solid red, no white or black to be seen. They were the eyes of a demon—the eyes of a monster.

"Jax..." I wanted to touch his cheeks, to trace the contours of his handsome, beautiful face. He was alive. He was in front of me. He wasn't dead. "Jax—"

Before I could finish my sentence, he shoved his fist in my chest. I could feel his hand around my heart, crushing the sensitive organ with each press of his fingers. A cold, malevolent grin lit up his face. "I am gluttonous for your blood. To drain you dry until you're nothing but a husk."

With a harsh laugh, he ripped my heart from my chest.

And...

And I died.

THIRTY-EIGHT

DEVLIN

"Why isn't she waking up?" I demanded, pacing the room. I rounded on Bash, who was perched on the edge of her bed. "And why the fuck didn't you tell us about the poison sooner?"

Poison.

Coursing through my mate's body.

Killing her.

I couldn't focus on that. *Wouldn't.* If I did, I would go insane.

Fuck.

This entire day had been a clusterfuck of epic proportions. Jax had *died.* Died. His heart had stopped beating.

Even from a distance, I could see the life drain from his eyes. Blood had coated his shirt and Z's hands. My brother, my best friend, had died.

And then, he was alive again.

I didn't know how to describe it. Light seemed to emit

from Z's pores like a golden sheen. I'd had to close my eyes against the sheer brilliance of it. So. Much. Power.

When my eyes finally readjusted, I'd watched Jax's chest rise and fall steadily as his eyes popped open. It shouldn't have been possible. The world worked because the dead stayed dead. Not even nightmares were immune to it.

We'd carried Z's unconscious body back to the car, and Dair had quickly driven us away.

Away from the gargoyles that had been reduced to piles of stone.

Away from the blood that soaked the front steps of the mansion.

Away.

Away.

Away.

It was only when we'd arrived at an inn on the outskirts of the city that Bash disclosed the truth about Z.

She was dying.

"It doesn't make sense," Killian rambled, forking his fingers through his dark red hair. "She was able to bring Jax back to life. How come she can't heal herself?"

"Because the poison was given to Zack by Aaliyah," Bash responded tiredly. His eyelids drooped with exhaustion. He'd been attempting to heal her for hours now, and I could see the effects it had taken on him. Dark shadows marred the skin beneath both his eyes, and his face appeared haggard.

"How long?" Lupe growled, his eyes flashing. He, more than any of us, was having trouble controlling his sin. Controlling his wrath.

"How long what?" Bash sounded resigned, as if he already knew what Lupe was going to ask before he asked it.

"How long have you known about the poison?"

"I suspected it after the fight with the kraken when I first healed her," he admitted. "I was only able to confirm my suspicions after the basilisk attack."

Surprisingly enough, it wasn't Lupe who lost his shit. It was Dair.

The normally gentle and kind man rolled his chair—which Ryland had stolen from a local human hospital—closer until he was directly in front Bash.

"You fucking asshole!" he hissed, punching Bash square in the face. The mage's head whipped to the side, blood dripping from his nose, but he didn't raise a hand to fight back. It was almost as if he thought he deserved it.

Which he did, of course.

But the beating would come *after* he healed our mate.

"Enough!" I snapped, stepping between them. Dair trembled with barely contained fury, eyes spitting hate. When he looked as if he wanted to punch Bash again, I placed a hand on his shoulder to stop him, imploring him with my eyes to trust me. "Enough."

Dair's sea-blue eyes locked with my violet ones, and the air around us practically crackled with electricity. It was a battle of wills, each of us attempting to assert our dominance.

And while Dair was strong, he was no leader. That role had always been reserved for me.

With a growl, Dair turned away, focusing his vitriol instead on the hideously patterned carpeting.

"Fighting will get us nowhere," I said to the room at large. Ryland was balancing on the windowsill, while Killian leaned against the wall beside him. With Lupe, Dair, and Bash around Z's bed, the only person we were missing was...

"Where the hell is Jax?" I questioned.

Jax.

The dead man.

The not dead man.

As if he'd been summoned, the door to the room was thrown open, and a very naked Jax stepped inside. I exchanged a wary look with Lupe, who was nearest to me, before focusing back on my vampire brother.

"Blood runs red. Blood. So much blood. My blood. My. Blood." He grabbed at his light brown hair, pulling at the strands until they were sticking out in all directions.

"What's wrong with him?" Killian asked nervously. "When he was with Aaliyah, he drank blood daily. He shouldn't have the madness anymore."

"It's a different type of madness." Ryland's voice now came from the desk sitting opposite the bed. "His brain has always been fragile, but with everything that happened..."

"My blood doesn't tingle anymore," Jax whispered as Killian helped him into his pants. "My blood doesn't tingle."

"We don't know what happened to him when he..." Lupe trailed off, swallowing. "When he..."

"When he died," Bash finished candidly, ignoring the fierce glare Lupe threw his way. "We don't know what Z's magic did to him."

"And we don't know how her condition is affecting him," Killian pointed out as he helped Jax into his shirt.

"She'll wake up," Lupe asserted, softly brushing at her golden hair. She looked so fucking beautiful, even when she was asleep. Her face was serene, soft, and appeared years younger.

Fuck, I loved her. I loved her so damn much that it almost didn't seem real. This type of love shouldn't exist. It shouldn't be possible. It destroyed me in the best way.

And now, I might lose her.

"We need to find that bitch," I growled out. "And demand that she give us a cure."

"And how do you suppose we do that?" Bash drawled. "We only found her before because she *wanted* to be found."

"Then we'll heal Z ourselves!" Lupe roared before taking a deep breath, hands clenching and unclenching as he attempted to control his rage.

"What is she?" Ryland whispered, now appearing at the edge of her bed. "She's not human."

"So she's an alien?" Bash snarked, and this time, I didn't stop Dair from punching him in the face.

"Can't you take shit seriously for once in your life?" Dair shouted, hands balling into fists as if he wanted to hit the mage again.

But when Bash released a self-deprecating laugh, voice heady with self-loathing, Dair relaxed, loosening his muscles incrementally.

"If I don't joke, I'll fall apart. And if I fall apart, I don't think I'll ever get put back together again." He rose to his feet abruptly, eyes spewing lightning. "I can't fucking lose her. I can't. I can't." He shook his head vigorously. "I should've told you guys the truth sooner, but I didn't want to break her trust. She hates me, and I thought that maybe..." He turned towards her, his expression for once unguarded. Without even being awake, she was capable of breaking through all of his defenses. "I thought maybe she would come to love me like she loves you guys."

Silence ensued as we all processed his words. It was Dair who broke it with a harsh snort.

"You fucking dumbass." He snorted again, the noise turning into a harsh bark of laughter. "Asshole, the girl is crazy about you. She just doesn't know how to admit it. You have a stick so far up your ass, it could be considered a colonoscopy. You're seriously an idiot sometimes."

Bash appeared shocked, stricken almost, as he gaped at the golden-haired mermaid.

"He's right," Killian whispered quietly, and Bash's head whipped in his direction. "Z loves us all. I can feel it." He closed his fist and placed it over his heart. "I feel it here."

Love for this incredible woman suffused me. Love for her jagged edges that somehow fit perfectly against my own. Love for her tainted light that somehow made my own shine brilliantly. Love for her darkness that made her a warrior, a survivor. She'd faced unspeakable horrors in her life, yet she still managed to emerge strong and compassionate.

Overcome by the strength of my emotions, I pressed a kiss to her clammy forehead.

"Wake up, baby. Please wake up."

"The kings," Jax murmured, and I whipped my head in his direction.

"Killian, help put him to bed," Lupe said dismissively, but before the incubus could take a step, Jax began speaking again.

"The kings," he repeated. "They were there."

We all turned to stare at him.

"What?" I asked, my eyes hurling daggers. He couldn't possibly mean...

"They were there. With Aaliyah. They were there." He began to tap a staccato against his leg, already lost in his own mind.

"What the hell were the kings doing with that...that monster?" Lupe roared, pacing. I spotted fur on both his arms and neck. It wouldn't be too long before he lost control completely.

"The vampire king..." Dair mused, eyes wide. "He mentioned something strange when I was with Atta. He said something about...something about living forever. A deal with the devil."

I exchanged another look with all of my brothers.

"You don't think the kings made a deal with Aaliyah in exchange for immortality?" I whispered, shock sizzling through my veins.

Bash turned to focus back on Z, stroking her cheek. "If that's the case, then we're fucked."

"No," I said adamantly, shaking my head. "No. We're alive. All of us." I pierced each of my brothers with an eloquent look. "All. Of. Us. I don't know what Z is, and I don't care. She brought my brother back, and that's all that matters. We *will* save her, no matter what it takes."

The tension in the room lessened infinitesimally, as if my brothers could hear the promise in my words. The vow. "We have two days. Two days to find a cure before she's scheduled to arrive back at the capital. Two days. We'll get her a cure, or we'll die trying. Whatever it takes."

"Whatever it takes," they echoed.

I gripped Z's cold hand tightly.

Hang in there, Z. We're going to save you.

Then, we'll kill the kings.

EPILOGUE

I stared intently at the glass vial Hans had given me. What I'd traded in exchange for it...

Fuck, this better work.

When I closed my eyes, I could see Z's face staring back at me, her animosity saturating the air. If she knew the truth about what I did, that I'd betrayed her to that vampire who ran the carnival, she would never forgive me.

Shaking my head vehemently, I focused back on the vial. A purple mist swirled inside, darker shades of indigo woven throughout.

A soul.

His soul.

She would come to understand the reasoning behind my decision. I knew that her mates would do whatever it took to get her out of there. Losing her trust was a small price to pay for what I'd gained. She'd forgive me. She had to.

Or she'll hate you forever.

I hit the brakes on that thought so fast that skid marks appeared on the asphalt and the air was perfumed by the smell of burning rubber.

Taking a fortifying breath, I dropped the vial onto the floor. Immediately, the purple mist rose until it was approximately my height. It solidified before my very eyes, taking the form of a broad-shouldered, brown-haired man.

Tears flooded my eyes as I dropped to my knees, gazing at the man as if he were a mirage that would disappear at a moment's notice.

"Brother," I choked out as emotions assaulted me.

S stared at his hands as if he didn't recognize them. Wonderment, shock, and confusion flitted across his face.

"T?" he whispered brokenly. He took a step forward, wobbling slightly, as if he'd forgotten how to use his legs.

"It's me, brother. It's me." I wrapped him in a tight hug, sobbing into his shoulder. He was here. He was alive. He was with me.

His next words were a metaphorical bucket of ice water being dropped over my head. "Where's Z?"

Fuck.

ACKNOWLEDGMENTS

As always, I would like to thank my family first and foremost. I don't know where I would be without your love and support.

Thank you to my incredible readers for sticking with me! I know you guys have been eagerly awaiting this book, and I pray it doesn't disappoint. I put my heart and soul into Gluttony! I thank each and every one of you for reading.

I would also like to thank my kickass team for helping me make this book the best it can possibly be. From the bottom of my heart, thank you. You guys are amazing.

Finally, I would like to thank all of my author friends who stuck with me whenever I dealt with imposter syndrome or writer's block. You guys are seriously incredible, and I thank the stars for you.

ABOUT THE AUTHOR

Katie May is a reverse harem author, a KDP All-Star winner, and an USA Today Bestselling Author. She lives in West Michigan with her family and cat. When not writing, she could be found reading a good book, listening to broadway musicals, or playing games. Join Katie's Gang to stay updated on all her releases! And did you know she has a TikTok? Yeah, me either. Follow her here! But be warned...she's an awkward noodle.

Together We Fall (Apocalyptic Reverse Harem,
COMPLETED)

1. The Darkness We Crave

2. The Light We Seek

3. The Storm We Face

4. The Monsters We Hunt

Beyond the Shadows (Horror Reverse Harem,
COMPLETED)

1. Gangs and Ghosts

2. Guns and Graveyards

3. Gallows and Ghouls

The Damning (Fantasy Paranormal Reverse Harem)

1. Greed

2. Envy

3. Gluttony

Prodigium Academy (Horror Comedy Academy Reverse
Harem)

1. Monsters

2. Roaring

Tory's School for the Trouble (Bully Horror Academy Reverse Harem)

1. Between

2. Beyond (Coming Soon)

Supernaturalette (Interactive Reverse Harem)

1. Introductions

2. First Dates

3. Group Outing

4. Game Night

5. Exes

Kingdom of Wolves (Shifter Reverse Harem Duet)

1. Torn to Bits

2. Ripped to Shreds

CO-WRITES

Afterworld Academy with Loxley Savage (Academy Fantasy Reverse Harem)

1. Dearly Departed

2. Darkness Deceives

3. Defying Destiny

Darkest Flames with Ann Denton (Paranormal Reverse Harem)

1. Demon Kissed

1.5. Demon Stalked

2. Demon Loved

3. Demon Sworn

STAND-ALONES

Toxicity (Contemporary Reverse Harem)

Blindly Indicted (Prison Reverse Harem)

Not All Heroes Wear Capes (Just Dresses) (Short Comedic Reverse Harem)

Charming Devils (Bully/Revenge Reverse Harem)

Goddess of Pain (Fantasy Reverse Harem)

Demon's Joy (Holiday Reverse Harem)